Also by Richard Daybell

VOODOO LOVE SONG

CALYPSO: STORIES OF THE CARIBBEAN

NAUGHTY MARIETTA AND OTHER STORIES

TERRY AND THE PIRATE

A NOVEL

BY RICHARD DAYBELL

CARIBE BOOKS

Lincoln, Vermont

Library of Congress Control Number: 2015937762

ISBN-13 978-0692419045

ISBN-10 0692419047

For Morgan,

a pirate at heart

Chapter 1

"Rain."

It was the first word uttered during the past hour, and even it was unnecessary – not to mention understated – since the dark sky had ruptured, and a heavy downpour pummeled both the beach and the choppy sea that stretched away from it. The sun had been playing hide-and-go-seek for a week now, its occasional appearances bracketed by rains such as this one. Rain is, of course, a word of four letters, and it was spoken in this case in the tone of voice reserved for four-letter words. Albert Lafitte, the speaker who had so eloquently described the spectacle they now witnessed, sat between two other men. The three of them sat in distressed director's chairs and remained for the most part dry, thanks to a large thatched canopy held above them by four wooden corner posts. From this vantage point, they settled in for what would likely be an afternoon of silent observation of nature's life-giving, but occasionally irritating, miracle.

For when the rain was this plentiful, the visitor's weren't, and Albert's Booby Bay Cafe was lifeless; they might just as well shut the doors, if it had any. Actually the Booby Bay Cafe was pretty much lifeless rain or shine. The tiny island of Soleil, whose windward beach it graced, was a long ten miles from its nearest neighbor, an island whose seaport, Bluebeard's Reef, had at one time been small but bustling. Back then, Albert's cafe had been a popular watering hole for a steady parade of seafarers, from vacationing sailors to fishermen to the pilots of odd junk crafts whose reason for being at sea remained a mystery. That was until Hurricane Glenda, which had been following a ladylike northward course through the islands, not threatening anyone, turned fickle and suddenly westward, nearly eliminating Bluebeard's Reef. And with Bluebeard's Reef all but gone, the journey from civilization to Booby Bay became more trouble than it was worth.

Occasional visitors did allow Albert to eke out a simple existence. All he really needed was the liquor to stock his bar, a commodity he purchased on other islands at prices low enough that he refused to talk about it. (He poured the contents of the bottles that came without labels into bottles with labels as necessary so as not to upset the more fastidious of his customers.) And although Albert's enterprise was called a cafe, he didn't serve food unless a patron were persistent enough to persuade Albert to produce a sandwich – not a Croque Monsieur or a BLT, of course – baloney if you were lucky, peanut butter if you weren't. Gastronomically, Albert himself fared better than his clientele because his neighbors all shared their meals with him, taking pity on his status as a lone, elderly male, although receiving in return alcoholic quid pro quo at the Booby Bay Cafe. As a result, the island community was basically a cashless society.

Nonpaying though they were, Albert's fellow islanders were the core of his clientele, his regulars, one of whom, Basil Ringrose, sat in the chair at Albert's left and another of whom, Mutton O'Malley, sat to the right. Neither responded to Albert's meteorological pronouncement. Perhaps that is why Albert felt compelled to clarify and expand upon his earlier statement: "*Il pleut, Il* motherfucking *pleut.*"

Yes, Albert Lafitte was French as well as foulmouthed. Most of the refined touches of his native language had disappeared through years of contact with those who spoke only the crudest form of whatever their mother tongue happened to be. In fact, he rarely spoke French at all – generally only when

3

vilifying someone or something that irritated him: a biting *"baisse-toi"* or, referring to the current situation, a disgusted *"Il pisse comme une vache."*

It wasn't that Albert hated rain; he was rather fond of it most of the time. But it had been raining steadily with only infrequent sunny interludes for too long now. And that meant no visitors. More importantly, it meant that he couldn't work on his project, the construction of his galleasse, a replica of a 16th century Mediterranean sailing ship – much smaller, not fitted out for indentured oarsmen, but every bit as much a work of art.

"Thank your lucky stars we're on solid earth," said Basil. "Nothing worse than a storm like this at sea, I hope to tell ya. Tossed around like a tub of coleslaw as if the gods were just letting you know what an insignificant little bit of cabbage you are." Basil carried most conversations to the sea and its magnitude, strength, beauty, vastness, cruelty, justice or loyalty. Basil Ringrose had, in his distant more worthwhile past, written a book about the sea – more specifically about pirates and even more specifically about one pirate in particular, Bad Basil Ringrose. "Tales of the Last Buccaneer" was the supposedly autobiographical account of Bad Basil's nefarious career. A reasonably close reading of the books would suggest, however, that if this particular Basil Ringrose were the chronicled Bad

Basil, he would now be at the very least 150 years old. Nevertheless, Basil believed himself to be the last buccaneer, the son of the elder Basil Ringrose (1799 - 1857), at least when rum wrested control of the man, which was every day after about two o'clock. By four he was swaggering, and by seven he was ready to run through anyone who crossed him. Physically, he could be threatening, easily topping six feet and weighing in at well over two hundred pounds. He had thin, sandy hair with a tendency to matting and an errant beard covering a good part of a blowzy complexion that was almost as red as his eyes.

Mutton O'Malley equaled Basil in girth but was more youthful and robust. He didn't drink much, but his mind was every bit as clouded without alcohol. The name Mutton was a nickname from his days of college football during which he had served as a human battering ram, and what little he learned in the classroom was quickly knocked out of his head on the field. In one particular game, almost everything was erased from his mind. All he remembered afterward was the Oklahoma steamroller that hit him and every contour of the pretty, but frightened cheerleader that he ended up on top of. He carried these scant memories and an inexplicable ability to recite *The Rime of the Ancient Mariner* in its entirety into his post-college wanderings. A few years in Jamaica where he associated freely with native ganja turned him into an itinerant beachcomber and finally a resident of Booby Bay. Mutton opened his eyes, stared for a moment, then said: "It's raining."

"And on what do you base that acute observation?" Albert responded.

"I can see the rain falling, and the beach is wet."

"*Il est fou.*"

"The boy needs some sea time," offered Basil. "Breathe a little salt, clear the cobwebs out of that empty skull."

Albert found it necessary to point out that neither Mutton nor anyone else could go to sea because of the fucking rain and was so doing when they heard the scuffle behind them.

"So here you sit like old men and swear at the rain. A fine bunch." The speaker was Peaches Verney, an abundant dark-skinned woman in her fifties. She was St. Kittian (she thought) and would not reveal how she got the unlikely name of Peaches. The men mumbled in reply.

"You just close your eyes and curse the darkness. You ought to open your eyes and smell the roses." Peaches had a poetic streak. She particularly fancied anything British, and her favorite lines, which she quoted often, were "Tiger, tiger, burning bright, in the jungle late at night." They were the only lines she could remember from this particular poem, but she did recall that the tiger was afraid of cemeteries.

"Why is the tiger on fire?" someone would invariably ask.

"It's all metagorical," she would answer.

"What does that mean?"

"It means things stand for other things. It means the tiger isn't on fire."

"Then why say it is?"

"Because it's poetry," she would say, bringing the conversation to what she felt was a more than satisfactory conclusion.

Peaches lived with her two children, Remy, who was 25, and Christian, who was 19. She also treated Albert as though he were a child, and rumor suggested they had, at one time, been lovers.

"Albert, you're an old fool," she said as he and the other two men ignored her words of wisdom.

"Something's out there," Albert mumbled, staring out to sea.

"I don't see anything," said Basil, "except rain."

"Me neither," Peaches agreed. "You're seeing things."

"You are a pathetically nearsighted and ugly woman," Albert decreed. "How could you not see it? It is as plain as the nose on Mutton's face."

"What?" said Mutton, opening his eyes.

"There's something out there."

Mutton stared blankly into space. "You mean aliens?"

"No, imbecile. In the water."

"I think I see something now," said Basil, probably lying. "Maybe it's a shark or a dolphin."

"Don't think so," said Albert. "It seems to be floating."

"There it is," said Peaches. "I see it now. I apologize for doubting you, wise keen-eyed old man."

"Apology accepted," said Albert graciously. "It's floating in to shore."

"The sun came up upon the left," said Mutton. "Out of the sea came he."

"*Merde.*"

"And he shone bright, and on the right, went down into the sea." Even though Mutton could recite the "Ancient Mariner," he didn't really understand it. Peaches, as the acknowledged poet laureate of Booby Bay, charitably explained to him that it was about why we should be kind to animals.

"I think it's a someone," said Peaches, her eyes now locked on the flotsam in question. "It's a person."

"Yea, slimy things did crawl with legs, upon the slimy sea," added Mutton.

"Probably a corpse by now," said Basil. "Shouldn't doubt it."

"The many men so beautiful and they all dead did lie. And a thousand thousand slimy things lived on; and so did I."

"Keelhauled, of course," Basil continued. "Then cut loose and left to drift like so much seaweed. By savage men committed to the savage sea." Basil Ringrose could be as lyrical as the next man, Coleridge included. "Well, I think I'll pour myself a little something to prepare my nerves for the ugly ordeal we're about to face." He stood and walked away in the direction of the bar.

"It's almost here," said Albert, standing. "I guess we're obligated to drag it in." They walked the twenty yards to the water's edge through the driving rain, Albert cursing all the way.

"Water, water everywhere and yet the boards did shrink," Mutton intoned as they stood waiting for one or two more waves to wash the package ashore. "Water, water everywhere nor any drop to drink." They could see now that it was indeed human – a man fused to a large slab of wood, looking much the worse for his journey, if not dead. Finally, a large rolling wave deposited their guest on the sand at their feet, and Albert rolled him over.

"Is it dead?" asked Mutton.

"Absolutely," said Albert. "Which brings up the problem of what to do with it.

We could just set it afloat again, hoping it would become somebody else's problem, but it would probably just float right back."

"We need to do the proper thing," Peaches remonstrated.

"But of course," said Albert, frowning. "I was just about to suggest doing the proper thing."

"Do dead people ever move?" asked Mutton.

"Sometimes," answered Albert. "Some corpses even sit up. It's a medical phenomenon."

"Like rigor mortis?" asked Peaches.

"I hope this corpse don't sit up," said Mutton. "I'm glad it's just breathing so far."

"What," said Albert, looking down. They all watched as their corpse's eyelids quivered for a moment then slowly opened, revealing eyes that stared at them with apprehension. Then his tight body began to relax, and he released his grip on the rude vessel that had carried him to safety.

"I don't think we're in Kansas anymore," he mumbled, then closed his eyes again. They carried him back up to the dry pavilion and plopped him into one of the beach chairs. Peaches wrestled a tattered blanket away from the dog, who snarled briefly in irritation, and wrapped it around the shivering stranger.

"My God, you'll catch your death," she clucked as she tucked here and there in her most maternal manner. The man opened his eyes and offered a weak smile in appreciation. At the same moment, Basil returned carrying two drinks. Although both had most likely been intended for personal consumption, Basil, upon seeing that the corpse lived, pushed one of the drinks into a cold hand. Then he sat down in the chair next to him, gulped down a good part of his own drink and stared at the new arrival.

"Now tell us lad, did they keelhaul you or just toss you overboard?"

"Nice of you to float by," said Albert taking his chair.

Excerpt from the Booby Bay Chronicle by Basil Ringrose, retired buccaneer (unfinished)

The islands of the Caribbean stretch from Trinidad in the south to Jamaica in the north like a string of pearls adorning the bosom of a dowager. But in this case the dowager is blue – a vivid aqua blue – and these sceptered isles, these petite pearls, these tiny individual Edens, are green – lush, tropical, verdant.

Midway through this shimmering band lies Booby Bay, at one end of Soleil, a tiny cay off the islet of Pointe Francoise, which is 90 miles ESE of L'Orient in the southernmost French West Indies.

Formed over thousands of years by the horrendous thunder of volcanic activity and spewing lava, Soleil is an island Janus. At the east lies Booby Bay, a long, inviting strand of pure white sand basking under the warm golden glow of the tropical sun; at the west looms a forbidding, rocky facade known as Pirate's Perch. Booby Bay is named after the booby, an aquatic bird that visits the cay with regularity for the noble purposes of procreation; that is, to lay young booby eggs. In reality a tern, the booby is so named because it is an incredibly dumb bird. Dumb though the booby may be, if Soleil were a nation, the booby would be the national bird.

In addition to being the booby breeding ground for hundreds of years, this tiny cay was for a few hundred years the home to a good many pirates, the most noted of which was Crimson Jack, scourge of the seven seas for most of the late eighteenth century. Crimson Jack had the cunning of a Corsican, the nerve of a Moor and the heart of a Barbary corsair. In short, he was a tough customer (possibly not as nefarious as the infamous Bad Basil Ringrose but a ne'er-do-well just the same). He plundered and pillaged with impunity, remaining safe between forays atop the rocky fortress that eventually took the name Pirate's Perch.

Only a few hundred people populate tiny Soleil. Coming from different cultures and backgrounds they are a heterogeneous group – warm and friendly, with the possible exception of one crotchety old frog – who, despite being a Frenchman, is a good man in his own way and generous with his rum.

"Terrence Bonney," said the stranger from within his blanket cocoon. He had, thanks to a second drink graciously provided by Basil Ringrose consisting primarily of Albert Lafitte's liquor, taken a few steps back from death's door.

"My bonnie floats over the ocean," mused Basil as he sipped. "My bonnie floats over the sea."

"But please call me Terry," he continued, learning as everyone eventually must that Basil was generally best ignored. "I certainly appreciate your hauling me in. I'd pretty much thought I'd had it."

"It was nothing," said Albert magnanimously, then with a sweeping gesture added: "Welcome to friendly Booby Bay. I, sir, am Albert Lafitte, proprietor of the Booby Baby Cafe, renowned throughout the West Indies." Having delivered his commercial message, Albert sat back and twisted a curly lock of the gray hair that bushed around his ears then grew quickly sparser until disappearing entirely at the top of his crown. His little satisfied smile did not erase the symmetrical furrows that years of scowling had etched across his forehead.

"*Albare*," said Terry, struggling with the pronunciation.

"A - L - B- E - R - T, *Albare*."

"French," said Terry.

"The man is a genius," said Albert. "He floats, he speaks, he reasons." His eyes narrowed momentarily. "Our wallet did float in with us, did it not?"

Terry laughed. "Yes. It's contents are wet but negotiable. And there's plenty of plastic, of course. Non-biodegradable Visa, American Express. . . ."

"Did you see a sign on the beach as you floated in that said American Express welcome here? Albert and American Express parted ways years ago. Cash is always welcome, however. Any currency is fine – francs, dollars, pounds – no euros however. The exchange rates are quite reasonable."

"And his prices are fair," said Basil. "Albert is no pirate."

"Glad to hear it," said Terry. "Any chance of buying something to eat? I'm incredibly hungry."

As if waiting for her cue, Peaches returned to the pavilion, carefully carrying a steaming bowl with both hands. "I brought you something to eat, " she said, handing him the bowl. "It will fill you up and warm you up too, poor boy. It's bouillabaisse."

They watched in silence as Terry gulped down the soup. "It's very good," he said, finishing up his bowl. "How much do I owe you? I don't want to fall behind."

"It's on the house," said Albert. "This bowl is medicinal. When you're healthy, you pay."

"Thank you."

"Well, now that you've eaten," said Basil, "you seem to have your wits about you." Basil had been sitting quietly but fidgeting impatiently while Terry ate; it was now time to get on with more important matters. "Now you can tell us your tale. What did the scalawags do to you? Don't leave out any of the loathsome details, no matter how horrific. We can take it, says I. Were you an innocent victim or did you have it coming to you?"

"There weren't any scalawags," said Terry. "It was nothing like that. It was just an accident, a stupid boating accident." Basil sighed and took a drink.

"I was out alone in a speedboat, lost control of it and got thrown overboard. The damn thing just kept going and there I

15

was, in the water, looking forward to a certain death by drowning. Fortunately, I spotted that hunk of wood, swam to it and adopted it as my own. And it appears to have been a wise choice. That clever hunk of flotsam found its way here."

"What were you doing out there in the rain?" asked Albert, his voice pregnant with reproach. "That's foolish."

"Of course it was," said Terry. "But it was starting to clear a bit and after all the rain I was ready to jump at any opportunity."

"Damned unusual," said Basil, standing. "I can understand the feeling." He headed once again for the bar.

"I know I just arrived," said Terry, "but I'm wondering how I'm eventually going to get back to one of the larger islands. Do you have any suggestions?"

"If it ever stops raining – and I begin to have grave doubts – there will be visitors," Albert said. "I'm sure you'll be able to work out arrangements with someone. If not, I'll be going to L'Orient next week. From there you can continue on to wherever you wish to go. If you're very anxious, you can hire one of the Dutch jackals or one of the Swedes to take you. I wouldn't recommend it. The Dutch are profiteers who will exploit you without mercy, and I wouldn't set foot in a boat with any one of the crazy Swedes." Soleil was not exactly a melting

16

pot. A small Dutch community encircled the harbor area, and a Swedish clan commanded the other end of the island. Booby Bay was under French influence (Albert Lafitte, in particular). The three ethnic groups rarely associated and agreed on next to nothing – other than the unanimous opinion that their mother countries should have no part of a shared currency.

"So for the time being, I guess I should just relax," said Terry.

"And spend money," Albert added.

Basil returned, followed by Mutton who had disappeared during the fuss over the new arrival. The former bore a large drink and the latter bore news. Basil settled into a chair, and Mutton spoke: "I saw a patch of blue sky."

Having delivered his important message, Mutton took up a cross-legged position on a dry patch of pavilion and waited for the murmurs of approval and the sunshine. Since no one really believed Mutton, no murmurs were forthcoming. Mutton was vindicated within five minutes, however, as the clouds overhead slowly thinned, and the sky began to tease the observers with tiny patches of precious blue.

"At last," said Terry.

"Don't count on it," said Albert. "It won't last."

They sat in silent anticipation as the patches of blue

became larger and the elusive sun finally began to actually shine, making the wet sand glisten.

"I give it ten minutes," said Albert.

"I'll take it," said Terry, removing his blanket. "Even ten minutes of it." He started suddenly and sat upright as a figure came from behind, passed by him and strolled down the beach away from the pavilion. She glided across the sand, long dark hair swaying across her light brown back. At her waist the light brown skin gave way to a short sarong with vivid splashes of orange and yellow before reappearing and stretching away from the bottom hem in the form of perfect legs, complete with perfect feet and presumably perfect toes.

"What – who was that?" Terry gasped, staring after her as she continued along the beach.

"Remy," said Albert.

"My God, " said Terry. "Is she as attractive coming as she is going?"

"Yes," said Albert simply. He was calm and unemotional in stark comparison to Terry who had begun to shiver once again, his drink sloshing wildly in his glass.

"A lass to tear your very heart from its socket," said Basil, his worried eyes watching the dancing liquor.

"She's very pretty," said Mutton.

"Pardon me for asking but . . . uh . . .is . . . does she always dress that way?"

"Only when the sun is shining," said Albert, "which has only been for two minutes in recent memory." He watched Terry for a moment, then added: "Don't get any strange notions. We all feel pretty strongly about Remy." Pretty strongly was a pretty weak description of the attitudes they had toward Remy. She was probably the primary reason Mutton had taken up permanent residence on the island, and he was the picture of unabashed if incoherent adoration. He had given expression to his feelings only once; she had let him down lightly with a kiss but he had been a prisoner of love ever since. Even Bad Basil Ringrose had a soft spot in his hard buccaneer's heart for the fair Remy, although he only made it public in the most obscure ways. Albert's feelings toward Remy took on a more fatherly nature but they were every bit as strong.

"Please no, I wouldn't," said Terry. "I was just taken back a bit by the surprise and, hell, she looked great and there's nothing wrong with saying so."

"Of course not," said Albert, seemingly satisfied with the explanation.

"Just bear't in mind, matey. The young gal is under the fearsome protection of Bad Basil Ringrose."

"I certainly will," said Terry, looking curiously at Basil, having never before witnessed the metamorphosis from man to scourge of the high seas. The group fell silent once again and each in his own way basked in the warmth of the sunshine, which, as Albert had predicted, turned out to be fleeting. Albert's ten-minute projection fell short, but only by a matter of minutes; fifteen minutes later, clouds once again began to thicken, crowding pieces of blue into tinier and tinier allotments of sky. And once again the rains came.

The resumption of wet weather actually raised Terry's spirits at first for he assumed that the heavy rain would drive the beguiling Remy back toward whatever shelter she had earlier departed, requiring a second pass by the pavilion. After ten minutes of downpour, however, he realized that it was not to be, that she had selfishly selected another route. The steady rain also forced him to return to reality and the nagging question of where he would lay his head that evening. He hoped that he would not be relegated to spending the night in the chair or, worse yet, with the dog, an ill-tempered Basset Hound who now lay on the blanket next to him and stared up without compassion, daring him to retrieve it.

Albert, never noted for his intuition and certainly not for empathy, nevertheless showed that his mind was traveling the same route as Terry's by saying: "Well, it looks as though you'll be spending the night."

"It looks that way," said Terry. "Under the stars, I guess. Although I doubt there will be any."

"I have a room," said Albert.

"That's very generous of you."

"To rent."

"Of course," said Terry. "*Merci.*"

Albert grinned. "Reasonable, monsieur. *Tres raisonable.*"

"The shadows be getting long now," said Basil, his voice noticeably more gravelly. "Time to take a bite to eat. A simple meal of meat and potatoes and rum is all this seafaring man will be aneeding, sure enough." He stood and staggered away.

"I wonder what Peaches will be cooking," Albert mused.

Albert was a man of many habits; he adhered with obsessive regularity to his many personal rituals, one of which he now – dinner successfully completed – undertook with great solemnity: his after dinner cigar and cognac. Albert puffed and sipped but rarely spoke throughout the ritual. It was a time of reflection, and his reflections were rarely shared with his dinner companions until they had been nurtured into a body of philosophy, at which point he was prepared to pontificate freely.

Terry, having accepted Albert's generous offer of cigar and cognac, puffed and sipped along with Albert, aping the silence if not the reflective state of his host. Peaches, on the other hand, bustled. She moved here and there erasing all traces of the recently completed meal, which was, as far as Terry was concerned, the best he had ever eaten. Either Peaches was a world-class chef or his appetite had been honed to its most appreciative by the day's adventures. Once her bustling was completed, Peaches joined the smokers although substituting for the cigar a short oval English cigarette and for the cognac a bottle of ale.

They sat at one of the six tables that ringed the bar of the Booby Bay Cafe. Dining was alfresco; three sides of the building were completely open. Only behind the bar stood a wall shared with Albert's living quarters and Terry's newly acquired rental unit. Outside, clusters of red bougainvillea and violet water hyacinths, cascades of yellow cassia, and a rainbow of hibiscus ringed the cafe, a tapestry bursting from a lush green background. Birds called, crickets chirped. Terry's imagination could easily supply the only missing elements: beautiful women in splashy sarongs and handsome men in cool white, crowded around the small tables, making love with their eyes as they sipped tropical punches.

Terry's thoughts and Albert's reflections were brought to an abrupt end – they each still had two inches of cigar and a half-inch of cognac – by the return of Basil Ringrose. Basil was followed by his loyal puppy Mutton.

"Tis a fine evening, t'be sure," said Basil heading toward the bar. Mutton sat at the table and grinned.

"An excellent smoke, don't you agree?" said Albert as he extinguished his cigar.

"Yes, it is," said Terry.

"Cuban," said Albert, "Cuba is to a cigar what France is to wine. Look at the leaf; somebody who cared rolled these cigars. I guess you don't see any of these in your part of the world, Cubans and Americans getting along as they do. Fortunately, we French don't have that problem. We get along with everyone." Terry coughed on his cigar and Albert shot him a suspicious glance but evidently decided the cough was an innocent physical reaction by one unaccustomed to the best cigars.

"What do you do when you're not floating around the West Indies?" asked Albert.

"I write mostly."

"A writer, says he," Basil had returned from the bar and sat across the table from Terry. "I was a writer meself once upon. Never made any money at it, though. I was always a poor writer what never had a plot to piss on."

"Do you write poetry?" asked Peaches, lighting up.

"No, I'm afraid not," Terry answered. "I've read some. That's all."

"Maybe he doesn't have his poetic license yet," said Albert.

"No," said Terry, "but I'm working at it."

"Have you read tiger, tiger, burning bright?" asked Peaches.

"A long time ago. Written by Blake, I think."

"And a gentlemen he is," said Peaches. "A very astute poet." She looked at Albert and added: "English. People here don't understand him. It's nice to have a literary person to discuss such things with."

"Thank you," said Terry.

"Now tell me, why do you think the tiger is afraid of cemeteries?"

"Afraid of cemeteries," Terry repeated, unsure of the question. Then it struck him. "Oh, you mean 'fearful symmetry.'"

"Exactly," said Peaches smugly, having now been vindicated by an outside expert while those who doubted her knowledge of the poem looked helplessly on. "Why is he fearful of a cemetery?"

"Well," said Terry, "I'm afraid it's not. . . ."

"He's not really afraid of cemeteries," Albert mocked. "The poet (he almost spat the word in a tone usually reserved for creatures that slithered and enemies of France) just says that because it's metagorical. He probably means that he loves cemeteries. *Merde.*"

"Cemetery," said Basil, looking at them through red eyes. "There's many a fine seafarin' lad as lays in a watery cemetery today. Oh the vasty deep."

"I'm afraid of cemeteries," said Mutton.

"Good, Mutton," said Albert. "Are you afraid of tigers?"

"No, I'm afraid of the dead people."

"It has recently occurred to me," said Albert, having had his fill of poets, tigers and cemeteries and anxious to get on to more important matters, in particular those he had recently been reflecting upon, "that the Americans are a strange lot. For the most part, they're rude and churlish, yet on occasion they can be decent and mannered like our guest here. One might never guess he was an American except for that terrible accent."

"Thanks," said Terry, "I think."

"You think," said Albert, waving his finger in the air. "Therein lies the difference. Most Americans don't. They form the few thoughts and opinions they have based on inane television programs; they speak in sports cliches and fret when other folks are too happy." Albert paused and the others hoped his lecture had been completed. "What is your heritage, young man?" he continued.

"Mixed pretty much, I guess," said Terry. "Mostly Scandinavian, I believe."

"But no English, I would imagine. That, I would say, is the source of most of the American cultural deprivation – passed down through genetic wrongdoing by the English. The Germans, too, perhaps, but the English are most culpable."

Basil sat upright, waved an arm and growled: "Beware o' the black'eart with a scar upon 'is cheek. He be a cowardly, cruel backstabbin' dog. An' he be English. Cap'n Low, by name."

"Ned Low is dead, Basil," said Albert.

Basil cocked his head and looked confused. "He be dead? Now o' what did he die? Was he kilt or was it disease? I hope he died with the terror in 'is 'eart. A black'eart he was – one to stab you in the back before your very eyes. His own crew set 'im adrift, finally."

"And the French picked up the English scoundrel and hanged him," said Albert. "You'll note upon reading any history of piracy, including Basil's, the regularity with which English names appear: Kidd, Teach, Rackham, Reade."

"That be true," said Basil, "But there was plenty o' frog picaroons, too."

"Yes, there were French privateers," said Albert. The distinction between picaroon, privateer, and pirate was lost on Terry, but he guessed that a privateer was somehow classier. "Men such as Pierre Le Grand who captured a Spanish galleon with just a handful of men. And, of course, Jean Bart and Jean Lafitte." He gave particular emphasis to the last who bore his own family name. "Considered heroes by most."

"Ho, ho, ho, Albert," said Basil gleefully. "What about old Lollynoise?"

"L'Ollonois," corrected Albert. "His French ancestry is, I am sure, questionable."

"Oh, he be French all right and a real bad one. He sometimes cut out 'is captives 'earts and ate 'em." Basil began to laugh loudly, then added: "But 'e got 'is, all right."

"Have another drink, Basil," said Albert.

"Mighty kind, Albert, " said Basil, heading off to the bar

27

without further comment or thought about L'Ollonois, Ned Low or the others.

"I don't understand," said Terry.

"L'Ollonois was one of the infamous Tortugans. He was as cruel and bloodthirsty as they come. And what Basil said is true: He came to a rather ironic end when he was captured and eaten by the Carib Indians."

"I see," said Terry. "I knew Basil was an aficionado, but you seem to know a thing or two about pirates yourself."

"Albert knows a thing or two about almost everything. Now, as I was saying. . ." Once again Albert was interrupted, this time by a voice from about twenty feet away.

"Hello, everyone." The speaker was at Terry's back but after two words he was absolutely certain it was the earlier vision from the beach even though he had never heard Remy speak.

"Hello, dear," said Peaches. "Did you have a good time?" Albert harrumphed, unaccustomed to being interrupted twice during one speech. Remy walked over to the table. She smiled at Terry and he was instantly an awkward teenager again, not sure whether to speak or bolt from the table. But neither was possible; he had lost all motor ability. She was even lovelier coming than going: Her dark hair billowed about a radiant face

28

with large eyes and a smile that crippled. Once again she wore a sarong-like wrap although this one revealed only bare shoulders and bare legs.

"You haven't met our stranger," said Peaches.

"Howdy, stranger," said Remy.

"Howd..., I mean hello. I'm Terry."

"I'm Remy. Happy to meet you. It looks like you're deep in intense debate with the ornery Frenchman."

"Hmmph," said Albert.

"Well, I'd like to stay and talk," she said, turning away. "But I can't. Maybe I'll see you tomorrow."

"Maybe," said Terry and he watched her leave as quickly as she had entered. Will our encounters always be so brief, he thought, as Albert began to resume his discourse on the shortcomings of the English.

Chapter 2

Terry held the fair Remy tightly in his arms. She was soft and warm, and her softness and warmth reinforced his own strength and masculinity. After a long embrace, he released her and she slowly backed away from him. He looked at her and discovered that she wore a black patch over one eye and held a long, steely sword in one hand, a sword with which, under the tutelage of Bad Basil Ringrose, she was about to cut his heart out. As she thrust, he parried – onto the floor next to the small cot where he awakened into the reality of his tiny room and the sounds of Albert's restless sleep in the next room. He got up, and peering outside, found to his surprise that it was morning and the world was no longer gray and wet.

Terry quickly dressed, abandoned his sleeping landlord, and headed toward the beach where after a brisk walk and a quick, refreshing dip in the morning sea, he sat cross-legged at the edge of the water and mindlessly tossed pebbles out to sea. He also indulged in the Albertian tradition of reflection. Booby Bay had become a paradise now that the sun had resumed its dominion over the sky and now that Terry knew of the lovely creature who helped inhabit the island.

O brave new world that has such people in it, he mused. Had Peaches cast this poetic influence over him on behalf of her daughter or had he grown lyrical all by himself? The word goddess drifted into his mind, but although apt in a way it was somehow too much like cold, polished marble for the earthly Remy. Yes, she was pretty – beautiful – but she was no goddess. Terry took pride in that assessment. It showed him to be objective, not given to giddy excess.

Visitors would be coming now that the rain had stopped, he realized, and he would have no excuse for lingering here in Eden. Eden? With Eve? "And I suppose you're Adam?" he said aloud. "You consider yourself a writer when you can't even think yourself beyond cliches. At least, thank God, you don't have a pen or pencil or any other way of committing this blather to permanent status."

"Are you talking to yourself?" said a voice from behind him. The speaker was a handsome young man who had the same light brown skin color as Remy and the same predilection for wearing next to nothing on the beach.

"No, I'm fishing," said Terry absentmindedly.

"By throwing rocks?"

"I think it's very sportsmanlike," said Terry. "Sort of equals the odds."

"No, it doesn't. The fish can't throw rocks at you."

"I suppose you're right. I guess the only really fair thing would be for me to go swimming and try to catch them in my mouth. By the way, I'm Terry."

"I know. I'm Christian. I've heard about you."

"Good things, I hope."

"Good things," said Christian, laughing.

"From whom? Your sister maybe?"

"My sister?" Christian looked bewildered, but only for a moment. "Oh. You mean Remy. She's not really my sister."

"She isn't?" Now the bewilderment was all Terry's and he had every right to it. People talked as though they were siblings. They looked like brother and sister. They both lived with Peaches and called her mother, though in fact she was only natural mother to Remy. Christian was actually the son of a cousin to Peaches who had died when Christian was an infant. Peaches had naturally taken the child and raised him as her own, as Remy's brother.

The nature of this relationship was no secret on the island, although for many years Christian remained completely unaware of it. No one had thought to tell him the truth of his parentage during his childhood and he was sixteen before he learned it. When he did, Christian reacted rather unexpectedly to the news. He reacted with neither anger nor sorrow upon learning that Remy was not his sister; rather, a wild passion crept into his eyes, a passion that had been submerged in deference to their relationship since he had first been capable of such passion. He immediately chased Remy for a mile down the beach and finally wrestled her to the sand, pawing wildly. Remy, upon realizing that Christian's passion was not sibling playfulness and that he was quite determined to have his way with her, had no choice but to deck him. Thereafter, his bestial behavior remained in check, but his passion never abated.

To Terry, this young man with his harmless good looks had suddenly become a possible suitor to Remy, and he eyed Christian warily, quickly tallying pros and cons about his features and his manner.

"But, yes, she did speak of you," said Christian, interrupting Terry's appraisal.

"Did she speak well of me?" Terry asked casually, feigning, he hoped, indifference.

33

"Not really," Christian answered.

Terry's heart froze. More cautiously, he asked: "You mean she spoke ill of me?"

"No." Christian grinned. "I just asked her if she met you and she said she did. I asked what your name was and she couldn't remember. I asked what you were like and she said you were all right she guessed. Mother, however, thinks you're a very astute gentleman. Basil says with a little training you might have the right stuff. I don't think Mutton actually realizes you're here. And Albert says you're not bad for an American. That's quite a compliment, by the way."

"All right, she guessed," Terry mumbled under his breath. Obviously he had made a fantastic impression on the young lady; she couldn't even remember his name. The vivid picture of Remy that had permeated and controlled his mind began to fade as this insensitive young man who stood before him shattered his spirits as idly as he might shatter a conch shell with a careless foot. Of course, Christian had no way of knowing this, and the little bit of logic that Terry had left told him that the young man's intentions were benign.

"All in all," Christian continued, "I guess you've been accepted. That's not particularly easy, especially with Albert. Do you plan to stay long?"

"Probably not, " said Terry. Was there any longer any reason to stay? "Of course it all depends on hitching a ride with someone."

"I imagine you find it a little quiet here."

"After yesterday's ordeal, a little quiet doesn't bother me at all. It's really peaceful here."

"It's boring as Hell," said Christian. "Your arrival is the most exciting thing that's happened all month. It doesn't seem to bother the others. They're all boring, too. Except Remy."

Terry's eyes turned green and narrowed as he stared at this young man who wasn't Remy's brother, and he wondered just why she too wasn't boring to him. "What do you and Remy do for excitement?" he asked, speaking as calmly as he could.

"Swim, visit people, other things." Did Terry detect a taunting glint in this callous young rogue's eyes that gave hidden meaning to "other things?"

"Well, maybe you can help liven the place up while you're here." Christian continued casually. "I've got to move on now. I'll probably see you later." He strolled off down the beach.

Terry uncrossed his legs, lay back with his hands behind his head, and closed his eyes. Had some mystical influence of this island or his ordeal at sea sparked such passions in him? In the past 24 hours, he had experienced feelings he hadn't had for years, feelings that ranged from lust to jealousy and several that he couldn't even name. Lying there, he reviewed the events from his arrival to the present, eyes closed, counting passions as one might count sheep and, under the soothing heat of the sun, promptly fell asleep.

"You're going to float out to sea again if you're not careful."

Terry awoke with a start to find himself lying in two inches of water that swirled around him and lapped at his ears as each wave pushed up the beach. His back was completely soaked, but the water was warm and not uncomfortable. The speaker stood above, only a shadow against the bright backdrop of the sunny sky and the dazzling reflection from the water. He strained without success to bring the figure more clearly into focus.

"Most people prefer boats. They don't get nearly as wet that way." As she spoke again, he recognized the voice that had haunted him for the last twelve hours but still couldn't see the physical incarnation that had haunted him for even longer. "Not that I'm criticizing."

"I must have fallen asleep," said Terry, praying for the return of his sight. "I guess I'm lucky you came along when you did; I had my fill of floating yesterday." Slowly, very slowly, vision began to return, and the silhouette became a being with dimension and discernible features. As it did, it sent chills throughout his wet torso. Long, dark hair highlighted by reflected sunshine, dark wide eyes and full lips appeared. She wore a tiny monokini and a simple bracelet around one ankle; all else was smooth, light brown skin. She smiled down at him and he was humbled.

"Chances are, I saved your life," she said, kneeling on the sand near him. He stared at the water swirling around her knees and toes, afraid to stare elsewhere, afraid even to make eye contact lest the gods punish him severely for his trespass.

"Does that mean that from now on I'm responsible for you or that you're responsible for me?" Remy asked.

It doesn't matter, he thought, *as long as it requires me to spend the rest of my life right here on the beach with you.* He said: "I think historically the saver becomes responsible for the savee except in the Old West when they hate each other. Then the savee owes the saver one and can't kill him or her until he or she saves his or her life in return." *God, am I really saying this?*

"I'm glad you cleared that up," said Remy laughing. "Are

37

you enjoying your stay here?"

I have gone to my reward and lack only a harp to make death perfect, Terry thought but said: "Yes, I am. Everyone's been very nice."

"Mother says you're a literary giant."

"She's very kind. Actually I'm only six-foot-one – in height, that is. Literarily, I'm closer to four-foot-two."

"What is it you write, shorty?"

"I'm writing a novel, of course. But I've been working writing news features, human interest stuff," said Terry, looking up from the beach for the first time since they had begun talking. He gulped only twice as his eyes hastily devoured all they could before looking directly into hers. "You know, cute pets, cute kids, cute serial killers, cute aliens."

Remy laughed. "Illegal or extra-terrestrial?"

"Either. Both."

"Do you make it all up?"

"Of course not. Completely factual – although there is a lot of creative interpretation."

"Elvis sightings as well?"

"Of course, frequently," said Terry, relaxing and unconsciously easing his strict eye-to-eye stare so his eyes might wander at will.

"I thought so. I know how crazy Americans all are."

"Sounds like you've been listening to Albert."

"No. He finds Americans completely useless. I just think they're crazy."

"Thank you."

"I didn't mean it as an insult. After all, I'm responsible for you now. By the way, do my responsibilities include just keeping you alive or am I responsible for your proper upbringing?"

"Both, I'd say," said Terry laughing. "Have you ever been to the U.S.? His eyes had inadvertently settled their gaze upon the hypnotic rise and fall of Remy's breasts.

"I went to college in Virginia," Remy answered.

"Virginia," Terry repeated, mechanically.

"Richmond. May I ask how long you're going to stare at my breasts?"

Guilty as charged, Terry turned crimson, averted his eyes, and stammered "I'm . . .I'm sorry. . . I . . ."

"It's all right," said Remy. "I was just wondering how long it will take to get it out of your system."

I will continue to stare at you until the day they place small change on my cold, dead eyes, Terry thought but remained silent.

"How much have you seen since you've been here?" Remy asked.

"I...uh..."

"Of the island, I mean," she said, laughing at his discomfort. "You really ought to explore the island. I'm sure you'd love it." She stood. "You can come along with me if you'd like."

"Sure," said Terry. "Where are you going?"

"To the harbor. It's only a half mile – a pleasant walk."

"Lead the way." *To the harbor, into shark-infested waters, into the fires of Hell. Whither thou goest. . .*

They walked along the edge of the beach where the water massaged their feet and erased each footprint behind them. A steady breeze rolled in with the waves and caressed them as they walked, mitigating the heat of the sun, which for the first time in a week was under no threat from any cloud.

"Are you on vacation?" Remy asked.

"Not really. I should have been more precise and said I used to write human interest for a newspaper. One day, several of us were informed that the newspaper would be strictly online and that our services, while appreciated, would no longer be required. So we did the obvious; we all booked a Caribbean vacation. The others went back a few days ago, but I decided to take some extra time to relax and maybe write something of a little more substance."

"Really? What have you written?"

"Nothing," Terry confessed. "I wrote the first day or two. I started on an adventure that quickly became a mystery and then science fiction. Suddenly it had no identity so I stopped."

"That's terrible. Where's your discipline? You should write for two hours every day before you do anything else."

"I know I should," said Terry. "But now I can't. I didn't bring a pencil with me."

"That's a pretty lame excuse," said Remy, suddenly kneeling down and writing in the wet sand with her fingertip: *once upon a time* . . . "You can write anywhere with anything if you're committed. Go ahead. Write something. Show me what you've got."

Terry knelt down and thought for a moment.

"Well?" Remy demanded. "I'm beginning to think you're a fraud, that you can't write at all."

We came from two different worlds, Terry wrote, *hers being Jupiter.*

"Keep going."

And when she gazed at me with those twelve baby blues, I was jelly.

Remy laughed and stood. "I think you're off to a great start. And this beach stretches on for a full mile. You could probably do an entire short story right here."

"But the tide would just wash it away."

"Only the stale ideas and excess verbiage. I think you're making excuses again." She started down the beach and Terry, jumping to his feet, fell into place behind her. He was perfectly happy in his subordinated position, walking behind her and watching the relaxed sway of her body as she lilted across the white sand.

"I hope you're not back there staring again." She turned around suddenly, catching him in the act.

"Of course not," he said looking down at the beach. "I'm very carefully watching where I step."

"That's very smart," she said, now walking backwards, her breasts swaying provocatively, taunting him. "This beach is crawling with vicious crabs that love to grab your ankles." She turned forward and Terry was just slipping comfortably back into his routine when she announced that the harbor was just ahead. Terry looked up the beach and saw several small, crude buildings and a bit of activity – bustling in comparison to the beach that had been theirs alone. As they approached, a young boy with two friends in hot pursuit raced between them and

42

around them, then once again tore off in the direction from which they had come. They were the first inhabitants Terry had seen other than the close-knit clientele of the Booby Bay Cafe.

Albert Lafitte's galleasse stood unmistakably ahead of them in the water, commanding the full length of a 70-foot pier that jutted into the harbor. Even in its unfinished state, the galleasse had a majesty that turned the otherwise ramshackle setting into a picture postcard view. Its three masts shot twenty feet upward, long, skinny fingers piercing the cloudless blue sky. It had no sails as yet and, as they started along the pier, Terry noticed the lack of other finishing touches, a testimony to the fact that it was still under construction.

The rough board that served as a temporary gangplank wobbled and groaned underfoot as Terry followed Remy across the four-foot span between the pier and the deck. The unpainted wood around them smelled new, the upper ends of the curved ribs that formed the skeletal framework of the hull were still exposed, and a large portion of the main deck gave way to a yawning hole, but the galleasse was afloat – the point of viability for a boat, Terry guessed – and well on its way to completion. Albert was fussing over a long strip of polished oak at the far side of the deck and did not look up as they greeted him.

"Prepare to be boarded," said Remy as she bounced

43

across the deck, perilously near the edge of the opening to the dark bowels of the craft.

"You've got quite a boat here," said Terry.

"The galleasse is a sailing ship," said Albert.

"A French sailing ship, no doubt," said Terry.

"Actually, no." Albert stood and turned toward them, looking just briefly at Remy with the look a parent might give to a child who came to dinner barefoot. "It was originally developed by the Venetians. The French naturally did a great deal to perfect it over the years. The Venetian galleasse relied primarily on oarsmen, using sails only secondarily. The later galleasse was longer and narrower, a true sailing ship capable of sustained voyage."

"How many people will it carry?"

"My model will sleep twelve comfortably," said Albert.

"Have any voyages planned yet?" asked Terry.

"Nothing specific," said Albert. "Guadeloupe, Martinique perhaps."

"Come on, Albert," teased Remy. "You know you want to sail across the Atlantic, thumb your nose at the British as you pass through the Straits of Gibraltar, and sashay triumphantly into port at Marseilles."

Having no rejoinder, Albert harrumphed. Terry

suspected that Albert, whether he had considered it or not, knew Remy was absolutely correct, would love nothing more.

"And if I do want to sail her to France," Albert said finally, "I will sail her to France. Or to China. Or around the world. This is a sailing ship. Her lines are clean; her hull is fair. *Elle est merveilleuse.*"

"That she is, skipper," said Remy. "Are you going to name her after me?"

"But of course."

Remy hugged him. "You're such a sweetheart for an ill-tempered old Frenchman. How about a carving of me up front?"

"On the bow," Albert corrected. "I haven't decided on the figurehead. First I must finish the decks and the planking."

"Sure. I'll bet you end up with a mermaid with a gigantic bosom. You men are all alike."

Terry feigned a look of insult at having been lumped into her stereotype. "Not me. I think a man would make a much better figurehead."

"I'd sail on your ship," said Remy. "As long as the wooden dude was anatomically correct."

"With me on board?" asked Terry. "Why would you need a wooden dude?"

"Well, with a wooden guy," Remy said playfully, "if it's up, it stays up forever."

Albert clucked disapprovingly.

"Okay," said Remy, "we'll head back now. Leave you alone to paint my name on the back."

"Stern," said Albert. "Actually, I'm going back to the cafe now myself. Would you like a ride?"

"Not me," said Remy. "I'll take the beach."

"I guess I'll walk back too," said Terry. Albert looked at him suspiciously.

Remy led the way back across the narrow gangplank with Terry and Albert close on her heels. Albert headed for a banged-up red minimoke parked near the end of the pier, and Remy and Terry stood watching as he boarded and pulled away, the jeep-like vehicle jerking repeatedly under his less than sure control. What Albert lacked in driving finesse, however, he more than made up for in recklessness as he honked and swerved, kicking up clouds of dust, until out of view.

"He's quite a piece of work," said Terry, as they turned away and started back down the beach.

"The king of his world," said Remy.

"Sure of himself. A little cocky, maybe."

"A little cocky?" Remy laughed.

"Do you really think he'll sail to France?"

"I don't know," said Remy. "Maybe after he gets tired of strutting through the West Indies."

They walked silently for a short time until Terry pointed at a small gray-green mass jutting awkwardly up from the horizon and asked: "What island is that?"

"That's Pointe Francoise," Remy answered. "It was once quite a place. It's main town, Bluebeard's Reef, was a funky, exciting little seaport. Ships coming and going. A lively open-air market. After the hurricane hit, it pretty much died out. People just gave up finally and took off for greener pastures. Too bad; it's a pretty place. About all that's left now is the old harbor area, and that's practically all prostitutes and sailors who haven't got anything left to sail. It's got a reputation of being involved with anything you can think of that's unsavory. Basil visits once in a while to soak up the atmosphere."

"I imagine he soaks up a lot more than the atmosphere," said Terry. "How did he come to be here?"

"I was fairly young when he arrived so I don't know all the details. I understand he was somewhat of a writer. Like yourself."

"Thank you."

"He published several books about pirates. I guess he

was always a bit eccentric – really got into the whole pirate thing. He had spent several years kicking around the islands before he got here. I guess he just liked it and stayed. Over the years, the rum pretty much clouded his brain and he became one of the characters he wrote about."

Remy looked out to sea again and Terry, seeing her concentrate on something out there, did the same. He finally spotted the speck on the water's surface and watched it as it grew steadily larger. At first he thought it might be a shark, but then he gradually realized it was a boat. "Someone's coming," said Remy.

"A boat," said Terry. He hadn't thought one would come so soon. They continued to walk as they watched the boat's inevitable approach, even though Terry convinced himself for a moment that it really wasn't getting closer, that maybe it was just passing by. Reluctantly, however, he had to accept the fact that the boat's destination was Booby Bay, and perhaps the cafe itself, and that it was very possibly his ticket out of here.

"I'm heading up this way," said Remy. "I'll see you in a little while." As she crossed the beach and disappeared into the heavy foliage, Terry trudged the remaining distance to the pavilion. Albert had already arrived and was watching the approaching craft with interest.

"It looks as though you may have an opportunity to get on with your travels," said Albert as Terry joined him.

"Looks that way," said Terry without enthusiasm, listening to the hum of the boat's outboard motor, as it steered its way to the end of the rickety pier. The engine whimpered into silence, and two men busily tied the boat at both the front and rear then hopped onto the pier. They were young and husky and wore almost identical flowered shirts and long white pants. A third man stepped onto the pier after them – a short man, improbably attired in a gray overcoat despite the glaring sun and 85-degree temperature. The man in the overcoat took the lead with the other two falling in behind him in positions of inferiority as they strode the length of the pier and up the beach to the pavilion.

"Good afternoon," said the man in the overcoat. "Sammy Apollo's the name. Lovely day, what?"

"Hello," said Albert. "Welcome to the Booby Bay Cafe. Lafitte. Albert Lafitte, proprietor." He carefully emphasized the French pronunciation.

"Terry Bonney," Terry added, extending his hand. Sammy Apollo shook it weakly. His two companions did not introduce themselves, and Sammy Apollo, obviously in charge, did not introduce them either; nor did he acknowledge their

49

presence.

"Terry." He nodded and turned to Albert. "Al." Albert winced. "I hope your establishment is open and ready to serve a little refreshment to a weary traveler, what?"

"But of course," said Albert. "Step to the bar and become refreshed." They all followed Albert the short distance from the pavilion to the Booby Bay Cafe, where Albert took up an authoritative position behind the bar, and Sammy Apollo sat on a stool facing him.

"Please," said Apollo, motioning to Terry to sit with him. "The drinks are on me." Apollo's two companions did not join them; they remained standing at the cafe's perimeter.

"What will you have, Terry?" said Apollo.

"A Bloody Mary perhaps?" He looked inquiringly at Albert, unsure whether his request was a possibility at the Booby Bay Cafe. Albert showed no concern.

"Good," said Apollo. "And I'll have a Sombrero, Al." Apollo was still looking toward Terry so he didn't see Albert's patronizing look as he quickly and efficiently began to mix the drinks.

"And you too, Al," said Apollo. "I'm buying." Albert placed the two drinks on the bar then poured himself a small glass of red wine.

"What would your friends like?" Albert asked.

"They're not thirsty," said Apollo lifting his glass. "Here's to sunshine and turquoise waters." He sipped. "Ah, great drink, Al. This is really a lovely spot, what? I'm surprised you ain't three deep at the bar."

"Booby Bay is a little out of the way for most people," said Albert. "And we have no duty-free shopping or toney casinos."

"Yeah, I see your point, Al. Tourists can't seem to do without such things, can they. Or air conditioning."

"Are you wearing something under that coat?" Albert asked.

Apollo laughed. It was a gravelly, forced laugh. "I sure am. I ain't no flasher."

"Expecting rain?"

"You never know," said Apollo, who evidently didn't consider his attire unusual. "So I guess as the proprietor of this establishment, you're a citizen of this lovely isle, what?"

"Such as citizenship is," Albert answered.

"And how about you, Terr?"

"No, I guess I'm just a tourist – one who can live without duty-free shopping."

"Where you from? The U. S.?"

"Yes," Terry answered. "New York."

"Well, I'll be damned, Terr. I was a New Yorker for a long time. Born in Brooklyn. Could have fooled you though, I'll bet. Not a trace of Brooklynese left, what?" Actually, it had been obvious to Terry almost from Apollo's first words.

"Where do you live now?" asked Terry.

"I kind of float around these here lovely islands," Apollo answered. "San Juan – that's Puerto Rico – is more or less my home turf."

"Don't you miss the Big Apple?"

"Guess not," said Apollo, trembling a bit. "Too cold for me. How many people are there on this island, Al?"

"Two hundred, probably," said Albert. "They're mostly clustered at either end."

"That's great. Nice spacious place. No crowds. I like that."

"And what brings you by?" asked Albert. "On your way somewhere?"

"Actually, Al," Apollo started but then stopped short as Remy joined them. Now in a long flowered shirt, she looked fresh and radiant as though she had just stepped out of a shower.

"Hello there," said Apollo, leering out from under his thick eyelids.

52

"Hi," Remy answered, taking the stool next to Terry. "Into the booze already, I see. And Basil isn't even here."

"My fault," said Apollo. "Can I buy you a drink?"

"No thanks. I'll be the designated driver."

Apollo shrugged and turned back to Albert. "Well, Al . . ." Remy giggled, and Albert gave her his angriest look. "As I was saying, this here is a real nice quiet place. I've been looking for a spot to have our company's . . . uh . . . sales meetings. Nice and quiet, what? I think this may be the place, Al."

"The Booby Bay Cafe is certainly nice and quiet," said Albert. "And we're almost always open. You and your associates are always welcome. What is it your company sells?"

"Sells?" Apollo replied. "Oh yes, what we sell . . . which is . . . hardware. Kitchen hardware. Spoons, thermometers, egg timers . . . you know, hardware."

"The Booby Bay would be happy to host your meetings," said Albert. "We're always anxious to further the use of egg timers in this haphazard world."

"Well," said Apollo slowly, studying Albert as he spoke, "you see, what we'd like is maybe for you to be closed when we get together. Sort of a private sales meetings like. You know . . . the competition . . . eyes and ears everywhere."

"I see. Egg timer espionage."

"Now, we wouldn't expect you to . . .uh . . . turn away other customers without we make it worth your while. You know, like we rent the establishment for maybe a couple hours once a week. And then you leave us be so we can . . . uh . . . do our Dale Carnegie motivational stuff, what?"

"I don't know," said Albert, studying Apollo back.

"Now don't say no too fast, Al. I'm talking like, let's say two hundred bucks for just a couple hours – maybe, not even that long."

"I don't think so." Terry and Remy both watched the tug of war closely. Terry wondered what Albert was thinking, how he was analyzing Apollo's offer. Terry knew how he himself analyzed it – fishy, name your favorite species.

"Two hundred and fifty," said Apollo. "I'm talking each and every time we meet, Al."

"No, thank you."

"You're a hard bargainer, Al. I'm impressed. Now Mr. Keyes didn't authorize me to go any higher than that, but I think maybe I can convince him to go, say three hundred, what?"

"Who?" asked Albert, his eyes narrowing.

Apollo grew wary now, too. "Mr. Keyes. He's like the president of our company."

"Would that possibly be Murchison Keyes?" asked Albert.

Apollo's eyes said it all: he had blown it with the mention of the name. He merely stammered and mumbled an inaudible reply. With great ceremony, Albert poured his own remaining wine into the sink, snatched Terry's half-finished drink and poured it as well. Apollo's glass was empty and Albert let it be. "Murchison Keyes." His voice quivered with anger. "We don't drink with the likes of Murchison Keyes and his friends. Please leave now. You needn't pay; I don't accept money from Murchison Keyes either."

"C'mon Al, I don't understand the problem here," said Apollo, but he had lost his oily confidence.

"The problem is you and your kind," said Albert angrily. Apollo's companions had noticed the change in the tone of the conversation and now watched attentively, looking, Terry realized, very much like henchmen. "You're scum. I can't stop you from doing your dirty business but you'll not use my cafe as a convenient rest stop to exchange your egg timers, launder your dirty money and whatever other despicable activities your *hardware* company is involved in."

"Now see here," said Apollo.

"I know who Murchison Keyes is," said Albert. "I know

what he is. No matter how fancy he's become with his millions, he's still just a barbarian. And he's not welcome here."

"Listen, old man," Apollo said, his voice and color both rising.

"No, you take your two thugs and get out of here." Apollo stood, and as short as he was, he still held a slight height advantage over Albert. Terry started to intervene as it looked as though Apollo were about to punch the defiant little man in the face, but then Apollo stepped back.

"Mr. Keyes will not be pleased," he said.

"*Je l'emmerde,*" Albert replied.

"What ?" said Apollo. "Don't jabber in some foreign language. Speak English damn it."

"*Va te faire foutre.*"

"What's he saying?" said Apollo, looking to the others for help.

"I believe he said to go fuck yourself," said Remy politely.

"*Parfaitemente,*" said Albert.

"I thought you were nice people," Apollo whined. He motioned to his two companions, and Albert, Remy and Terry watched in silence as the visitors marched away. A few minutes later, they heard the boat's motor start up and then grow steadily more distant.

"That was a bit foolish, talking to him like that," said Remy.

"It's nothing to worry about," said Albert. "Sammy Apollo and his type don't do anything spontaneously. He's on Murchison Keyes' leash and he won't bite unless Keyes tells him to. And Murchison Keyes doesn't care about one grumpy old Frenchman. He'll just find another island to push his drugs and whatever else he's into these days, a place where no one has heard of him yet or where they're willing to look the other way. We're too much bother."

"I hope you're right," said Remy.

Albert looked at her incredulously. "Of course, I'm right."

"Walking the plank," Basil intoned, "was a very ceremonial punishment. Meant to set an example t'others as much as t'im what was doin' the walkin'. Most of the time you just wouldn't bother with a plank; you'd just fling the rogue overboard."

Terry had listened patiently to Basil for nearly an hour as he lectured on the various forms of pirate punishment. During that time, Terry had finished his first drink of the day (other than the aborted Bloody Mary of their earlier encounter with Sammy Apollo) while Basil had polished off four rums, presumably not his first of the day since he had almost completely metamorphosed into Bad Basil Ringrose, the fearsome buccaneer.

Albert had kept himself busy behind the bar, skillfully steering clear of the pirate's monologue. Peaches fluttered here and there but seemed to be completely immersed in a culinary undertaking. Terry had not seen Mutton at all, Christian since morning, or Remy since they had parted shortly after the Sammy Apollo affair. Terry reluctantly admitted to himself that he missed her already. He was overjoyed that Sammy Apollo was a drug runner and therefore not a fit traveling companion, leaving him here with no arrangements for leaving at hand.

As Basil demonstrated in mime exactly how one goes about throwing a rogue overboard, Remy reappeared almost as if Basil's piracy lesson had finally put Terry to sleep and her ethereal entrance – an apparition in a silky, yellow halter top and white jeans –was a dream.

"Tie him to the yardarm, Basil," she said cheerfully as she joined them, leaning a hand on Terry's shoulder and forcing an involuntary shudder.

"Ma'am," said Basil, "you points the rascal out and I'll tie 'im to whatever you wish."

"Thanks, Basil," said Remy, then turning to Terry: "See my power. You better watch your step, buster."

"I certainly will," said Terry.

"I'm going over to Pirate's Perch to watch the sunset. I haven't seen one in over a week. Would you like to come along? It's really impressive."

Does a chicken have lips? "Sure, if it's really impressive."

Best sunset in the West Indies," said Remy. "Or double your money back."

"Great. How do we get there? Walk?"

"No," said Remy. "We have to cross a mountain to get there. We'll take the moke."

"Okay," said Terry, the picture of the moke bumping and grinding with Albert at the wheel looming in his mind. He hoped Remy was a better driver, but he really didn't care. He felt he could fly over if necessary.

"It's parked out behind those trees," said Remy. "I'll go get Christian and meet you there."

Terry's spirits immediately flagged as she casually walked away to invite another man to their rendezvous. He shuffled slowly out to the moke and stared at it dejectedly, realizing they'd probably make him sit in the back seat while they flirted shamelessly up front. He leaned against the dusty vehicle and felt incredibly sorry for himself as he waited for the two young lovers to come skipping into view – laughing, holding hands and exchanging conspiratory glances. *Life, a smoldering pit of sorrow.*

Instead, Remy appeared alone and climbed into the driver's seat of the moke. "Looks like it's just you and me, kid." she said. "I couldn't find Christian, so to hell with him."

Terry barely had time to climb in before Remy had started the engine and the moke had jerked forward into Albertesque motion. They rumbled ahead less than a hundred yards before the road, which was dirt and rock and not much wider than the moke itself, began to climb rapidly. It rose steadily until cresting at the top of one hill where it switched back 180 degrees in a tight hairpin curve, one that Remy negotiated much too cavalierly for Terry's liking, and started right up a longer, steeper hill. They clung to the side of the hill like an ant to a garden wall with not a guard rail or even a tree or shrub between them and the depths below. Terry couldn't help thinking that on an island this size it would be easier to go around mountains than over them. "What happens if someone is coming the other way?" he asked.

"One of us has to back up," Remy answered, and Terry shut his eyes. The incline had become precipitous, and Remy was forced to grind the transmission into its lowest gear, stalling momentarily and nearly stopping Terry's heart completely.

One more hairpin and a tormenting snail-like pull up one more incline, with Terry pushing his body forward in an effort to impart momentum to the moke and chanting to himself the line from one of his least favorite children's books, *I think I can, I think I can*, and they crested the hill to arrive at the highest point on the island. Terry expected them now to begin an equally harrowing descent, but instead they passed over a few gently rolling hills with the comfort of real land and trees on either side of them. Finally they drove into a clearing where the dirt road began to meander along the edge of huge rocky cliffs. The road was too close to the edge of the cliffs for Terry's liking, but the view out to sea was spectacular.

Remy suddenly hit the brakes, almost sending Terry through the windshield, and announced: "We're here. Just a short walk now." She set the parking brake and bounded out of the moke toward the edge of the cliff. As Terry climbed carefully out of the moke, he watched her suddenly jump over the edge and disappear. He ran to the spot from which she had disappeared and peered over the edge. She stood just five feet below him on a wide rocky ledge.

"Jack be nimble," she said and motioned him to jump. He jumped, stumbling just a bit as he landed and rekindling his fear of rolling over the edge like a suicidal potato bug. Remy led the way along the ledge to a point that jutted out, hanging almost magically over the water some 300 feet below. In the center of this terrace, the rocks had been formed into a perfect settee or love seat as though a piece of furniture had been carted up here eons ago and become encrusted into the landscape through millions of years of settling dust. Remy sat down and said: "Well, this is Pirate's Perch. Are you impressed?"

"Deeply moved," said Terry, sitting next to her.

"Actually, the whole area is Pirate's Perch. This is my special part of it. We got here just in time. The sun will set in ten minutes." It now hung above the horizon, a giant, angry red balloon, swollen to the point of bursting.

"Do you think those men will come back?" she asked suddenly.

"No, I don't think so. I guess I agree with Albert. Sure, if this Keyes is a drug kingpin, he's ruthless. But why buy unnecessary trouble when they have so many other alternatives."

"I hope you're right," said Remy, not thoroughly

convinced. "I'm glad you were there today. I worry about Albert sometimes. That French lip of his is bound to get him in trouble sometime."

"*Merde*," said Terry, in a poor impression of Albert. Remy laughed and held his arm tightly, then released it after a moment.

"There it goes," she said. The ball was now being gobbled up by the voracious sea but not without first defiantly spreading its color across the water's surface. Vibrant reds and oranges mixed with the now dark blue water in an incredible light show before the sea swallowed the sun entirely. As it disappeared, Terry, almost without realizing what he was doing, leaned over and kissed Remy. It wasn't a long kiss but it was long enough, and she didn't pull away – nor did she prolong it. After he pulled away, she said: "What did you do that for?"

"I don't know," said Terry. "Maybe the sunset made me do it. I'm sorry it upset you."

"It didn't upset me," said Remy. He leaned toward her again but she pulled back. "Why don't you stop while you're ahead. The next one might upset me."

He turned away, trying to hide his look of disappointment.

"Don't mope," she said cheerfully. "The sunset was

beautiful and you kissed me. The moment was right, and that's fine. But does it have to lead somewhere? We really just met this morning. You're still the floating stranger."

"I thought maybe you found more in me than that," said Terry, a bit sullenly.

"Maybe I did," said Remy. "Look, I've enjoyed spending time with you. I brought you to my special spot, didn't I. I didn't slap you around when you got frisky. Relax a bit. Adjust to our pace. You're still caught up in the rush of the real world. You want to kiss, fondle, make me, have kids, raise them and part friends after the kids are grown – and you want to get it all done by Tuesday."

"I resent that."

"Okay, Wednesday. Slow down. Let's get to know each other. Maybe something will happen, maybe it won't." She smiled at him. "If it does, it will be worth the wait."

"But I don't know how long I'll be here," Terry complained.

"See, that's the real test. If it doesn't fit conveniently into your tight schedule, we'll find out how important it is to you."

"Then there's a chance if I work at it?"

"There's a chance of anything if you work at it," said Remy.

"That sounds fair," said Terry, brightening a little. "But what are the odds? Ten to one, a hundred to one, a thousand to one?"

"My God, are you a writer or some kind of bookie. What if I said a thousand to one? Would you give up, lose interest?"

"Of course not."

"That's the proper attitude," she said, then having completed her lecture, did the last thing he would have expected. She put her arms around his neck, kissed him, then pulled back and grinned.

"How come you can do that and I can't?" said Terry.

"It's my island," Remy answered lightly, standing up. "We better go now before it gets too dark. The lights on the moke don't work that well, and I imagine you'll be nervous as hell."

Terry followed her as she retraced their earlier route. They scaled the five-foot wall and walked to the spot where their carriage awaited. Climbing in, Terry said: "You didn't answer my question, and I think you should answer it before we go, in case we don't make it."

"You're a persistent little devil, aren't you?"

"The odds."

"Exactly what do you want the odds of?" said Remy, starting the engine.

"A lasting friendship, a sordid affair, or marriage, kids and a ranch house. Take your pick."

"Okay. For marriage, kids and a ranch house, I'd say a million to one. Even money on making it to the bottom of the hill. And the other two are somewhere between." She backed the moke right to the edge of the cliff as she turned it around.

"If we plunge off the edge, I'm going to kiss you whether you like it or not," said Terry, looking straight ahead.

"Relax and pray," she said as they lurched forward. Then she geared down, the moke whined in response, and they descended through the near darkness.

History rarely records exactly when a watershed moment occurs in trifling human affairs, and it did not make note of the exact point at which the conversation at the Booby Bay Cafe evolved from a philosophical premise that the island might be better off without certain individuals to a concrete scheme of cold-blooded assassination. Aided and abetted by rum, the conspirators grew steadily more cognizant of the threat this stranger posed to the precarious balance of power in relation to

Remy's attention and affection. They agreed that the bottom line was that Remy could not be spread any thinner and that, even though the three of them were competitors for her heart, it was in their mutual interest to form a temporary coalition to address this new threat. The enemy of my enemy and all that.

"He's been here a day and a half and already she's spending all her time with him," whined Christian, his boyish voice blurred. "He's a rake."

Mutton looked at him in confusion.

"A rake," said Christian. "A philanderer."

"You mean he builds libraries?" asked Mutton.

"Whether he builds 'em or don't," said Basil, "when some black'eart tries to take 'imself another man's treasure, seafarin' men knows how to deal at 'im. Such a dishonorable scalawag ain't above bein' run through."

"Maybe seafaring men have the right idea," said Christian.

"Maybe seafaring men have the right idea," said Mutton.

"I've took such a fondness to that dear child, sure enough. It gives me the horrors t'see a rogue after her. What's say we put it up for discussion like that this devil be due his due."

Terry's defense was not bolstered by his strolling in with Remy on his arm long after the sunset had been completed. Neither Terry nor Remy took the time to explain their flat tire and subsequent stroll on the beach with Peaches. Instead both said goodnight and departed, and when Mutton, Christian and Basil turned in a half-hour later, Terry's death sentence had been decreed.

Chapter 3

The merciless band of conspirators had second thoughts during the morning hours. Under the benevolent brightness of the island sun, Terry didn't seem quite the villain he had the evening before; the adopted course of action now loomed overly harsh; and a dozen other doubts, intensified by the throbbing after-effects of spirits, clouded their scheming minds. But as afternoon superseded morning and Basil's rum began to tame the dogs that had bit them the night before, their determination began to reassert itself. Of course it was a drastic move, but the bastard was insinuating himself into the delicate balance of Booby Bay relationships. More importantly, they had made a solemn pact the evening before, and as Basil was quick to point out, a seafarer never breaks a solemn pact; a seafarer is as good as his word. So once more after a brief reprieve, Terry's fate was sealed.

"How goes we about it?" said Basil. "Shall we bash his skull in?"

"Have you ever bashed a skull before, Basil?" Christian asked.

"Be I a swarthy pirate or a schoolmarm?"

"What's it like?" asked Mutton. "Does it hurt a lot?"

"Well," said Basil, "first he looks at you all twirly like, eyes wigglin.' And sometimes they just stays open and keeps wigglin' while the brains squirts outen 'is skull and flies all over tarnation."

Christian blanched and choked slightly as though he were about to lose his rum breakfast.

"But it don't hurt none," Basil concluded.

"Couldn't we be a bit more humane than that?" asked Christian, taking a quick sip of Basil's rum to erase the mental portrait of a bashed skull. "He's not really a horrible person."

"'At be true," said Basil. "I guess we ought let him 'ave an honorable end. That's fair."

"Yes," Christian agreed, "let him hold his head up to the very end."

"And not wiggle his eyes," Mutton added.

"Walkin' the plank be rather honorable," said Basil.

"We haven't got a ship," said Christian.

"Or a plank," said Mutton.

"Hangin' be a proper death. Or how about we shoot 'im. Not weaselly like in the back but man-to-man like, facing him front on and puttin' the bullet atween 'is eyes."

"Ugh," said Christian. "Isn't there any way we can do it without watching him die, yet still be honorable?"

"Hmmm." Basil thought.

"Maybe we could just make him go away," said Mutton.

"How, Mutton?" Christian asked.

"Sometimes when I want something to go away, I just close my eyes and it's gone."

"Hmmm," said Basil. "Here we go. We knocks 'im in the skull. But this time we bashes 'im nice and gentle like – just to knock 'im out, not spill 'is brains. Then we puts 'im to sea in a boat. And maybe he dies at sea, but maybe he don't. Maybe he survives and floats to another place. It's sportin'. If he's got the real goods, he saves hisself."

"I like that," said Christian. "And when people ask where he is, we won't have to say we killed him. We can just say he left. We could even pack him a lunch."

"Like a picnic," said Mutton.

"That be it," Basil agreed. "We'll even send him with a drop a rum to tidy hisself over until he reaches some other place.

It'll be awful sporting."

"We'll use that old rowboat out behind Albert's place," said Christian.

"It leaks," said Mutton.

"Twon't matter," said Basil, "if he's got the real goods."

"Let's do it while he's on the beach," said Christian. "Then we won't have to carry him that far."

"If he was asleep we wouldn't even have to hit him," said Mutton.

"Okay," said Christian. "We'll wait until he takes a nap on the beach."

"But if he don't take a nap," said Basil, scowling, "we gots to bop 'im."

"Okay," Christian conceded, "but we'll wait a while. He fell asleep on the beach yesterday."

"That be fine, but if he don't fall asleep, who bops 'im?"

"I guess I thought you would," said Christian.

"Now y'did, did ya. Why be that?"

"Because you were the first to talk about hitting him over the head, and you're the only one that's ever done it before. You've got experience."

"Hmmm," said Basil. "So be it. This'n won't shirt his duty."

Terry splashed around in the water which was refreshingly cool when compared to the warmth of the air. He glanced frequently beachward at his clothes, a neat little pile safely out of reach of the occasional energetic wave that stretched beyond the normal line between wet and dry sand. He wasn't sure why he watched them so closely; he couldn't imagine anyone wanting to steal them. It was probably just the self-consciousness of being completely naked in a public place, a place where a Girl Scout troop could parade by at any moment and subject him to their questioning adolescent minds. He also had the strange feeling that someone somewhere was watching him.

He swam for a few minutes longer and then, abandoning the security of the protective water covering, began to wade back to shore, carefully checking both directions for any sign of Girl Scouts or a ladies' auxiliary shell-hunting expedition. Careful as he was, however, when he reached a point of no return where the waves lapped at his calves and he was pretty much committed to land, Remy appeared seemingly out of nowhere and headed toward him or, more specifically, toward the same pile of clothes he sought. *If a train traveling sixty miles an hour left point A at the same time another train traveling eighty miles an hour. . .* He didn't need an algebraic equation to figure out that she would reach his clothes before he would.

She stopped a few feet short of the neat pile – *would she grab his clothes and run away, leaving him stranded in nakedness? –* and he reached the same spot a few seconds later.

"My goodness," said Remy who was perversely fully dressed in white pants and a red T-shirt just to underscore his lack of apparel. "A naked man." Terry reached down and hastily grabbed pants, fumbling badly and frantically dancing on one leg as he sought the opening for the other. "What's a young lady to do?"

"What this beach needs is a door for people to knock on before entering," said Terry, donning his shirt with a bit more dignity and aplomb.

"I did knock. I also rang the bell. You just didn't hear me. I even shouted 'Are there any naked men on this beach?' as I always do before venturing out."

"You've been in the bushes watching me, haven't you?" said Terry.

She laughed. "You've got to be joking. Either that or you're suffering from one dandy delusion of grandeur."

"Is that an insult?"

74

"Of course not. With a body like that, you could go places, kid."

"Well, I felt like someone was watching me; that's all. As a matter of fact, I've had that feeling all morning – like someone is following me, watching. Even right now, it feels as though we're being watched."

"Just because you're paranoid, it doesn't mean that someone isn't out to get you."

"I guess it is a bit silly," Terry admitted. "You look like you're all set to go to the big city or something."

"I would be, but we haven't got a big city. Right now I'm looking for Christian. He's supposed to be going with me. Have you seen him?"

"No, I haven't."

"Albert said he was with Basil earlier, but I can't find either one of them."

"They're probably off privateering somewhere," said Terry. "Do you need a stand-in?"

"No, but thanks anyway," said Remy. "You'd be bored silly. Well, I'll continue my search. Enjoy your beach. I won't look back if you want to take your clothes off again."

She sauntered off down the beach, and Terry fought the impulse to tag along with her, like Mutton following Basil, and make a complete nuisance of himself. Instead, he sat down on the beach, stared out at the water, letting its smooth undulation rock him into a peaceful hypnotic state. After a few minutes, he lay back and closed his eyes.

"See," said Christian from his careful concealment behind a hibiscus, "nap time."

"Hard to tell," said Mutton. "I can't see his eyes very well from here." Mutton had hidden himself behind Basil who grudgingly knelt behind a large poinsettia where for the past hour he had shown little tolerance of the waiting game.

"You'da never caught Blackbeard skulkin' behind a bush waitin' for 'is victim to fall asleep," Basil grumbled. "It don't seem right."

"But we agreed, Basil," said Christian. "It's the most equitable way."

"But equitable ain't pirate-like. By rights, we oughta storm right up to 'im and face 'im face to face. We coulda faced 'im and told 'im flat out 'you be sailin' away now, laddie, or we'll run you right through. He'd have a choice still. But instead here we are sneakin' about in the pansies, waitin' to tiptoe up on 'im, tryin' not to disturb his sleep."

"It's our plan."

"Okay, but if'n he wakes up, Basil ain't gonna bop 'im with no rock. Basil's gonna stare 'im down and tell 'im to get into the boat friendly like or he'd be wishin' he was facin' the devil instead of Basil Ringrose."

"Okay, Basil," said Christian. "Let's go." Christian led them out of their ambuscade onto the beach, and the three ruthless killers staggered on tiptoe toward their quarry, Mutton dragging a rowboat behind. The Booby Bay basset hound strutted after them, head held high, as if knowing that Terry's time had come and determined to witness the happy occasion. Terry had indeed fallen asleep and, when the three assassins approached, was unaware of their presence.

"He be sleepin' like a babe," Basil bellowed.

"Shh," said Christian. "You'll wake him. Get the boat into the water and hold it. Mutton, you take his arms and I'll take his legs. We'll lift him gently into the boat." Basil did as ordered without further comment, and Mutton took up a position near Terry's head. When Basil had completed his task, Christian and Mutton carefully lifted Terry and carried him into the water toward his waiting vessel. As they reached the boat, Terry began to stir a bit. He opened his eyes and looked sleepily and questioningly at Christian who stood awkwardly with one of Terry's legs under each arm and a terror-stricken look on his ashen face. Just as Terry began to speak, however, Mutton stumbled.

"Whoops," he said as he lost his footing entirely and dropped his end of the load into the boat, wrenching the other end of the dead weight from Christian's grip.

"I'm sorry," said Mutton, looking down at Terry whose motionless body was sprawled across the boat and whose eyes were once again closed. "I tripped."

"Well, I guess he's really asleep now," said Christian.

"Be he dead?" asked Basil.

"I don't know," said Christian. Basil leaned over Terry and listened; with breaths held and eyes wide, Christian, Mutton and the dog all watched.

"He's breathin,'" pronounced Basil. "He ain't done in."

"Okay," said Christian with a quick shudder. "Mutton, go back up and get the lunch basket." Mutton trudged back up the beach and Christian called out: "Hurry, so we can shove him off before he wakes up. I don't think he's going to be happy."

"Ar," said Basil, "but happy at bein' saved. He got 'imself a fair shake for a desperado."

Once Christian and Basil saw Mutton reemerge from their earlier place of concealment lugging the picnic basket,

78

which Christian had filled with at least a week's supply of food, they began to push the boat out into deeper water. They turned back to their chore too quickly, however, or they would have seen Remy heading for them as well, just twenty feet behind Mutton. When Mutton reached the edge of the water, Basil and Christian were standing in three feet of water, holding the boat. Mutton waded in toward them, so that all three conspirators were at the scene of the crime when Remy arrived. She immediately spotted Terry lying in the boat and said: "What the hell are you doing?"

Christian stammered and Mutton just stared down at the water. The dog, sensing censure in the air, beat a retreat up the beach and into the trees. Only Basil dared to answer: "It be for 'is own good."

"What be for his own good?" Remy demanded.

"His settin' out to sea. He be a rogue what was takin' advantages of yer dainty nature."

"A rogue? Taking advantage of my dainty nature?"

"Ar. With no good purpose upon 'is mind, t'be sure."

"What are you talking about?" Remy shouted. "Are you insane?" She looked at the motionless Terry again. "What have you done to him?"

"I sort of dropped him," said Mutton. "I didn't mean to. But he's not dead."

"You oaf," said Remy. "Christian? Don't you have anything to say?" He didn't. Remy waded into the water and pulled the boat toward the beach. Each of the conspirators tried to help but to do so in a way that did not attract Remy's attention and give direction to her anger. Once the boat was beached, Remy knelt next to it, leaning over Terry and touching her hand to his face. She shook him and he groaned slightly.

Christian stood a few feet away, eyes down, nervously kicking at the sand. Mutton absentmindedly opened the picnic basket and began chewing on a sandwich. Basil spotted the small bottle of rum in the basket, retrieved it and took a swig. "The lad won't be aneedin' this now," he said.

Remy turned to Christian and stared at him intently until he had turned bright red and begun to sweat. "I expect a lucid answer from you. What were you doing and why?"

"We didn't want to hurt him," Christian said tentatively, looking once again to his feet for inspiration. "We just wanted him to leave. We even packed a big basket so he wouldn't get hungry before someone rescued him. We were afraid that he was trying to hit on you."

"Doesn't it occur to you that, if he were, it would be my business, not yours?"

"We were just trying to protect you."

"As good seafarers is obliged to proteck young damsels such like yourself," Basil added.

"Shut up, Basil," said Remy, then turning to look squarely and harshly at Christian, she continued: "Let me assure you – all three of you – that I can take care of myself. You're not my bodyguards. If this man, or any other man, hits on me, and if I don't want him to, I will deal with it myself. Do you understand that?"

Terry sat up with a groan. "What's going on?"

"You had a boating accident," said Remy.

"Another one?" said Terry foggily. "Or is this the same one, and I dreamed everything else?"

"Another one," Remy answered. "But Christian will have to explain how it happened. I wasn't here at the time."

"Christian?" said Terry, looking at the red-faced young man who was now fidgeting violently. "What happened? Were you carrying me a few minutes ago?"

"I think . . ." Mutton suddenly began, but was hushed by Remy.

"Go, on, Christian," she said.

Mutton spoke again: "I think there's . . ."

"Please, Mutton," said Remy. "You'll have your chance."

"But there's really something . . ." Mutton persisted.

"Shut up, Mutton," said Remy angrily.

"Smoke," screamed Mutton. "There's smoke." He pointed up the beach, and they all turned to see black clouds billowing into the blue sky from somewhere near the Booby Bay Cafe.

"My God, the cafe," said Remy, jumping up and running in the direction of the smoke. The others stumbled after her.

Peaches merrily hummed "London Bridge" as she sat at a table near the bar and polished the last of six miniature vases that were actually small Perrier bottles with their labels removed. She then carefully placed a pink hibiscus blossom and several leaves in each of the vases. There was no reason the cafe couldn't look a little cheerful, she reasoned, even if its owner rarely was. After each refrain of the song, she sipped at a bottle of ginger ale and puffed on an oval English cigarette. After completing her floral arrangements, she carried one vase at a time to each table. It was a small contribution perhaps, but it did add a pretty touch that refined customers would appreciate, should there be any. After the vases had been distributed, she returned to her seat, finished her drink and cigarette, and admired her decorative touches. As she did, she suddenly realized that she had prettied the place just in time, for what should be approaching at this very moment but a rarity – not one, but three visitors, perhaps even paying customers. Naturally, when you needed him, Albert was not here where he should be; naturally he was working on that boat.

"Good afternoon," said Peaches cheerfully, grinning broadly at the three men who had just entered the cafe.

"Ma'am," said one of the trio, a strange, short man – kind of ugly, Peaches thought – all bundled up in a gray overcoat and not sweating a bit. As he spoke, the other two men retreated to a spot just outside the cafe.

"What can I do for you?" Peaches asked. "Maybe get you a drink?"

The man thought for a moment, then smiled. "Yes, a drink would be lovely, what?"

"What will you have?" said Peaches as she quickly moved around behind the bar.

"Sombrero."

Peaches looked at him apologetically. "I'm afraid I don't know how to make those. I'm not really the bartender, you see.

He's away at the moment."

"Anything then," he said, smiling. "That bottle there will be fine." He pointed to a bottle of Scotch. Peaches quickly grabbed the bottle and poured a generous helping into a glass, about three times that which Albert usually served.

"My name is Sammy Apollo," he said, sipping and wincing. "Is my friend Al Lafitte around?"

"No," said Peaches, "he's down at the harbor working on his boat. I tell you, him and that boat."

"Fancies his boat, does he?"

"Fancies?" said Peaches. "It's a royal passion, I'll tell you. He's sort of obsessed with it."

"Men do have their hobbyhorses, what?"

"Their what horses? Albert doesn't have any horses. He hates horses."

"Hobbyhorses."

"He doesn't like hobbies either."

"Well, maybe I'll just take a walk down to the harbor and try to find him," said Apollo, standing. "I did so want to see him. But if I should happen to miss him, please tell him that Murchison Keyes sends his regards."

"Murchison Keyes," Peaches mumbled. "Murchison

Keyes. I should write that down so I'll remember it. Murchison Keyes."

"You'll remember," said Apollo, picking up his glass and slowly pouring the remaining Scotch onto the floor. Then he dropped the glass to the floor where it shattered, and he turned and began to walk away.

"Hey," said Peaches. "Why did you do that? You had no call. There's nothing wrong with that Scotch." She began to follow him, speaking to his back. "You gotta pay for it, you know. And the glass, too. They don't grow on trees." Apollo continued to ignore her as he walked past his two companions without looking back, snapping his fingers as he passed. When Peaches reached the two men, she pleaded her case with them. "He's gotta pay. It isn't right."

They too ignored her, but instead of following their boss, they walked the opposite direction into the cafe. Peaches stopped now, unsure whether to follow Apollo or to keep her eyes on his two companions. Maybe they were remaining to pay for the damages their ugly little friend had caused, she thought, and started back into the cafe. She quickly realized that the two men had no intention of paying either as one of them picked up a bar stool and flung it into the shelves behind the bar, shattering glassware and bottles of liquor.

Peaches gasped and ran toward them. "Stop that," she shouted, grabbing one man's arm. "Stop that. Get out of here." As she began to pound her fists against his back, the other man grabbed her and pushed her roughly against a table which came tumbling down around her as she fell to the floor. She sat in a daze and watched helplessly as one of the men pulled a small can out of his pocket and sprinkled its contents all along the length of the bar. Then he stepped back, lit a match and tossed it gently onto the bar which exploded violently into flames, instantly engulfing its entire surface and jumping at the roof above. The two men turned and hurried away. Even before Peaches could pull herself to her feet, the flames reached the thatch roof and spread rapidly over the entire cafe.

On her feet, Peaches fought her way behind the bar to find a pail but the heat became intense, and a burning ball of thatch fell to the bar next to her, searing her arm with pain. She backed away from underneath the flaming roof and into the open, sobbing.

Remy reached the cafe first, a few steps ahead of Terry, with Christian, Basil and Mutton taking up the rear. Peaches had found a bucket and was now feverishly dashing back and forth between a small cistern where she filled the bucket and the cafe where she emptied it into the flames. Without pause, the others scouted up an odd assortment of containers and fell naturally into a bucket brigade rhythm. Fortunately, Peaches, in her solitary firefighting effort, had done a remarkable job of keeping the fire from spreading much beyond the bar and thatch roof, and with reinforcements, the blaze was rapidly reduced to smoldering. When they finally paused to survey the damage, they found that, although the thatch roof was completely gone and the bar a shambles, the remaining damage was limited to a large blackened hole that peered into Terry's rental unit. The fire out, Peaches sat down on a nearby rock and began to cry softly.

"What happened?" Remy asked quietly.

Peaches looked up, sniffed once and spoke: "These men came – there were three of them. The little ugly one asked for Albert and told me to tell him a Mr. Murchison said hello. Then he poured his drink on the floor and smashed his glass. The other two threw things and started a fire on the bar. Why would they do such a thing?"

"Where's Albert?"

"He's not here, thank God. For once we can be happy that he's working on that boat. Oh dear." A frightened look crept across her face. "I told the ugly little man about Albert and his boat. Do you think . . .?"

"The galleasse!" Remy shouted.

"Let's go," said Terry, starting back toward the beach.

"No, in the moke. Christian, stay here and make sure this one doesn't start up again." Remy ran to the moke, jumped into the driver's seat and started the engine. Terry managed to get one leg into the vehicle before it lurched forward, and they started down the dirt road with Terry fighting to hang on while being slapped by passing foliage. By the time he had planted himself firmly in his seat and begun a futile search for the seat belt, they rounded a corner and spotted the smoking galleasse ahead.

On closer inspection, they discovered that the smoke was now actually steam spewing more from the water than the galleasse itself. The galleasse had evidently listed to the starboard side as it burned, rolling away from the pier into the water, and by so doing extinguished the flames on its own, preventing it from being extensively damaged, if not entirely consumed, by fire. Even though reparable, the galleasse, lying on its side, its long masts now pointing toward some distant spot on the horizon, was a sorry sight – a picture of majesty humbled.

A small crowd had gathered, and they lined the pier, silently watching the steam rise and listening to the low hiss each time the water lapped against the charred galleasse. They could do nothing more now than speculate in hushed voices about what had happened, what had caused the fire and whether the ship could be salvaged. Remy pushed past them with Terry following closely behind. She spoke briefly to a man in what Terry guessed was German or something close to it, and the man responded by pointing toward the end of the pier where a lone figure sat on a chair, looking small and fragile against the wide backdrop of the Caribbean Sea. They hurried along the pier toward him and saw that, as promised, it was Albert, staring at the fallen galleasse.

"My God," said Remy as she reached him. "Are you all right?" Albert nodded his head slowly and mechanically without taking his eyes off the ship.

"Are you sure you're not hurt?" Terry asked. Albert just nodded again, his eyes vacantly reflecting the blue of the water.

"What happened?" Remy asked. Albert didn't answer, but a man who had followed them to the end of the pier attempted to explain what little he knew. Three men had arrived at the pier a short time ago and boarded the galleasse. He had thought little of it since he knew Albert was on board and so went back to his own business, repairing a net. He had looked up briefly once more as the three men passed him again, this time in much more of a hurry. He had thought it odd, but then Albert himself was odd. A few minutes later, he heard the crackling of the fire – before actually seeing it or smelling the smoke. He ran to the galleasse at about the same time as several others arrived, and they had all boarded it and attempted to douse the flames with bucketfuls of sea water. But then the galleasse had begun to heave and roll upon its keel, so they had dragged an unwilling Albert off the craft just before it went onto its side. Albert had refused to leave the pier, so someone brought him a chair.

"Come on, Albert," said Remy, guiding him up out of the chair. "The fire's out. There's nothing more you can do here for now." Albert allowed himself to be pulled to a standing position and led away from the galleasse. Once his gaze was unlocked from the galleasse, he didn't look back but just stared vacantly ahead as they headed slowly for the moke, Terry and Remy nodding to the murmurs of sympathy from those they passed. Terry wondered if Albert were in shock and if there was something specific they should be doing for him, something that was neatly outlined in that medical emergency manual he had been promising to read for years.

Although Peaches had been through nearly an identical ordeal and she had certainly been frightened and confused by it, she somehow seemed all right. Albert, however, was different; he looked as if a fire within him had gone out at the same time the fire on the galleasse was extinguished. The impatient, impudent, and sometimes intolerant little Frenchman had been replaced by a detached, spiritless cardboard figure. There should have been anger – sound and fury – but there was nothing.

"Why?" said Remy, almost whispering, choking slightly on her words. "Why him? Sure, he's difficult at times, but he doesn't really bother anyone. He lives here on his tiny island, away from civilization where he can't even get in people's way inadvertently. And life goes out of its way to hurt him. It's not right."

"No, it isn't," said Terry. He sat next to Remy on the cot that had been hastily set up for him on the porch just outside the small building that Peaches, Remy and Christian called home. Christian had given up his bed to Albert who already occupied it, sleeping fitfully, and volunteered to sleep with Basil, a gesture for which Terry would be eternally grateful.

"Unfortunately," Terry continued, "he did inadvertently get in someone's way – someone named Murchison Keyes. But

91

it's done with now; they've had their revenge. There's no reason for them to come back again. And it could have been worse. Things were destroyed, yes, but no one was hurt or killed."

"But his cafe," said Remy. "And his boat. That boat was his dream."

"It's not totally lost. There was a lot of damage, but he can repair it; he doesn't have to start over. And we'll start working on the cafe first thing in the morning. It won't take long to get it rebuilt."

"Thank you," said Remy, smiling at him. "Thank you for being here."

"Don't worry," said Terry, looking into her eyes and noting the vulnerability that had not been there before.. He wondered if that was what made her even more beautiful tonight. He hoped not. Forcing an air of cheerfulness into his voice, he added: "Albert will be himself in the morning – full of vinegar and ready to take on the world."

Chapter 4

But Albert was not himself in the morning; nor was he the next afternoon. He had cloaked himself in a deep Gallic sulk, demonstrating no concern with any part of the tiny island world that continued to rotate around him the day after the two fires. He spent most of the day alone on the pavilion, staring dispassionately out to sea and responding to attempts at conversations by others with only a shake of the head or a grunt.

Likewise dinner: He nibbled at his food with complete detachment, and at one point, his hand actually crept onto his plate where, for several minutes, he unconsciously stacked green beans in a Lincoln Log manner. After dinner, he sipped his sherry in silence and smoked only half a cigar before crushing it out. The others observed his silence, remained silent themselves, and watched him, waiting for the sudden moment that he would snap back with anger or another emotion; any emotion would be welcome. But he finally broke the uneasy quiet by complaining of weariness, excusing himself, and going to bed.

Fortunately, the rehabilitation of the cafe progressed more rapidly than the rehabilitation of its owner. Under Terry's command, all hands, even Basil, performed their tasks with steady determination and a reasonable degree of effectiveness so that, by the afternoon of the second day after the fire, most of the structural repairs had been completed and the decorative phase was underway. Here Peaches assumed command, having strong opinions on the appearance of a proper cafe and a detailed analysis of the ambiance this one previously lacked. Albert continued to sit on the pavilion staring seaward, thereby giving Peaches carte blanche with her decorative innovations.

Only one minor catastrophe occurred during the rebuilding of the cafe – unless one were to count Basil's accidentally drinking his paint instead of his rum – when Mutton, atop the cafe, lost his balance, fell through the new thatch roof and crashed to the floor, bringing Terry down behind him and Remy down behind Terry. Mutton took the worst beating in the accident, first landing on the hard floor, then taking the full weight of Terry and Remy in quick succession. Lying on top of Mutton, hopelessly entangled with Remy, Terry couldn't really think of it as a catastrophe – actually it was an experience well worth at least one roof.

"Fancy us both dropping in at the same time," said Remy, giggling and rolling off the pile. Terry followed her to her feet, and they both helped Mutton, who looked confused but not seriously hurt, to his feet.

"I'm sorry," said Mutton. "I sort of slipped. I'm so clumsy. I guess the roof is broken, isn't it?"

Terry looked up through the roof at a three-foot patch of blue sky and said: "A little, but it's all right. Maybe we're all getting a little tired. How about a half-hour break?"

"I'm for it," said Remy, not waiting for further discussion, dashing off for the beach instead.

"Me too," said Christian, not pausing either, heading off in hot pursuit, followed by a lumbering Mutton.

"Ar," said Basil, his tongue still a subtle shade of Frosty Lilac, despite several rum mouthwashes. Bottle in hand, he staggered off toward the pavilion to continue stripping his tongue. Peaches sat down at a nearby table with a sigh and gazed at their handiwork thus far. Terry admired the resiliency she had demonstrated since her harrowing ordeal. Peaches stood in sharp juxtaposition to Albert who had totally withdrawn since the event. It was almost as if they had undergone a complete role reversal, she gaining the strength he had given up. Terry walked over to her table and sat down.

"It's going to look very nice when it's done," she said.

"Yes," Terry agreed. "I'm sure Albert will be very pleased.

"I certainly hope so," said Peaches. "He's not right. He should be yelling and cursing. I wish he'd at least complain about something."

"I know. Passion of any kind would be good."

"He's like an ugli fruit that no one wants to eat." Terry agreed once more even though the comparison completely eluded him. "I sometimes feel like kicking his little ass," Peaches continued, "even though that's not very ladylike."

"I guess it's not really the Florence Nightingale technique, but if you thought it would help, I'd join you. I think we all would."

"That would be quite a kicking," said Peaches, grinning at the thought. "And he's got such a little ass." She paused, and the grin faded as she stared intently at Terry. Then she spoke abruptly: "What are your feelings about Remy?"

"What do you mean?" asked Terry, knowing full what she meant.

"I don't want her to be hurt. I don't want her to make the

kinds of mistakes I made when I was young.

"As far as I know, we're just friends. I think that's what she wants."

"Go on," said Peaches skeptically. "There's more there than that."

"On my part, you mean?"

"On her part."

"On her part? I guess I wish you were right – for my part. But I don't think you are."

"You like her?"

"Yes," Terry answered.

"What are your intentions?" Peaches asked, studying him.

"Intentions?" Terry thought for a moment. "I don't know. I don't think our relationship has progressed enough to have intentions. It's just sort of a day-to-day thing. I suppose that's a weak answer, and I'm not trying to be evasive. I do know I wouldn't consciously do anything to hurt her."

"I didn't think you would, but a mother's got to check on these things. It's the right thing to do." She paused, then added: "God knows I've done enough wrong things already."

"How?" He suddenly realized that Peaches was leading the conversation toward a specific destination.

"Well, she hasn't ever had a proper family like other people do."

"I think you and Christian make a perfect family. And she's got Albert and Mutton – even Basil – it's as much an extended family as anyone could hope for. Maybe it's not the traditional textbook family, but sometimes not being so makes a family stronger."

"I guess so, but with no father. . ."

"What happened to her father?"

Peaches looked down as if she were afraid to answer, but Terry was certain this was exactly where she wanted the conversation to lead. When she spoke, she stammered a bit. "That's a story. And I handled it bad, I'm afraid."

"Is her father alive?"

"Yes," said Peaches. "But I've never told her the real story."

"Has she asked?"

"Oh, yes, she did, but I made stuff up. I kept it a secret. She doesn't know who her father is and her father doesn't know either. Nobody knows, except me. Yes, she asked. But I made up a story about how he went away. Once, when she was ten or eleven, she asked if Albert could be her father, and I said yes, if he didn't mind. After that she stopped asking about who her real father was. I've just kept it a secret. It hurts to do that. I think it's being unfair to both of them, but with Albert being a pretend father, maybe it's all right. Maybe – I just don't know what else to do."

"Tell her," said Terry.

"But it's so hard, and she hasn't asked lately."

"Tell her anyway."

"Maybe it will make her unhappy."

"Maybe it will," said Terry, "but it won't last. She has the right to know. Whether you tell the father or not is another thing. Maybe Remy can help you decide that."

"If I tell, I've got to tell both."

"Can you reach him?" Terry asked.

"Yes," said Peaches. "He'll hate me. Maybe Remy will hate me too for not telling her sooner. I'm afraid." She began to sob.

"Remy won't stop loving you," said Terry. "She may be angry for a while, but she won't stop loving you."

"You think so?" She looked at him, the need for reassurance etched in her face.

"I'm sure of it."

The workers reappeared even before the scheduled half hour of break time had elapsed, anxious to get back to the job at hand. They worked throughout the afternoon, and by early evening, Peaches placed a ceremonial vase of flowers on the brand new bar of the resurrected Booby Bay Cafe. Remy went for Albert while Terry poured glasses of sherry for everyone, and Basil poured himself a glass of rum "to tidy 'imself over until the sherry was ready for the drinkin."

A few minutes later, Albert, wearing a bathrobe, shuffled in under Remy's guidance. He looked around mechanically but registered no surprise at the transformation of the Booby Bay Cafe. He just smiled weakly and murmured a thank you. Terry handed him a glass of sherry, raised his own glass into the air, and when the others followed his cue, gulped at the sherry. Albert sipped slowly along with them.

"An here's a toast straight from old Basil t'old Albert," Basil added, sending his rum in pursuit of the sherry.

"The cafe really looks quite nice," said Albert, setting his glass of sherry on the table. His words were unconvincing.

"There's more color to it now," said Peaches. "It really needed some color. Do you like the color?"

"Yes," said Albert. "It's a fine color."

"It's not exactly the same as it was," said Peaches. "But

it's close. And you'll get used to it. Before long it will be like the ugly fire never happened."

"I'm sure it will," said Albert. "It already fades from mind."

"You have a right to be angry," said Remy. "You should let your anger out."

"Ar," said Basil. Albert gazed at Basil's oddly colored tongue as he spoke. "Let the rogues have for it with some nasty words from ol' Albert's vocabulary of cursin'."

"Anger," said Albert quietly. "Anger is pointless. It solves nothing."

"But a good curse is cathartic," said Remy.

"Besides bein' that," Basil added, "it's good fer ya."

"Perhaps," said Albert. "But one does get past anger. At my age, it's more tiring than productive. One reaches a point in one's life where he must cease to care about certain things. It's more sensible. It smooths out the ups and downs."

"So everything is just flat," said Remy with exasperation.

"Yes, I guess so," said Albert. "One day – when you're older – you'll see that that's not necessarily bad."

"Albert, you're just feeling sorry for yourself," said Peaches.

"No," said Albert. "I'm really not. I am feeling quite

weary, however. I hope you'll excuse me, and I do thank you for your efforts on my behalf." With that, he forced a quick smile, stood and shuffled out of the cafe.

"Damn it," said Remy. "Goddamn it He's being such an ass."

"Remy!" Peaches chided.

They all fell silent, reflecting on the man who had just left them, the automaton who claimed to be Albert Lafitte. In spite of their earlier accomplishments, a gloom hung over the newly restored Booby Bay Cafe and refused to leave.

Remy leaned back on her elbows, gazed at the stars that crowded into the sky above the beach, and listened to the gentle slapping of the nearby waves. She didn't acknowledge Terry as he approached and took up a position looking down at her.

"Is this seat taken?" he asked after a few minutes.

"No," Remy answered, looking up, only now aware of his presence.

"Do you mind if I join you?" Terry asked.

"Be my guest," Remy answered, snapping out of her reverie. "It's the best seat in the house." Terry sat down next to her, and they both looked upward again.

"I've never seen so many stars in one place at one time," he said. "Are you watching any in particular?"

"Orion."

"Why? Because he's strong and virile?"

"No," said Remy. "Because he's easy to find – and always there. I like that in a constellation."

"How about the Big Dipper?"

"I never liked the Big Dipper. It bores me. I realize that's very arbitrary. If I gave the poor thing a fair chance, it might be very entertaining."

"Or it may be just another Little Dipper puffed up by its own importance."

She turned to look at him. "You know, you're right. You're very observant when it comes to stars. One of these days you'll have to give me your analysis of Sagittarius." They both laughed, then Remy added in a hushed voice and more solemn manner: "I want you to know how much I appreciate what you've been doing. We all do. You're just a passer-by, sort of, and you had no reason to have to do what you've done."

"I just floated up onto the beach one day," said Terry, "yet Albert – and everyone – treated me like a returning son. I was immediately accepted here and treated as though I'd always been here – with the possible exception of the attempt on my life, but then people don't normally kill passers-by anyway. I guess I do feel a responsibility."

"I didn't mean that as an insult about being a passer-by," said Remy. "I just meant that . . . well, I mean . . . I'm just thankful you were here when all this happened. I don't know what we'd have done – what I'd have done – without you."

"I just wish it could have been more," said Terry. "I wish the new cafe had jarred Albert back to his normal self."

"I do too," said Remy. "I don't know. I guess maybe it's the boat, too."

"Well, we'll just have to rebuild that as well."

"You're kidding."

"No, I'm not," said Terry. "Why shouldn't we? I think it's a great idea."

"But none of us know anything about building a boat."

"Well, we'll just have to get a how to build a boat book."

"A book? That sounds a little too easy."

"Then we'll just have to find someone who can guide us through it," said Terry, not about to be deterred in his plan. "Maybe Basil would know someone."

"He might," said Remy, thinking about it. "There might be a shipbuilder of sorts among his Bluebeard's Reef cronies."

"There you have it," said Terry. "We'll get started on it tomorrow."

"You're really something," said Remy. She smiled and brushed a solitary tear from her cheek. "And I'm the one who's supposed to be responsible for you."

"Well, you did save me from being cast adrift by the members of the Booby Bay Welcome Wagon Committee."

"I did, didn't I?" said Remy. "I guess that means we're square, pardner."

"Not really," said Terry. "Now I owe you one."

"One what?" A mischievous smile played on her lips as she leaned closer and looked at him with eyes that seemed to capture reflection of the entire Caribbean sky. Then she leaned back on her elbows and looked into that sky, letting her hair fall back and brush the sand below.

"Don't toy with me," said Terry. "We're all alone here, and I've never been known for my will power."

"How about your won't power?" asked Remy. She sat upright, leaned into him, and putting a hand behind his neck, kissed him lightly."

"Is this gratitude?" Terry asked.

"Does it matter?"

"I guess it does. I guess I don't want it out of gratitude."

Remy laughed. "The other night you would have taken it any way you could get it."

"Not me. I've got scruples."

"Oh swell," said Remy. "It's a starry night on a sensuous beach, I'm feeling frisky and the only man around has scruples." Then she leaned closer again and, with her face a few inches from his, said softly: "I am grateful, but this has nothing to do with gratitude."

She kissed him again, and he knew it wasn't a thank-you kiss. This time there was passion. He wrapped his arms around her and prolonged the kiss in a bold demonstration that passion could be a two-way street. Finally she pulled away and he realized that his reckless passion had probably sent hers running, leaving behind only cold feet and certain censure for having crossed that invisible line she had drawn between them.

But Remy only pulled back far enough so that she could look into his eyes, and Terry once again saw that Orion, the Big Dipper and all their friends were sparkling there. She buried her face in his neck and returned the tightness of his embrace. She rubbed his back gently then pulled his shirt free of his pants and slipped her hand up underneath to caress his bare back. He, in turn, let fingertips roam across the back of her shoulders and down to the point where her sarong stretched across her back.

His hand occasionally brushed against the sarong and it grew steadily looser until finally only the closeness of their bodies held it in place. And at every such step, he expected her to stop, stand up and tell him to get lost.

Once again, Remy pulled way, letting the sarong fall away and drop to her waist between them. Terry's eyes followed it down and he stared momentarily, mesmerized by the rise and fall of her breasts. He hastily looked up again, but she smiled at him, no chiding this time. She kissed him lightly again then dropped back onto her elbows. Terry leaned over, placing his hand first on one breast then the other, then he slowly let his hand slide down across her body to where the sarong lay loosely covering her. He lifted it and gently tossed it aside.

They each leaned on one elbow, and Terry, using his free hand, continued to explore her body as it glistened under the soft moonlight. He leaned closer to kiss her once again when he heard a low, angry growl from somewhere just behind him. He looked back over his shoulder and there, sitting in the sand next to Remy's sarong, with teeth bared, glaring at him with disapproval, was his canine nemesis.

Remy giggled. "Don't worry. She won't bite."

"She?" said Terry with astonishment. Not knowing the dog's true sex – nor really caring – he had given it a decidedly masculine character. "I'm not sure about that. It . . . she hates me."

"She doesn't hate you," said Remy. "She just has no use for you." The dog growled in agreement. "Stop it, Barbie," Remy said sternly.

"Barbie?" said Terry laughing.

"I named her when I was ten years old. She was my Barbie Dog."

"Yes, I see the similarity now," said Terry, pulling his lip up in a silent snarl at Barbie.

Remy leaned into him once again and said: "She won't bother us, I promise." She initiated the next kiss, and Terry began to forget Barbie. As he began to caress her again, she tugged at his belt and whispered: "Take your pants off."

"Are you sure Barbie won't bite me in the ass?" Terry worried, but nevertheless began to struggle awkwardly out of his pants. He was naked for no more than a second or two before they heard the voice.

"Ar, I think maybe they be down in this here direction."

"Oh shit," said Remy, as Terry, panic stricken, lunged for his pants. Barbie Dog had anticipated his need a second earlier than he acted, and Terry ended up clutching at sand while Barbie nonchalantly dragged his pants away. Terry leaped up after her and within ten feet had caught up with her. He wrenched the pants from her mouth, and after a quick, malevolent look, she trotted away.

Heading back toward Remy, Terry danced feverishly on one leg then the other as he clawed at the pants trying to pull them up his legs to his waist. Remy tried to help him zip them up but was laughing so hard that she wasn't much help. "This isn't easy, you know," she said. "There's more of you going back in than there was coming out."

"I spies them," shouted Basil. "Yo matey, yo lass. What be y' doin' out here all alone?

Terry finished dressing just as he spotted Basil and Mutton in the distance. Remy, with a little more ease and a lot more dignity, stood and wrapped herself quickly in the sarong. "Hello, Basil," she said. "Hello Mutton. We were just stargazing."

"Ar, the sailor's best friends. The dear little navigatin' stars. Find your way anywhere, if you can read 'em. Peaches be lookin' for you lass. Now you go mind to your mother. We'll sits here and look to the stars with the lad. 'Splain as how they guide your way."

Remy looked at Terry and they both shrugged. "Night," she said, kissing him lightly on the cheek, then trudged up the beach and out of sight.

Mutton sat down on one side of Terry and grinned. Basil plopped down on the other side and said: "Swig o' rum?"

"No thanks," said Terry.

"No grudge about the other day, be there?"

"No grudge," said Terry with a sigh.

Mutton, who had been staring quizzically at Terry's attire, asked: "Why do you have pockets on the outside of your pants?"

Terry didn't see Remy again until the following afternoon. Basil, accompanied by Christian, had gone to Bluebeard's Reef to find a master shipbuilder Basil claimed to know. Terry had roamed the beach for most of the early part of the day, hoping to avoid Mutton who, he feared, would follow him around like a puppy dog whose boy is off to school. The solitude also helped him to re-enact in his mind the felicitous events of the previous evening here on this very beach with Remy. He also hoped that she might appear so they could begin once again – a passion replay, wickedly in the full light of day.

Finally giving up the beach, he passed her just before he reached the cafe. It was quickly obvious that her thoughts had not followed his back to their evening on the beach; she barely acknowledged him. She smiled at him almost as weakly as Albert had smiled during their celebration of the rebuilding of the cafe, mumbled a greeting and kept on walking, leaving him standing there looking hopelessly after her. He thought about going after her but decided it was unwise and continued on to the cafe.

Peaches was there alone. Terry slumped down at the table where she sat with needle in hand, deftly stitching double letters 'B' on a lavender napkin, the picture of domesticity except for the oval cigarette hanging in defiance of gravity from her lower lip.

"How's everything?," he asked, trying to adopt a cheerful voice.

"Just fine," Peaches answered. "Everything's just fine."

"I just passed Remy," Terry ventured. "She seemed a bit distracted. Do you know if anything's wrong?"

"I told her last night," said Peaches. "Just like you said."

"You did? How did she take it?"

"I'm not really sure. I was nervous as can be. Fearful like the tiger in the cemetery. At first she laughed – thought I was making a joke. But I told her I was telling the gospel truth and she started getting serious."

"Sometimes the truth can be unsettling," said Terry.

"Yes," said Peaches, lighting up. "Unsettled, that's what she was. She didn't seem angry. She sat without saying much, like she was trying it on to see if it fit. Then she remembered things from her childhood and talked about how strange and different they seemed now that things were this way. I said they were always this way, really. But she said they weren't because not knowing something was a certain way meant it really wasn't that way. Do you understand that?"

"I think so," said Terry.

"I don't know if I do," said Peaches. "It's sort of philosophy, isn't it?"

"I guess it is."

"Anyway, she cried some and then she laughed some."

"Most things are too complicated to evoke a single emotion," said Terry, admitting to himself that he didn't know what he was talking about.

"Yeah, a bunch of emotions, that's what she had. Me too. But mostly fearful. I still am a little, but not as much. I asked her if she was angry at me, and she thought for the longest time. Then she said she wasn't. She said she understood why I did it. I was so relieved I cried. She hugged me and we even giggled some – like little kids – before she went to bed."

"And you're not sorry you told her?"

"Good heavens, no," said Peaches, puffing resolutely at the last little cigarette remnant, then letting a broad smile creep across her shining face. "I'm happy. Thank you for making me do it."

"I didn't make you do it," said Terry. "I just suggested."

"I know, I know. But you gave me the courage."

"As the great Oz pointed out, it was there all the time." Peaches looked at him questioningly, and he quickly went on: "Thank you for telling me about it. I was afraid she was mad at me about last . . . something or other."

"You mean last night on the beach?" said Peaches. Terry flushed, and she continued: "Remy told me about it. We most of the time talk about things." Terry's discomfort was apparent. "Don't worry," she added. "She didn't tell me all the details. I told you she likes you. And I don't think she's mad at you. She's still just unsettled."

"That's certainly understandable. I'll just stand back for a while and let her sort things out." Terry was curious about the details of Peaches' revelation that had had such an impact on both of them but realized that, if Peaches had wanted him to know, she would have told him. And the details couldn't change Terry's feeling for Remy – he didn't care if her father were a

113

drunken sailor, Murchison Keyes, or the devil himself.

"Ar," said Basil, taking a swig of rum from the dirty mug.

"Aye," answered Barnaby Stout, taking a swig of rum from an equally dirty mug.

Christian, who formed the third point of the triangle at the wooden table whose top was pockmarked with cigarette burns, just stared blankly at his dirty mug – or more specifically at the two dirty mugs he saw circling each other on the undulating table in front of him. Basil and Christian had been sitting at this table in the Narcissus, a run-down rum house in the seediest part of the Bluebeard Reef harbor district, for three hours. Two of those three hours had been in the anticipation of the arrival of Barnaby Stout, " a mariner what know'd everything and all about sailing vessels and how they's constructed together." During these two hours, they had been regularly ingesting the coarse house rum as they waited and watched a steady parade of derelicts, drunks and wastrels swaggering or staggering in and out.

At one end of the long Narcissus bar, a black-bearded man, who was large enough that no one doubted his authority, lectured on the proper way to drink, belch, spit and shit. At the other end of the bar, a gaunt, washed-out woman swayed on her stool, giggling at the improper remarks made by a bevy of swarthy admirers. Occasionally she would wink in the direction of the table. Between the two ends of the bar, others laughed, argued or slept. For two hours Basil and Christian sat watching this vaudevillian spectacle, Christian drinking his rum defensively while frequently checking over his shoulder for the approach of backstabbers, Basil gulping his and basking in the nautical ambiance of their surroundings.

As the third hour began, the master shipbuilder arrived, and Basil and Barnaby Stout began the lengthy seafarer's reunion ritual in which the participating parties bring each other up to date on the status of various rogues and mercenaries of mutual acquaintance. At the same time, Stout made a gallant come-from-behind effort to reach rum consumption parity. As the ritual appeared to be reaching its finale, Christian, as if to punctuate the transition of the conversation from trivial to weighty, pushed back his rum and dropped his head to the table, and the two mariners broached the matter at hand.

"Now it be a well-known fact," said Basil, "that there be no one as can hold a candle up to Cap'n Barnaby Stout when it comes to buildin' a ship."

"Humble as I am," said Stout. "I can't deny it for a fact."

"Now here's what we be needin'." Basil lowered his voice so as not to be overheard by unsavory onlookers. "We needs a knowledgeable gentleman as yourself to 'elp us build a Frenchman's girlie ass."

"A Frenchman's girlie ass?" questioned Stout.

"It be a boat with three masts, give or take – the girlie ass, I mean. The Frenchman be a funny little frog whose boat it be."

"You mean galleasse," said Stout.

"That be it," Basil shouted gleefully and thumped the table upon hearing what he now remembered to be the French pronunciation of the vessel under discussion and realizing that he and Christian had indeed sought out the right man.

"Not sure I can do that," said Stout. "That's one I don't know so well."

Basil's grin disappeared. "But sure, matey, you can do it. It be sort of put together already. Just needs fixin'. And we got a picture of what it oughts look like."

"Ah, a picture," said Stout. "That's a difference, then." He paused and thought for a moment. "What are the terms of payment for this undertaking?"

"I can't rightly say," said Basil. "You'd have to work it out with that Bonney chap or this 'ere lad with his face in the table or with the lass what's sorta his sister." Basil chuckled.

"You talk with the lass and I wager you won't be sayin' no."

"Pretty one, huh?" said Stout. Basil nodded in return and Stout continued. "Well, I guess I'd be willing to discuss the matter."

Christian stirred, raised his head off the table and mumbled: "Food, a place to sleep and fifty bucks a day. It shouldn't take more than three days."

"I'll need me six or seven men," said Stout.

"Find three men. There are four of us all ready to follow your instructions. But your men only get thirty."

"Thirty's fine," said Stout, looking down at the heavy-lidded negotiator. "But I'll need seventy myself."

"Okay, seventy."

"And food, including rum."

"You've got it," said Christian. With negotiations complete, he dropped his head with a thud to the table.

"Odd sort of duck, ain't he?" said Stout, nodding at Christian.

"Yeah. He's a good enough lad, but he hasn't quite got the hang o' tolerance to good spirits."

Stout gulped down the rest of his rum and stood. "I guess I'll be about putting together a work crew." He walked off toward the bar where, with the wave of a hand, he silenced the black-bearded lecturer and immediately had the attention of a dozen derelicts.

"I guess I got him for a pretty good price, huh?" said Christian barely raising his head. "Seventy dollars isn't bad."

"Seventy plus three thirties," said Basil. "That be more'n a hundred."

"But the rest is for the other men."

Basil laughed. "No. Old Stout'll keep it all. He'll just find 'im three drunks what'll work for nothin' but the rum. But it be okay, lad. We gonna make old Albert's boat all fixed up again."

"Hi there, good looking." It was the woman from the bar who had now freed herself of her fan club.

"What?" said Basil.

"Not you, fatface. Him. The cute one with his head on the table." She shook his shoulder. "How'd you like to come to a little party. I could show you a real nice time."

"Can't y'see the lad's not so well?"

"Looks fine to me. I'll bet you can still get it up, can't you, Dearie?"

"Go mind yerself. He's just a lad."

"If he's old enough to be with the likes of you," the

woman said angrily, swaying back and forth, "he's old enough to fuck, sweetheart."

Christian lifted his head, stared blankly at the woman, and threw up.

"See. What'd I tell ya," said Basil lifting Christian to his feet. "I think we best be leavin' now lad. Why don't you toss some money onto the table for our drinks and we'll be gettin' back with the good news." Christian emptied his pockets onto the table and Basil led him out into the night air.

Chapter 5

Captain Barnaby Stout and his crew of shipbuilders arrived the next morning just in time for breakfast. The first member of the three-man work crew that Stout had assembled overnight was a thin, cadaverous man whose scalp and facial hair had been reduced to random clumps. He spent the entire meal with his head back, staring vacantly at the roof. He was a zombie, aptly called Ghost.

Sitting to his left, testing the capacity of the Booby Bay furniture, was Zack, a furiously obese, bald-headed man with the face and rolling wrinkles of a bulldog. He may have lacked a few qualifying pounds for sumo wrestling, but he must have been a wrestler of some kind sometime for he sported two huge cauliflower ears. The last of the trio was a dark, muscular Indian who towered over everyone assembled and who never spoke but just glowered down at the others in what must have been a conscious attempt to instill terror. As Basil explained: "He be a Carib, only civilized language he speaks be a little Spanish, and it don't matter what he says anyhow." As far as anyone knew, the Carib had no name.

The three of them sat off by themselves, devouring anything sent in their direction. Stout huddled at another table with Basil who had produced all the papers he could find relating to the galleasse and Albert's construction methods thus far. Stout frequently stroked his chin and limited his conversational banter to "hmms" and "ahs" although on one occasion, he said loudly: "No, no. That's wrong."

Terry watched as closely as he could and tried his best to understand what wasn't being said by following Stout's frequent finger tracings across Albert's sketches. Stout seemed to know what he wasn't talking about, but on the other hand, Basil, more clear-headed than Terry could remember seeing him before, also looked as though he understood, and that worried Terry a bit. Stout's crew worried Terry even more; they were not his idea of the model workforce. He half expected Zack to start making canine overtures to Barbie Dog and expected Ghost – had he survived a nuclear disaster somewhere? – to float away. The Carib certainly looked as though he had ample muscle for any job, but Terry couldn't help thinking this was out-of-career employment, his preferred line of work being something in which he inflicted a lot of pain.

Terry buried his anxieties and biases about the work crew and decided to trust, for now, Stout's judgment and his assessment that the job would be done in the three days originally forecast, even though a single finger had not yet been lifted other than to point at Albert's blueprints.

Peaches shared none of Terry's apprehension. She loved having people sitting at the brightly decorated tables, and it didn't seem to matter much that they were the lowest echelon of Pointe Francoise society, less accustomed to bright tablecloths than to naked tabletops with knife points driven into them. As long as their forks, knives and fingertips remained active, she kept the food coming.

Remy floated through once in one of her increasingly rare appearances. As usual, all eyes turned toward her, openly lascivious, as she passed. She greeted everyone pleasantly without paying a great deal of attention to them, including Terry who had hoped, in vain, for something to set him apart from the others. Had whatever truth she had learned about her father changed her to this degree or had her attitude toward Terry simply changed? Or was he overreacting again? He had continued to hold back, not pushing her, assuming that she would make it known when she was ready to talk or to resume their budding relationship.

But what if she were holding back in the same way, waiting for him? Terry vowed, as he watched her disappear once more, that he'd make a point of talking to her before the day was out. His reverie was quickly broken by Stout, who stood and announced he was ready to begin.

Stout proved to be a real taskmaster on the job. He barked orders and the others obligingly jumped. Where earlier he had been nonchalant about the passage of time, he now squeezed the most from each moment. Shirking brought scowls; wasted motions, words of reproach. Zack and Ghost proved to be, as Terry had expected, pretty much useless, excess baggage, and Terry guessed that they served much the same function as deceased voters served in some elections: a little extra padding – in this case, an extra ninety dollars a day for Barnaby Stout. The Carib, however, performed the work of three men, so it was basically a wash.

They worked through lunch and on into late afternoon. Finally, when they were all tired and hungry and had begun to grumble, Stout relented and called it a day. Back at the cafe, they ate and drank as though eating and drinking were newly discovered pleasures – pleasures that would surely be taken away from them forever the moment they stopped. Remy hadn't joined them at the cafe, and Terry noticed with a start that Christian was missing as well. When Terry asked Peaches, she told him they had gone to Pirate's Perch together. His appetite vanished.

Terry sat on a large rock just beyond the glow of light from the Booby Baby Cafe drinking in the fresh night air as an antidote to that which he had been drinking for the past three hours in the company of Bad Basil Ringrose. Basil was neither a proper role model nor an apt drinking companion. However, since the only companionship Terry sought was that of evil rum itself, Basil was a satisfactory means to an end, as evidenced by Terry's decisive peregrination from the path of moderation. Now he sat alone, and the night air might have helped to clear his addled mind were it not for the countervailing force of the tableau vivant within the cafe: Remy and Christian frozen together in close conversation, foreheads almost touching. Terry watched helplessly as their tete-a-tete twisted his heart, and the jealousy welled up angrily within him. Finally they stood and delivered a finishing blow, as Remy put her arms – the arms that should have been for Terry alone – around Christian and held him tightly for what in Terry's mind measured easily an eternity. The anger overwhelmed him and, no longer able to watch this betrayal, he turned and stormed off to the beach.

The beach was dark and quiet but lacking the starry, sparkling sensuality of that evening of long ago. *(Had a mere 48 hours passed?)* The stars were out there, of course, but tonight they were misers, grudgingly giving off a lusterless light while selfishly keeping their twinkle to themselves. Terry paced, letting the angry feelings rise, nurturing them, then allowing them to bathe him in discontent.

You have no claim on her, said the miniaturized clone dressed as an angel that stood piously on this right shoulder.

Fuck off, said his devilish counterpart from the left shoulder. *Go on, feel sorry for yourself. You have every right. Sure, maybe you didn't have a verbal contract with the Jezebel, but her actions implied something.*

Maybe you read too much into her actions, suggested the angel.

Aren't we rational? answered the devil. *What a wuss.*

"Are you talking to yourself?" It was Remy, standing a few feet behind him.

"No," said Terry, not turning around.

"Want some company?" she asked, walking around to face him.

"Oh, is it my turn?" said Terry, stiffly.

"What do you mean?" She looked at him, perplexed by both his words and the edge in his voice.

"Nothing," said Terry, looking down at the sand.

"Yes you did. Tell me."

"I just thought that it was Christian's turn tonight. I had my turn two nights ago, remember? And tomorrow Mutton, I presume."

"You mean because Christian and I were . . ."

"Exactly," said Terry, turning away.

"You don't understand," said Remy softly. "There's something you don't know."

"But I'm beginning to guess. Once I was blind, Lord, but now I see."

"What's your point?" said Remy slowly, an iciness now creeping into her voice.

"The point is you want us all to follow you around like puppy dogs. Little Ken dogs to go with your Barbie Dog."

"That's not fair."

"Not fair?" said Terry. "But it's true." Little devil Terry

jumped gleefully up and down on his shoulder while little angel Terry, who had fallen from his perch, struggled in the sand.

"You flirt with us, charm us and keep us neatly in line – on a tether, unable to get too close but also unable to get away. Your coterie of worshipers. Well, I don't want to kneel at the altar."

Terry paused, perversely proud of the clarity of his reasoning and speech. Remy now glared at him. Her angel icon was groveling in the sand near Terry's; her devil icon stood defiantly on her shoulder, making obscene gestures at his.

"You bastard," she shouted. Terry smirked at the emptiness of her argument – but she wasn't finished. "What have I done that's worthy of your self-righteous scorn? Forgive me, I must have sinned. And how did I sin? My big sin was liking you. Being a friend. That's all I did. The orchestra section may now start casting stones." She paused for a moment, lowered her voice and went on: "And I let you get close. But that wasn't good enough for you, was it? You're frustrated because you almost conquered me, but not quite. And you've been here almost a week – mercy, what will the boys back home say about that? That's all you need. You just need to fuck me, to add me to that scrapbook in your swelled head – Ladies I Have

Laid by Terry the Stud. Check out Remy, she's page two hundred.

"You're a typical, true blue American male. Albert's right about all of you. No substance, just one hundred percent ego. We're number one. We have the biggest ships, the biggest bombs, the biggest pricks." She turned away and spoke to an unseen audience: *"Egoiste. Il ne se prend pas pour de la merde."*

"That's right," said Terry. "Revert to the romance language. Babble incoherently in French. Demonstrate the shallowness of your argument by speaking in tongues."

"Baises toi. Would you like me to spell that out for you in English?"

"It won't be necessary."

"I'm going back now." said Remy, storming off. "Don't drown."

Basil was attempting to explain to Christian and Mutton as clearly and concisely as possible how a shipbuilder plied his trade when Remy stormed out of the darkness toward their table. Each of them, seeing the look of intense anger on her face and assuming she was about to lash out at one or all over their previous blunder or some new inadvertent atrocity, cowered.

She plopped into an empty chair and mumbled: "Stupid American bastard."

"Who be that?" asked Basil.

"How many stupid American bastards are there on this island?"

"I guess I'm an American," said Mutton. "But I don't think I'm a bastard."

"What did he do?" asked Christian.

"He hurt me. He said some awful things about me."

"By any chance did you also say awful things about him?" asked Christian.

"Yes. But he deserved it."

"Perhaps we shoulda bashed him when we was about it," suggested Basil.

"Maybe you should have," said Remy. "He insinuated I was some kind of strumpet. Just because you and I were together."

"He thinks that we . . .?" said Christian. "Did you set him straight?"

"Why should I? He has no right to think – it's his problem."

"Of course," said Christian. "And naturally you aren't about to give an inch." Remy glowered at him so he looked away but continued: "Did you stop to think that maybe he was acting a little irrational because he was jealous?"

"A fat lot you know."

"And why don't you just shrug off his nastiness, the way you do when one of us is nasty?" Christian was clearly enjoying the surge of superiority he felt on those rare occasions when he could lecture Remy. "Why does it matter what he says? You know what I think?"

"Yes, I know what you think," said Remy, standing and walking away. "You think you know everything."

For the two days following his fight with Remy, Terry avoided her as much as possible and guessed that she was avoiding him as well. Guilt was his frequent companion; he had acted the fool and given quite a convincing performance. Yet anger dogged him too. Yes, he had overreacted and, yes, he could have imagined, blown out of proportion, Remy's transgression. But there were her words; she had said some pretty nasty things about him during their argument. Just as he had, she could have said things in anger that she didn't really mean. But on the other hand, perhaps her true feelings about him jumped out of hiding and into the ugly light of day.

Avoiding her was easy. They were all busy with the galleasse during the day, and during the evening, he simply gravitated to his new drinking companion, Basil.

While they struggled to restore Albert's dream and thereby, hopefully, the man, Albert himself continued in his hermit's ways, generally talking only to Peaches and even then only about his new preoccupation, the failing of his health. For Albert, the transition from melancholy to hypochondria was a smooth one. He suffered the onslaught of jaundice, food poisoning, the pain of a deeply imbedded brain tumor and the warning signs of an imminent heart attack with resignation. He spent the evenings wrapped in a blanket, the mornings with a cold cloth across his forehead and the time in between studying his heart beat, respiration and skin tone for possible irregularities.

"Albert, you're not sick," said Peaches, handing him an herbal tea. "You're just imagining these things because you know you should be back on your feet being a human being."

"We have no aspirin," answered Albert. "Are we a Third World country? How can a civilization have no aspirin?"

"Because no one's been to L'Orient for two weeks. We're running out of things."

"It is because we have no pharmacy," said Albert. "It's

the twentieth century. How can there be an island without a pharmacy?"

"You always said pharmacies are a plague of civilization," said Peaches. "That they create sick people, people dependent upon drugs."

"I had no need of a pharmacy when I said that," said Albert. "I was a well man. Now I need a pharmacy because I am not a well man. Is that so difficult to understand? Please speak, don't nod; my vision is blurred."

"That's because you're a cross-eyed old fool," said Peaches.

"Perhaps I am, perhaps I am," Albert said, softly. "And I'm a burden. But please don't think ill of me. I may only be a burden for another day or two. The tea is very nice. I appreciate your bringing it to me. Would you recite for me, please, the tiger poem? I'd like to hear it once more."

Peaches was dumbstruck. Albert was requesting her poem. Maybe he was dying after all. What other reason could he have? He needed a pretty thought to take him to heaven. Peaches couldn't deny his request, even if he were dreaming his illnesses, so she recited dramatically: "Tiger, tiger, burning bright, in the jungle late at night . . .uh . . . fears he nothing 'cept where they bury." She paused, then grinned suddenly and said:

"For this tiger is fearful of the cemetery." Peaches had, of course, ad-libbed the final two lines, but they were actually quite good, capturing the spirit, if not the exact wording, of the original. She repeated it once again, giving more emphasis to her newly created dramatic elements, then sat smiling with satisfaction, waiting for Albert to voice his appreciation.

"I think the dog is probably rabid," said Albert.

"Why do you say that?"

"He bit me."

"It's a she," Peaches corrected.

"It's my understanding that rabies is found equally among the two sexes of the species."

"Yes, but she doesn't have rabies," said Peaches. "She just wanted your attention."

"We would be able to find out for certain if there were a veterinarian on this island," Albert lamented. "But of course there isn't. There are probably a thousand veterinarians in Paris. But not here. We don't even have a doctor. This is no place to live. In France, there are specialists. If I have a heart attack, I have no chance. If disease sweeps the island, we'll all die."

"But you said doctors were worse than disease," said Peaches. "You said the only difference between a medical doctor and a witch doctor was their makeup."

"I have said a great many things in my life."

"And now they're coming back to haunt you."

"Situations change," said Albert, then he sighed. "I hope you'll excuse me. Conversation has made me weak. I must rest."

Albert closed his eyes, a clear signal for Peaches to leave, but she remained seated next to him. Finally, he was coaxed by her silence into opening one eye slightly to check on her whereabouts, and Peaches seized the opportunity to speak: "Albert, I have something important to tell you."

"None of its any good," said Remy in exasperation. "The old fool just sits there. The galleasse is everything he could hope for, and does he care? All he cares about or thinks about is when he's going to die. Hell, he's dead now; he's a damn zombie."

"I know," said Christian. "But what can we do about it?"

"He's got the curse of the black spot on 'im," said Basil, squinting his eyes. "The old pirate's death curse. They just sits there an likely as to fade away before your very vision. Lost 'is will to live, says I."

"Don't be so bleak, Basil," said Terry, walking toward them. He had hesitated before joining them, thinking at first that it might be better to stay away from Remy, but had at last decided that maybe he would give her the opportunity to recant. "I still think he'll get over it. Before long, he'll tire of self-pity and work himself out of it."

"The expert on human behavior has arrived," growled Remy.

"I just thought the jury that's about to pronounce him a carrot for life might like another opinion."

"And what have you got to base your opinions on?" asked Remy. "A few days of keen insight and in-depth analysis? What could you possibly know about his hopes and his dreams?"

"No, I haven't been here long," said Terry. "But I have talked to him and he's talked to me. You don't always need a lifetime to get to know someone. In fact, you can figure out some people – well, Albert has talked to me enough that I feel justified in having an opinion."

"Yes, he talked to you," said Remy. "On occasion he's talked to the trees. They probably understood as much but didn't have the need to pontificate about it."

"Remy," said Christian. "You don't have to be so nasty."

"Yes I do," Remy snapped.

"Yes she does," said Terry. "We mere mortals vex her."

"No, mere mortals are fine," said Remy. "It's mere morons that vex me."

"Jesus Christ," said Christian. "You sound like two kids having a playground argument."

"Mind your own business," Remy answered. "It's my playground."

"Ar," said Basil, "Perhaps the lad not be knowing how t'be talking of a lady."

"Perhaps, if the lady . . ." Terry stopped abruptly and changed course. "I still say he'll snap back."

"No, he won't," Remy insisted. "He assumes that they'll just come again. Burn him out again and maybe hurt someone this time. He figures it's no use."

"He assumes. He figures. Now who's pontificating? What gives you this great insight? Oh, you've known him a lot longer, sure. But do you understand him?" Remy glared at him, but Terry pushed on: "Actually, I think he's just a joke to you. You don't empathize with him. I doubt that you even like him very much."

"Like him?" Remy screamed. "Like him?" she repeated, her voice barely a whisper this time. Tears streamed down her face. "Damn it, he's my father." For two days Remy had kept secret what Peaches had bottled up for years, but now there was no longer any reason it needed to be secret. Terry gaped at her, struck dumb by the revelation, the color rising in his face as he realized what he had just done.

"I'm sorry," he finally mumbled. "I didn't realize."

"There are a lot of things you didn't realize," she said and looked away from him. She leaned her head on Christian's shoulder and might as well have, at the same time, plunged a knife into Terry's heart.

"Father," said Basil, digesting the news. "And daughter. Shiverin' timbers. What a strange tale tis told." He emptied his glass and went for another rum. The others sat silently, Terry guilty and embarrassed yet still hurt and angry.

"There must be a way to bring him out of it," said Christian finally.

"God, I wish I knew," said Remy. "If I could just get my hands around Murchison Keyes throat for a minute, I'll bet it would help."

"Stranglin' be too pretty for the likes of him," said Basil, returning with drink in hand. "Justice of the high seas, that be the ticket. Buccaneer justice. Cap'n Morgan or Cap'n Kidd woulda handled him just fine."

"And what about Bad Basil?" Remy demanded sarcastically, obviously fed up with his blustering. "What would Bad Basil do?"

"Bad Basil?" Basil roared and slammed his drink to the table, where it sloshed wildly, most of it landing on Christian. "Why he'd fit hisself a fine ship, get hisself a crew of upstanding cutthroats and go after the rascal – chase 'im down at sea. Board the bastard's ship and have to 'im." He danced in feigned swordplay.

Terry and Christian laughed, both shaking their heads, but Remy just stared at Basil as though she were fascinated by his gyrations. When she turned her head back toward the others she had a bemused expression and looked past them, her mind elsewhere. Finally she spoke. "We have a ship, Basil." She spoke slowly, as though merely thinking aloud. "It's a good ship. As good a pirate ship as ever sailed, I imagine. And cutthroats, well . . ."

Terry stared at her in astonishment. "Pardon me for the disbelief, but you're not seriously suggesting that we become pirates and go after Murchison Keyes?"

"Why not?" Remy countered.

"And cut his throat?"

"You don't have to cut it. Just hold him and I'll do it. The man's a drug smuggler for God's sake."

"And that's one very good reason for letting the authorities handle him," said Terry. "Several other good reasons are his goons."

"Look, I don't care if you approve or not," said Remy angrily. "I'll bet Basil's ready to become a pirate."

"Sail the high seas," mused Basil. "Just like in the days gone by. And we'd be goin' after a black 'eart, not treasure. T'would be good deedin' like. Hmmm. By gar, I'm with ya. Maybe this old rascal of a pirate will find hisself a place in Heaven yet."

"And how about you Christian?" said Remy.

Christian looked back at her nervously, whether because of his fear of undertaking battle or his fear of Remy's wrath uncertain. "Sure," he said after a moment. "What the hell. I'm willing to try it if there's a chance it might help Albert."

"Mutton?" Mutton raised his head from the spot on the table where it had been resting throughout the conversation and looked at her quizzically. "Would you like to be one of my pirates and go on a sailing adventure?" she asked.

"The ship was cheered," chanted Mutton, "the harbor cleared, merrily we did drop."

"See," said Remy smugly. "I'm a pirate and I have a ship and a crew of cutthroats. Basil, I'll have a glass of that rum." Terry shook his head in disbelief as Basil quickly fetched her a very large tumbler of rum and she took a big gulp. "Remy

Lafitte. The name will bring terror to blackhearts throughout the West Indies." She took another drink.

"Yo ho ho," said Basil gleefully, taking a drink himself.

"And there will be a reward for the man who brings me the head of Murchison Keyes."

"Reward, says you." Basil staggered over and looked down at her with deep red eyes. "What kinda reward has ya in mind?"

"Well, I don't know exactly," answered Remy, taking another drink.

"How's about a reward like only a fair maid can give to the winnin' cutthroat? Flirty, touchy sort of stuff."

"What?"

"Will ya bestow favors of a sexual nature on he what brings this scoundrel's head to yer dainty feet?"

"Don't be a jerk, Basil," said Terry.

"Don't pay him any attention," said Christian.

"Sexual favors?" said Remy, looking at him awkwardly. "I hadn't thought about . . ." She sat back and silently sipped her rum. Finally, she spoke slowly and with determination: "I want Murchison Keyes dead for what he's done to Albert, and I guess I'll do whatever it takes to get him dead." She looked at Terry and, seeing his look of disapproval, added angrily: "Yes, Basil, if that's what it takes, that will be the reward." She finished the rum and slammed her empty glass on the table.

"I don't believe this," said Terry.

"Why don't you?" said Remy. "You've already suggested that I'm some kind of whore. What's one more trick for a good cause? I'm just living up to your expectations."

"It's like Salome dancing for the head of John the Baptist."

"Maybe so," said Remy. "But I don't have any veils, and Murchison Keyes is certainly no John the Baptist."

"And you're actually going to go through with this?" Terry asked, still incredulous.

"Yes."

"Even if it's Basil?"

"Even if it's you."

"Well, you don't have to worry about that," said Terry icily. "I want no part of it."

"That's right. You don't like to work for it, do you?" said Remy.

"Don't worry," said Christian in a doomed attempt to help. "I'll be there."

"That's cozy," said Terry. He stood and walked away.

"Lad don't seem to have no pirate into 'im," said Basil. "Sorta thankless. Like a dog that bites the bowl what feeds him.

Well, some's got it, some don't. What's say we have another little sip or two for piratin'."

"You handled that well," said Christian, ignoring Basil and looking at Remy.

"Oh Christian," Remy said and sighed.

Since its volcanic creation millions of years ago, Soleil has evolved through a slow continuous process to become the island paradise it is today. Taking a cue from this steady, comfortable pace, the inhabitants of Booby Bay lived their lives in a slow motion, changing only gradually if changing at all. Yet like the occasional sudden cataclysms of nature, those upheavals that goose the evolutionary machinery into sudden spurts of change, Peaches' revelation left reeling principal players and observers alike.

Peaches had told Remy of her father, then Albert of his daughter, a long kept secret that became public in the passion of a moment. What hadn't become public, however, was yet another dramatic realignment of relationships. After Peaches had dropped her paternity bombshell on Albert, Albert, as though Peaches were Churchill and he De Gaulle needing to upstage this churlish Englishman, dropped a bomb of his own:

Christian was also his son, the result of a brief encounter with Peaches' cousin twenty years earlier. This confession might have hurt and angered Peaches, but so much time had passed, and she had herself done Albert a great hurt by denying him his daughter for twenty-five years.

Now, in a few short days, Remy had been given an instant family, statistically traditional, if not traditional in other ways – father, mother, baby brother. But tradition is a hard thing to grasp quickly. This family was not about to move to a traditional suburban house in the hills above Booby Bay and try to regain some of the quality time together they had missed. Like their island, they would have to evolve – slowly and comfortably.

Christian was understandably taken back by the fact that the object of his passion and pursuit had suddenly – once again – become his older sister, an older sister for whom he had shamelessly lusted in his heart, mind and other parts of his body throughout the majority of his lusting years. Now he faced the shame of that lust, but the looks of shame that stole into his eyes just possibly might have been less the ghost of passion past than the fact that such long-held desires cannot be turned off like water faucets when one no longer needs nor wants water. Chances are an errant lustful thought still crept up on him now and then. He was a young man who needed a respectable new direction in which to point his lust.

Albert's shock may have been the greatest, but he didn't run to Remy, hold her, call her daughter, and vow to be the father he had never been. He didn't even cautiously explore the new relationship. Instead he slipped deeper into reverie and became even more distant than before. Guilt was the likely motivator, but Remy assumed he now hated her.

Terry, upon learning that Remy was Albert's daughter felt as much shame and guilt as anyone. Not only had he said some very nasty things to Remy, he had timed them perfectly to add to the burden of her uneasy new relationship. More importantly, perhaps, Terry's lack of knowledge about the newly discovered relationship between Remy and Christian had led him to suspect a different relationship. This lack of knowledge had led him to create the cruel rift between them, and it now helped to widen it.

Had Terry known the truth, he most likely would not have adopted the plan of action he did. Had he known, he probably wouldn't have hired Peter Stander, the Dutch fisherman, to take him not just to Pointe Francoise but, at a very steep price, all the way to L'Orient. He told only Peaches he was leaving and, although he appreciated her concern and her attempts to convince him to stay, he remained resolute. So, as the others celebrated the completion of the galleasse and planned their pirate adventure, Terry, surrounded by darkness, rocked by unseen waves, staring silently at the stone-faced Dutchman, sailed away with his tail between his legs.

"He's gone?" said Remy, looking up at Christian with surprise.

"Total exit," said Christian. "He left this afternoon. Peter Stander took him to L'Orient. He must have been pretty anxious to go; I'll bet he had to pay old Peter a pretty penny to go that far."

"Who be gone?" demanded Basil as he and Mutton joined Christian and Remy.

"Mr. Bonney has sailed away," said Remy.

"Oh did he now?" said Basil. "Well, what makes we of that? It looks as like maybe he's a bit of a yellow dandy. No stomach for the noble duty of huntin' down scoundrels and belayin' 'em."

"Maybe I shouldn't have eaten his picnic," said Mutton. "He'll probably be hungry."

"Weasels has a way of finding themselves food," said

Basil. "Probly wrestle him down a little old granny lady and swipe her victuals."

"I don't think he ran away from being a pirate," said Remy. "I think he had other reasons for leaving."

"And why did he leave?" asked Christian, eying her sharply.

"Because he's stubborn," said Remy, "and self-centered."

"Oh, yes," said Christian, "I forgot how he selfishly pushed us to rebuild the cafe and the galleasse. Must have been something in it for him. And how he selfishly fell in love."

"You have no way of knowing if that's true."

"My God, Remy. It wouldn't be more obvious if he paced back and forth wearing one of those sandwich signs that said: 'The world will end tomorrow and I love Remy.'"

"Don't be silly," said Remy.

"And, of course, flexible, understanding Remy sees his pathetic jealousy and goads him along. Then you get angry about it. Why didn't you tell him the truth about us?"

"It shouldn't have mattered."

"Shouldn't have mattered?" said Christian, shaking his head in disbelief. Basil and Mutton observed them in silence, their heads turning back and forth from one speaker in the verbal tennis match to the other.

146

"If you think it's so important, why didn't you tell him?" asked Remy.

"Because it's not me he loves," said Christian. "And I probably would have told him if I got the chance."

"Tell what?" Basil asked. "What be all this talk about tellin'?"

"Remy really is my sister," said Christian. "Half-sister, anyway."

Basil's eyes clouded over with a pirate's fog as he attempted to absorb this detail. "Half a sister," he mumbled. "There be Albert and there be Peaches." He paused for a moment and then said, as though he had just discovered the secret of her existence: "An there be Remy. Now there be Christian." He returned to deep thought.

"It means," said Mutton, almost authoritatively, "that one of their parents is the same and one of them isn't."

"Very good, Mutton," said Remy. "Albert is my father and he's also Christian's father."

"Albert," said Basil, the cloud lifting, "be the father of both." He chuckled. "Pesky old Albert. Who else's father do we suppose he be?"

"He's not mine," said Mutton. "I was born in Des Moines, and Albert's never been there. He told me that."

"Oh, Christian," said Remy. "I was angry at the things he said and I had to punish him. I drove him away, didn't I?"

"Unfortunately, I guess so," said Christian. "Like ships passing in the night, just waving, then moving on. He'll get over you, and maybe that's for the best."

"Yes, I guess he will," said Remy. She dropped her head and studied the table. "I guess he will."

Chapter 6

Since the hours before noon were Basil's most lucid, they scheduled their maiden foray so as to take advantage of them, not realizing that the heady anticipation of a great buccaneering adventure would leave Basil restless and unable to sleep. As a result, the morning sun climbing upward from the horizon to herald the big day found Basil still sitting in the Booby Bay Cafe, one arm wrapped tightly around his bottle of rum, and loudly singing about the Three Whores of Winnipeg.

An hour later, Christian awakened to a strange swishing above his head and a gravelly voice exhorting him to rise "as they's fine ships t'be stormed and black'earts t'be kilt." He peered out from under the folds of his pillow and beheld an apparition in red velvet and a plumed hat, awash with Dutch courage, wildly waving a sword through the air.

After a breakfast of orange juice and three stiff martinis, Terry slipped silently into a melancholy and slipped frequently from the plastic seat of the rickety bar stool, only determination and his vise-like grip on the edge of the wooden bar preventing him from falling to the floor. He sat – and swayed – in the Club Nautique, a small bistro that usually catered primarily to the local fishermen of L'Orient but at the moment, it being several minutes shy of noon, catered primarily to Terry.

Through his clouded mind, Terry realized that his descent into dipsomania during the past few days had robbed him of whatever dignity he had been able to carry out of Booby Bay and that he was well on his way to becoming a hopeless barfly. The bartender, unaccustomed to morning customers, had tried to serve him the only morning drink he could think of, *cafe au lait*, but Terry would have none of it. A martini fixation had gripped him, and the feckless bartender was forced to succumb to his whim, even though the man had never heard of a martini. Terry led him through a crash course in mixology that resulted in the closest thing to a martini he was going to get out of this establishment – a glass of gin and two black olives.

Terry downed his drink, ate the olives and carefully placed the two olive pits in a little pile that had grown on his napkin. The bartender watched him blankly.

"A very good martini," Terry said, and when the bartender looked at him quizzically, he added: "*Un autre bon martini, monsieur.*" The bartender immediately began mixing another. This, Terry realized, was part of his problem – every time he complimented this man, he got another drink. The bartender placed the martini in front of Terry and studied him with awe as he sipped.

"*Monsieur est'il malheureux?*" the bartender queried. "He is ... uh .. note gay?"

"Not gay," said Terry. "There's a woman, I think maybe I love. But she hates me. *Je t'adore.*" The bartender's smile disappeared and he stepped back. Terry continued: "*Je t'adore jeune fille.*"

The bartender's eyes narrowed. "*Vous adorez jeune fille?*"

"*Oui,*" said Terry, feeling quite proud that he was almost communicating in another language. "*Tres jeune fille.*"

"*Mon Dieu!*" said the bartender.

"You, too? I mean, *avez vous jeune fille?*"

"*Monsieur!*" huffed the bartender.

"I'm sorry," said Terry. "I didn't mean to pry. *Pardonez moi.*"

Terry finished his drink in silence, and the bartender

151

kept his distance, busying himself at the far end of the bar. Suspecting that the bartender's attitude had changed during their conversation, Terry promised himself he would get hold of a French phrase book and find out if he had said something wrong. After a moment, he waved to the bartender and asked: "Do you have the time? Uh, *quelle heure est il, s'il vous plait?*"

"*Il est midi moins cinq,*" answered the bartender, approaching him.

Terry pointed to his wrist and made a circular motion. "Could you show me? The bartender held out his own wrist toward Terry, who noted that it was almost noon. "*Merci,*" he said.

Terry quickly finished off his drink and, eating the two olives, realized he was hungry. As he stood, he also realized that if he didn't get something more substantial than eight olives into his stomach, he'd most likely pass out right here or somewhere on the streets of L'Orient. He stood and looked toward the door – an action that transcended the barriers of language. It brought an immediate reaction on the part of the bartender who came around to the front of the bar, took up a position between Terry and the door, and smiled expectantly.

"*Soixante et onze,*" said the bartender after waiting in vain for Terry to make a gesture toward payment. Terry suddenly realized what the bartender wanted and pulled his wallet from his pocket. He fumbled through the bills, produced two twenties and held them out.

"Is this enough?"

"*Oui, monsieur*," said the bartender grinning. "*Merci.*"

"*Merci* yourself," Terry answered. "*Beaucoup.*"

Terry walked out of the bar into the bright sunlight, concentrating on each step he took in an attempt to maintain a reasonable carriage as he made his way back to his hotel. His hotel was only a block away, the village itself being only two blocks long. L'Orient qualified as a true Caribbean hideaway – not as hidden as Pointe Francoise, which gets no tourists, but nevertheless undiscovered as islands go. Its tiny airstrip was amenable only to planes that are small and daring, and its one hotel was not of the standard usually demanded by visitors to the West Indies. The only other tourist accommodation on the island was an exclusive, getaway spot called Eros Beach, populated by Americans away for a week to meet and mingle and, if one accepted the opinion of the hotel clerk, couple indiscriminately with peers they would never have to face again. Fortunately, their hedonistic excess kept them within their enclave, so Terry had no need to dodge mopeds. In fact, he could have crawled to his hotel and less than a half dozen people would have known.

At the hotel, Terry went directly to his room to refresh himself briefly before lunch in the unfriendly hotel restaurant but made the mistake of sitting down on his bed momentarily. It was after six when he woke up, two hours after the scheduled departure of his flight.

At ten a.m., they dropped the sails, and the galleasse, under the guidance of Captain Barnaby Stout, glided out of Soleil harbor, its crew of swarthy pirates – Remy, Christian, Basil and Mutton – looking excitedly across the bow at the infinite blue sea ahead where, somewhere, their first emprise awaited. With great ceremony, they hoisted the flag Peaches had made for them the night before using remnants of a tablecloth and, without his knowledge, Albert's French flag. As it rippled on high, the orange skull and crossbones against the bands of red, white and blue resembled a jack o' lantern and two carrots more than a pirate symbol, but broadcast its warning just the same.

They sailed past Pointe Francoise and toward L'Orient, Captain Stout certain that Murchison Keyes was to be found in these waters. The virgin buccaneers chattered in nervous anticipation and marveled at every sea creature they spotted from the dolphins dancing alongside to the Portuguese men-of-war, innocent floating bubbles hiding virulence below. They eyed each craft they passed, looking for the magic word Esperance that would designate it as the object of their search, and the passengers of each craft stared back at them in wonder – wonder at the sight of this sailing ship out of a distant past – and amusement at the sight of the fearsome pirate dressed for plunder and poised like a park statue atop the poop deck.

They had sailed for several hours before Basil spotted a large yacht in the distance, and placing a hand to his forehead and squinting, proclaimed it to be their enemy. Christian quickly viewed it through binoculars and confirmed the pirate's identification. They all stared in jittery silence as Captain Stout moved the pirate ship in for the kill. The galleasse was about the same size as the yacht but stood higher in the water so that as Stout skillfully brought her alongside, the pirates looked down onto the deck of their quarry.

The only enemy visible were two women in their fifties who sat on the deck in chaise lounges, one reading a book, the other carefully painting her toenails with a bright red polish. They looked up in astonishment as the galleasse suddenly appeared above them and gasped as Mutton, who leaped before he looked, came tumbling onto the deck.

The toenail painter uttered a feeble shriek and drew a red line across three toes. Her companion, dropping the book into her lap, attempted to speak forcefully but instead whimpered: "Who . . .who are you?"

"This soul hath been alone on a wide, wide sea," said Mutton, grinning. The ladies' expressions suggested they were not Coleridge fans, but it was just as well because, before Mutton could recite another line, three additional pirates dropped to the deck of the yacht. The fear deepened in the two women's faces as they studied the intruders, unsure whether they were lunatics on the loose or terrorists, but sure that they were unwelcome.

"Just keep calm," said Remy, trying to hide her own fear by approaching them with a bold stride. "We won't hurt you. We're just after Keyes."

"Keys to what?" asked one of the women.

"Please don't talk." Remy's voice was authoritative but not threatening and it calmed them a little bit, but they each kept a wary eye on the velveteen lunatic lunging with his sword at invisible rogues. "Christian, stay with the ladies. Basil, you check down below. Mutton, up front with me."

Mutton followed Remy stemward, while Christian gave

the two ladies his most disarming boyish grin. "Hi, I'm Christian," he said.

"I'm Patrice Arvis," said the book-reader and braver of the two. "This is Esther Lovejoy."

She motioned to her cowering friend. "You shouldn't be here, you know."

Christian ignored her and watched Basil who, swordplay complete, barged through the opening leading below deck. Once below, Basil pushed doors open one by one and lunged through each opening, sword extended. After thus besieging three cabins, he found behind a fourth door two occupants, naked bodies welded together on the small bed, writhing in passion and oblivious to their new audience. The party atop wheezed as he executed feeble pushups against his partner, flabby buttocks jiggling as he moved. He nearly smothered the other party who remained incognito beneath him, only her two long legs stretching out from the concealment of his corpulence. Her dainty feet with bright red toenails were planted firmly against his jiggling buttocks. Basil strode to the edge of the bed and poked the quivering posterior with the point of the sword.

"Yeow," screamed the man. "What in the hell?"

"On yer feet, Barnacle Bill," growled Basil. "Be ye the damnable rogue, Murchison Keyes?" The man rolled over and

157

into an upright sitting position, his angry face flushed. Anger turned quickly to fear as he saw the buccaneer and the sword that danced in the air a few inches from his face.

The secret partner, now on public display, was a young woman, only a third of his age. Fortunately, she had not been flattened by the weight of her paramour; her curves remained in their proper places now that she was covered only by a tan. Her blond hair strayed across the pillow in all directions, and a telltale smudge of lip color adorned her right cheek. She didn't move but looked up at the intruder through wide eyes, more curious than afraid even though he looked as though he had every intention of impaling her love mate, if not both of them. Basil's mouth dropped open slightly as she lay there in defiant nakedness, and he wondered momentarily if Remy might not let him keep her as a spoil of war.

A stirring brought his attention back to the rogue at hand. "What's the meaning of this," demanded the rogue, his face now mottled with red.

"Stand and deliver, Keyes," said Basil, prodding him with the sword. Under the pressure of the blade, the man reluctantly stood.

Basil looked back to the young woman and asked: "This man be a'bothering you, lass? If he do be, I'll gladly whack his wicket off so he'll do no more a'bothering." He pushed his sword toward the appendage in question.

The young woman giggled a little, then said: "Please don't hurt him."

"I'm afraid I be duty bound to cut 'is black'eart out. But I won't do it afore your tender eyes. Now updeck, you scoundrel. You too, lass, if y'please."

"For God's sake, let us get dressed first," wailed the man, his entire body now quivering.

"You'll not be needin' any clothes where you be headed, Murchison Keyes."

"Who's Murchison Keyes?" asked the man.

"Why you is, you snake," Basil answered.

"I'm not Murchison Keyes," said the man. "Please, think of the young lady."

"Like you be thinkin' of the young lady," scoffed Basil. "Doffin' away like there be no tomorrow. For shame." Basil moved around behind the man and poked him in the buttocks again. "Move it, matey." He turned to the young woman and said more politely: "After you, lass."

"Yes sir," she said, standing. "But please don't poke me in the ass, okay?"

The unusual procession, led by a naked man, with a

159

naked young lady following, and the overdressed pirate taking up the rear (as well as watching the rear end that wiggled ahead of him), marched out of the cabin and up the stairs. When it emerged on the deck, it was greeted by gasps from the two women.

"Harold!" said Patrice Arvis upon seeing her naked husband.

"Anna!" said Esther Lovejoy upon seeing her equally naked daughter.

"Basil!" said Remy upon seeing the fully clothed pirate and his two naked prisoners. "What are you doing to these people?"

"Capturing 'em be all," said Basil. "This here fat one. . ." He pointed at Harold with the sword. " . . be Murchison Keyes and he was tryin' to put the screw onto this pretty one." Anna waved meekly while Harold stared down at the deck.

Two more gasps. "Harold," shrieked Mrs. Arvis, "how could you?"

"My God," added Mrs. Lovejoy, "she's only seventeen."

"Want me to whack his wicket off?" asked Basil. "I be in a cuttin' mood and one little jab'd do ya. It'd take care of that troublemaker atwixt his legs for good so's it couldn't nevermore offend none of you ladies."

"Maybe you should," said Mrs. Lovejoy angrily. "You animal. You rapist. Oh my poor darling. Did he hurt you terribly?"

"It wasn't like that, mom," said Anna sheepishly.

"She seduced my Harold," said Mrs. Arvis. "I knew it. I always thought she was a tramp."

"Basil, let the young lady go back down and get dressed," said Remy.

"I'll go down with her," said Christian, jumping forward. "Just to make sure she doesn't try anything funny." Anna looked at him and smiled, then she turned and went below deck. Christian bounded after her.

"Now shall I cut this yellow dog's heart out for ya?" Basil looked to Remy. "So's I can get my reward."

"This lunatic is lying, Patrice," said Harold. "We weren't doing anything down there."

"Then why were you naked, Harold?" asked Mrs. Arvis.

"He made us undress. We weren't even in the same room."

"Oh Harold," Mrs. Arvis said, shaking her head.

"What you keep saying about 'arold?" said Basil. "This don't be a 'arold; this be a Murchison – of whom I is sworn to kill."

"I am not," said Harold.

"You is too," said Basil.

"I am not," Harold insisted.

"If you're not Keyes, then where is he?" Remy demanded.

"I don't know any Keyes," said Harold. "Can't I get dressed too?"

"Here," said Remy, picking up a towel and tossing it to him. "Wrap yourself with this. We happen to know this is Keyes' yacht, so you might as well tell us where he is."

"This is my yacht," said Harold huffily. "I've owned it for years. It's properly registered, and I paid the taxes.

"It's well known the Esperance belongs to Murchison Keyes," said Remy.

"That very well may be," said Harold. "But this is the Exasperation and it belongs to me. You're trespassing." The towel and the sense that there might be a mistake had rebuilt his courage. He walked over to the railing of the yacht, picked up a life preserver and tossed it at Remy's feet. "Exasperation."

"Merde," " said Remy, staring down at the life preserver. "Christian, Basil, you imbeciles. This is the wrong goddamn boat." Now Remy looked sheepish. "I guess we owe you an apology. I think we boarded the wrong yacht. I hope you'll see the humor in it."

"Nice ta meetcha, old naked 'arold," said Basil, lowering his sword. "Hopes there be no ill feelings about my pokin' y'in the ass. But I thought you was a rogue, y'see."

"Hard feelings," said Harold, speaking icily through a tight plastic smile. "Mistake. Boarding a person's yacht, nearly castrating its owner. By mistake?" He turned toward Remy. "If you don't remove yourself immediately and take this swine with you, I'll see that you spend the rest of your lives in jail, if they don't hang you."

"Yes sir," said Remy, backing away from him. "Well, we'll be going now. Have a pleasant day. She and Basil edged toward the galleasse where Mutton already stood staring vacantly out to sea.

"Don't forget the one that's down below," Harold snarled.

Remy ran to the doorway leading below and shouted: "Christian!" No reply came and she yelled once more: "Christian, get your ass up here." A moment later, Christian emerged, nervously tucking his shirt into his pants. Anna was a few steps behind him, now wearing a long T-shirt and a wicked smile. Christian and Remy hurriedly reboarded the galleasse where the others were waiting. Anna waved as they sailed away.

The explosion came from the direction of the beach. It reverberated through the Booby Bay Cafe, shaking those within out of their late afternoon lethargy. The five of them – Remy, Christian, Peaches, Basil and Mutton – hurried to the pavilion to find out what was invading their tranquility.

Mutton pointed out to sea. "Boats," he said.

"Boats?" said Remy, looking. A dozen massive gray ships dominated the normally empty seascape. "It's a fucking armada."

"What do you suppose they want?" asked Christian, looking at Remy with a touch of panic. A quick puff of smoke against one of the ships gave answer to his question. At almost the same instant, something whistled overhead and an explosion somewhere in the distance behind them once again shattered the calm.

"I'd say they want to blow us up," said Remy. "Who the hell are they, anyway?"

"You don't suppose that Harold guy was pissed off enough to sick the Navy on us, do you?" Christian offered.

"I guess he was that angry," said Remy. "But I can't believe he has a navy at his command.

"Looks t'be a navy, all right," said Basil.

"But whose navy?" asked Remy.

"Maybe Keyes has a navy," said Christian. "He found out we were looking for him and came to save us the trouble." Another whistle overhead, another explosion.

"*Mon Dieu*," said Remy.

"Do you suppose we should surrender before they find their range?" asked Christian.

"Surrender?" thundered Basil. "I say we fights 'em to the last man . . . uh . . . and gal."

"Forget it, Basil," said Remy. "That's a really well armed navy out there. We wouldn't have a prayer."

"Course not. But I reckon we can take a hundred of the rascals along with us to meet up with Davy Jones."

"Basil, if it's all the same to you, I'm not quite ready to meet Davy Jones," said Remy.

"Lookee there," said Basil, pointing toward the beach. Peaches had slipped away from them and now stood on the rickety pier waving a light pink tablecloth through the air above her head.

"Thunderation," cried Basil as he stormed down the beach, sword in hand, to join Peaches on the pier. The others watched as the two figures on the pier acted out their conflicting messages – Peaches waving her off-white flag of surrender and Basil waving a sword with one hand while shaking his free fist in the direction of the ships. Another puff of smoke in the distance, the ominous whistle and an explosion, this time just beyond the cafe, brought Albert in bathrobe and bare feet to the pavilion.

"Now, they're shooting at us," said Albert, as though the others had been waiting for him to explain what was happening. "Can't they leave a man to live out his last few weeks in peace. Ah, but of course not. That would be asking too much. *La demande deraisonnable.*"

Albert walked halfway down the beach where he spotted Basil and Peaches still signaling war and peace. *"Vous deux etes des idiots,"* he said, then looking out toward the ships, yelled: *"Tirez, messieurs.* I do not care. If it amuses you to bomb one insignificant Frenchman, go right ahead. Albert does not care. Aim your sophisticated military weapons at this world-weary soul and squeeze your motherfucking triggers. It is nothing to Albert. Albert is ready to die. Do you hear me? *Comprendez vous,* assholes?"

There were no further puffs of smoke, no whistles overhead, no explosions. The blast that had brought Albert to the beach to make his impassioned speech had been the last. Whether it was that speech, Peaches' flag-waving, Basil's threat or some unknown influence that had silenced the mighty guns, no one knew. But the guns were silent and so were those who stood nervously on the beach, watching and waiting. Finally, when Albert was satisfied that the firing had ceased, he said: *"Merci,"* turned and walked back up the beach, past the pavilion, to his room.

Remy watched until he disappeared then, turning back, spotted a small gray craft that had pulled away from the armada and was heading toward them. It reached the beach within minutes, and a young man in a white naval uniform stepped onto the pier, fidgeting slightly for a moment as his gaze alternated between Peaches and Basil.

"Does your army be in the employ of the scurrilous Murchison Keyes?" Basil demanded, breaking the uneasy silence. His sword hung menacingly in the air.

"Who?"

"Murchison Keyes, Murchison Keyes. Be ye deaf?"

"I've never heard of the gentleman," said the young man, eyes darting this way and that in confusion.

"Gentleman," huffed Peaches. "He's no gentleman."

"Then did old naked 'arold send you to get even with us for pokin' him in the ass?" Basil asked.

"I don't know a naked arold." the young man said, his words punctuated by a nervous cough.

"Then why is it as you're shootin' at us?" demanded Basil.

Remy and Christian now joined the summit at the pier. "Yes, why?" Remy added.

"Wh . . .why are you people here?" stammered the young officer. Even his freckles appeared to be quivering. His shoulder insignia identified him as a lieutenant, his overall demeanor as an inexperienced one. "What are you doing on this island?"

"Dodging your gunfire, primarily," said Remy.

The lieutenant looked at her and immediately blushed. "But you shouldn't be here," he said. "This island is uninhabited."

"I beg to differ with you, General," said Peaches. "We're as proper and upright as any folks you might find in the West Indies."

"What I mean is nobody is supposed to live here," said the lieutenant. "And I'm not a general, ma'am. Just a lieutenant."

"Well, it may not be living," said Christian, "but I personally have inhabited this island for every one of my nineteen years."

"We's all lived here for his nineteen years plus a good bunch of our own as well," said Basil.

"This can't be," said the lieutenant, shifting from foot to foot. "I have my coordinates. I checked them and double-checked them."

168

"Coordinates," boomed Basil. "What you do is you aim your guns when you can see your enemy close up enough to take a bead atween his eyes. If'n you do that, you can be certain you is shootin' the right rascal. Coordinates!"

"Oh dear. Was anyone hurt?"

"No," said Remy, taking pity on his discomfort and and ratcheting her tone down to a softer level. "Just a bit frightened."

"Oh dear." He looked at Remy again, blushed again, and looked to Peaches. "I had coordinates."

"Maybe you got hold of some bad coordinates, dear," said Peaches gently. "We all make mistakes."

"We don't all make mistakes with howitzers," said the lieutenant, wearing his guilt like a battle ribbon.

"Come, come," said Peaches, slipping her arm through his. "Why don't you come up to the cafe and have a little something to settle you down. What's your name, dear?"

"Trillig, ma'am. Lieutenant Trillig."

"Don't be so formal, Lieutenant Trillig," said Peaches, leading him off the pier. "What's your first name?"

"Horatio," he said meekly, darting a glance at Remy and grinning sheepishly.

"Welcome to Booby Bay, Hornblower," said Remy. He blushed again.

"Hornblower," mused Basil, taking up the rear of the procession, "a right seaworthy name."

When they reached the cafe, Peaches led Lieutenant Trillig to a chair and gently pushed him into it. Basil produced a stiff rum drink for the young man (as well as one for himself) and they all sat down around the table and ogled him as though he were the chief freak at a traveling naval sideshow. Trillig took a drink, coughed violently, then tried again. "I don't usually drink spirits," he said.

Each successive gulp, however, went down just a little easier than the previous one, and before long Trillig relaxed enough to let his gaze travel from one inquiring face to another. But whenever he looked directly at Remy, he quickly lowered his eyes as if looking at her were a criminal trespass, with consequences as ghastly as those of gazing upon Medusa. After a few minutes, he began to babble another apology: "I'm really sorry that we shot at you. Thank goodness no one was hurt or killed. I just don't understand it. I. . .I had . . ."

"We know, Hornblower," said Remy. "You had the coordinates."

"Like ol' Peaches was sayin'," said Basil, "someone musta give you some bad coordinates. You oughta try and think up which scalawag give you the spooky numbers."

"Are you in charge of all those boats?" asked Peaches. "Or just the one with the gun?"

"Oh goodness, no," Trillig giggled. "I'm barely in charge of one howitzer. I'm mostly a go-fer. That's why they sent me ashore to find out who you were. Nobody else wanted to do it." Trillig finished the last of his rum. His face was flushed, his eyes rolled before finding focus, and his speech was thickening. So Basil naturally brought him another rum, which Trillig began to drink as though it were water rather than the spirits he rarely touched.

"It's kind of funny," he continued. "Here I am, Horatio Trillig, shooting at people. I couldn't even shoot a shquirrel when I was a kid. I'm really a pacifist."

"What's a pacifist?" asked Mutton.

Basil, slightly confused by its relevance, nevertheless attempted to explain: "It be's a thing what you stick in a baby's mouth so's he won't cry."

"No, Basil," said Christian. "A pacifist is a person who doesn't believe in fighting."

"What don't believe in fighting?" Basil leaned back to the point where his chair tipped, and he stared at Trillig, his face screwed into befuddlement. "How can that be?"

"Some people are," said Remy.

"Hmmph," Basil snorted. "Then you might just as well stick 'em in a baby's mouth for all the good they be."

Ignoring the buccaneer, Remy prodded Trillig. "If you're a pacifist, why are you in the Navy?"

"I didn't really want to be in the Navy. My father wanted me to be in the Navy. And he was my father, so here I am. What else could I do?"

"Tis honorable to take heed of your father," said Basil.

"But even though I'm in the Navy," said Trillig, "I'm not going to kill a single living thing, not even a shquir . . . .shquir . . . .squirrel."

"Except you almost did," said Remy.

"Oh dear," wailed Trillig. "You'll never forgive me, will you?"

"Of course," said Remy, laughing. "We already have."

"Thank you, sho mush," said Trillig, looking at her with a silly grin on his face. Then he suddenly frowned as though an unwelcome thought had popped into his mind, and he looked down at his watch. He studied the watch for several minutes, moving both his wrist and his head, testing various distances between the two for the exact position that would enable him to translate the numbers and hands thereon. Finally, when everyone was certain that he had forgotten his reason for looking at it, he announced: "I got to get back to my shit."

Trillig stood falteringly and, swaying, thanked each one of them twice, Remy three times. Then he turned, took one step, and immediately fell to his knees. Christian jumped up and helped Trillig to his feet, then led him slowly away from the table. "Easy does it, Hornblower," said Christian. Peaches took his other arm and the trio moved slowly toward the door.

"I don't know if your general is going to be very happy," said Peaches. "Maybe we should send a note back with you explaining that everything is all right. We could tell him that something disagreed with you. I'm sure he'll understand."

"I think we're going to have to take him back," said Christian.

"Thank you, " Trillig mumbled. "But thashan't be necess . . . ess . . ." His head dropped to his chest.

When, after a labored journey, highlighted by a great deal of stumbling, they reached the pier, Christian looked out at the horizon, now subdued by dusk, and said: "Uh oh. Look."

Peaches looked up to see that the view had changed during the past hour; not a ship was in sight. "Oh dear," she said. "I'm afraid they sailed off and forgot to take you with them."

"Dinerez vous seul?" asked the waiter with an accusatory tone.

"Je ne parle pas Francais," Terry answered apologetically.

"Naturellement."

"Parlez vous Anglaise?" Terry asked hopefully.

"When necessary," the waiter sneered. "Will you be dining alone?"

"Yes please," said Terry. The waiter sniffed and led him to a table at the rear of the restaurant.

"Would monsieur care for something to drink?" the waiter asked stiffly as he held the chair for Terry.

Sliding into his chair and adjusting it, Terry answered: "Tomato juice, please." The momentary thought of alcohol set his stomach spinning.

"One *jus de tomate*," said the waiter as he walked away. Terry looked aimlessly around the restaurant and was surprised by the fact that every table was taken – although there were less than a dozen tables. He also noted that the waiter appeared to be working the room alone, an appearance that proved to be a reality as Terry waited fifteen minutes before the waiter reappeared with his tomato juice. Placing it in front of Terry, the waiter said: "Will monsieur mind if he is joined by two diners?"

His tone said monsieur damn well better not mind; monsieur is lucky to have a table at all.

"Of course not," Terry answered. The waiter pursed his lips into a stiff smile, then departed, returning a few minutes later with two women, one a well-manicured woman in her fifties, the other a fresh-faced young woman whose age Terry pegged at possibly twenty.

"You're so kind," said the older woman, sitting down across the table from Terry. The other flashed a quick, wayward smile and winked as she took the seat between Terry and the other woman. After carefully arranging her napkin in her lap, the older woman continued: "My name is Esther Lovejoy and this is my daughter, Anna. We're so happy you allowed us to share your table. We've had such a trying day and the thought of waiting and waiting for dinner is just too much."

"It's my pleasure," said Terry. "It's nice to have the company. I'm Terry Bonney. I hope you enjoy your dinner."

"Thank you, Mr. Bonney."

"Terry," said Anna, her eyes attacking his. "That's a cute name."

"Anna," Mrs. Lovejoy cautioned. "Don't be forward."

"I wasn't being forward, Mother. I was just being sociable. If you want people to be friendly, you've got to be friendly, too." She turned back to Terry. "At least that's what Misterogers says."

"Misterogers?" said Terry, laughing. "You watch Misterogers?"

"Doesn't everyone?" She dipped her fingers into her water glass, pulled out an ice cube and began sucking on it.

"Are you from the United States, Mr. Rogers?" asked Mrs. Lovejoy. Anna giggled and Terry just smiled.

"Yes, I am," Terry answered. "New York."

"It's so nice to run into a fellow American," Mrs. Lovejoy continued. "It somehow makes things more comfortable, you know, when you're around mostly foreigners."

"Mother, we're the foreigners here," said Anna, in a show of exasperation at her mother's parochial attitude.. "Honestly, you're so bourgeois. Do you speak French, Terry?"

"Don't be so familiar," said her mother. "He's an elder and very nearly a stranger. Show some courtesy."

"It's all right, Mrs. Lovejoy," said Terry. "I don't mind. No, Anna, I don't speak French – at least not enough to matter."

"I think people who visit other people's countries should learn their language," said Anna.

"Anna!" said Mrs. Lovejoy.

"I agree," said Terry quickly. "At least they should try. I

tried to speak French this morning and I fared rather poorly, I'm afraid. As near as I can tell, I told a bartender I loved him, among other things."

Anna laughed and said: *"Voudrez-vous etre mechant pendant diner?"*

"Anna has had five years of French," said Mrs. Lovejoy. "What does that mean, Anna?"

Anna gave Terry a lickerish look then turned to her mother and said: "I just said I hope he enjoys his dinner." Turning back to Terry, she said: *"J'ai de beaux nichons et un petit cul mignon."* Her words were followed by a foot brushing against Terry's leg. He shifted nervously, pretty sure Anna had not been talking about dinner, but rather something more in keeping with the playful foot under the table. He tried to avoid eye contact with her.

A moment later, the waiter returned and glowered at their unopened menus. "Would you like additional time to make a decision?" he asked icily.

"Not me," said Anna. "I just want a salad with vinaigrette."

"That sounds fine for me, too," said Mrs. Lovejoy, relieved at having the burden of translating the menu lifted. The waiter now stared impatiently at Terry, his eyes suggesting that

Terry be as easy to please as the two women and order a third salad.

"What do your recommend?" Terry asked.

"I recommend the salad."

"Fine," said Terry, adopting a tone equal to that of the waiter. "I'll have a salad."

The waiter smiled thinly but with satisfaction. He made a note and turned to leave. "And a steak," Terry added. The waiter stopped and without turning back made another notation on his pad.

"Our waiter isn't very friendly, is he, Mr. Rogers?" said Mrs. Lovejoy.

"He's an asshole," said Anna.

"Anna, don't talk like that. I must apologize, Mr. Rogers. The language that young people use today. We would never have thought of using such words in our day. I don't even know what half of them mean."

"Do you want me to tell you what asshole means, Mother?" asked Anna, with an innocent smile.

"What can I say, Mr. Rogers?" said the hapless Mrs. Lovejoy. Terry smiled noncommittally at her, then jumped as he felt the foot brush against his leg again.

"I want to tell you, I've had my fill of rude, unfriendly

people today," Mrs. Lovejoy continued, retreating to her previous thought. "Would you believe that we were actually attacked while sailing today. These horrid people just sailed right up and got right onto our yacht." She looked up briefly and said: Oh dear." A couple of about her own age were just passing the table.

"Hi, Mr. and Mrs. Arvis," said Anna. The man smiled weakly but the woman just sniffed and ignored her.

"Harold, Patrice," Mrs. Lovejoy stiffly acknowledged. The other couple nodded coolly and continued on without stopping.

"Actually, it's not our yacht," said Anna. "It belongs to Mr. Arvis, the man who just passed us."

"That's true," said Mrs. Lovejoy. "He's very big down here. Or so he thinks."

"Mom's right," Anna whispered to Terry. "He thinks he's big down here." She lowered her eyes quickly then looked back up at Terry. "But he's really not. How about you? *Est-ce grand?*" If Terry had missed the double entendre in her words and the added reinforcement of her eye motion, the hand on his knee would have made it quite clear. He coughed and fidgeted. The salads fortuitously arrived, and Terry prayed that Anna would give her full attention to eating.

Mrs. Lovejoy tore aggressively into her salad and, after several bites, returned to her tale of woe: "As I was saying, these terrible people came onto our boat . . ."

"It's called boarding, Mother."

"Boarding. These unpleasant people came boarding onto our boat. One of them even had a sword, and I'm certain he was as mad as a hatter. He dressed very strangely and kept talking about cutting people's hearts out."

"And their wickets off," Anna giggled. "At least Harold's little wicket. He was a pirate; they were all pirates. It was kind of exciting."

"Anna, stop that. We must just forget about the entire unpleasant incident. It was very trying."

Anna leaned closer to Terry and looked at him conspiratorially. "But he couldn't find Harold's wicket," she whispered and giggled.

Anna's playfulness had not registered with Terry. From Mrs. Lovejoy's first words about her ordeal, the countenance of Bad Basil Ringrose had risen immediately and absolutely in his mind. My God, he thought, they're actually doing it; they're going after Murchison Keyes. Was this a practice run?

"They were determined to kill us all," said Mrs. Lovejoy, having forgotten about the entire unpleasant incident for long enough.

"Actually, it was all a mistake," said Anna. "One of them – the young cute one – said they were looking for someone else."

"Nevertheless it was a terrible ordeal," said Mrs. Lovejoy, beating a dead ordeal.

"I'm sure it was," said Terry sympathetically, but he couldn't help laughing at the mental picture of Basil swashbuckling in full dress and the others trying to act like grownup pirates. Mrs. Lovejoy, unsure of the source of his laughter, looked at him sternly as she pushed her remaining lettuce into her mouth. Anna poked at her salad with the fork in her right hand and poked at Terry under the table with her left, watching him to see how he reacted. Terry tried to squirm free and ignore her the best he could as he conjured up the picture of Remy the Pirate. It was quite a handsome portrait, but it was continually violated by a leering Christian.

The waiter returned and silently removed two empty salad plates from the table. He then took up a position next to Terry and looked condescendingly down at him. "Shall I take away your salad, monsieur? Or would monsieur care to fondle it a bit longer?"

Suddenly realizing that the waiter was remarking on his left hand which was resting carelessly on his untouched salad,

Terry pulled it away, methodically wiped it with a napkin and, looking directly at the waiter, said: "I was just checking the lettuce. It's limp."

Not giving any quarter, the waiter replied: "I regret that. Would monsieur care to check the soup now?"

"Yes," Terry snarled.

Having finished her dinner, Mrs. Lovejoy was fidgeting as was Terry now that Anna was free of culinary distractions. "We should be getting upstairs," said Mrs. Lovejoy. "It's been an exhausting day. But dinner was quite pleasant, Mr. Rogers."

"Yes," said Anna. "It's been ever so . . . oh shit, I dropped my napkin." She leaned down and began fumbling under the table.

"Anna, your language," said Mrs. Lovejoy sternly.

"Anna!" said Terry sternly as her hand slid the length of his leg and into his crotch.

Anna sat up, wearing the smile of a good little girl, and held up the napkin. "Found it."

"They have busboys for that sort of thing," said Mrs. Lovejoy, standing.

"Now there's a novel idea, isn't it Terry," said Anna. "Oh dear, I think I forgot my room number, Mother."

"It's number eleven," said Mrs. Lovejoy.

"Room eleven," Anna repeated, turning toward Terry. "Mother and I have separate rooms because she insists on going to sleep right after dinner. I don't." Anna stood and stretched, and Terry realized what an attractive young woman she was. "So here I am, stuck all alone with the television and my vivid imagination." She gave Terry's leg a hard kick "Well, *plus tard,* Mr. Rogers. It's been a wonderful time in your neighborhood." Then softly singing "Won't you be my neighbor?" she stretched once again, winked, and strutted away.

As they disappeared, the waiter reappeared with a bowl of soup and placed it in front of Terry. "I'm sure you'll approve, monsieur. Mushroom bisque. It has a velvety texture. It slides sensuously through the fingertips."

"You realize, of course, that your gratuity has gone packing."

The waiter smiled back smugly. *"Service compris, monsieur."*

The Hotel L'Orient had eighteen rooms, six on each of its three floors. Terry's room, number 7, was on the second floor at one end of a dimly lit hallway, facing Room 12 at the other end. Rooms 8 through 11 lined one side of the hallway between them.

Terry returned to his room and alternately paced nervously and stared out the window toward a dark void that he knew was the Caribbean Sea. With a sigh, he turned away from the window and the little island he couldn't see and went to the bathroom where he showered, shaved and brushed his teeth, performing each ritual without giving it any thought.

Dressed, he opened the door to his room and stepped into the quiet hallway.

Chapter 7

"Oh, my gosh," wailed a pasty-faced Lieutenant Trillig. "I'm absent without leave. AWOL! And with stolen Navy property, too." They had led poor, inebriated Trillig back from the beach and put him to bed where he had remained for fourteen hours. This morning they had forced coffee and bits of solid food on him. He looked none the better for it.

"Now dear," said Peaches, "it wasn't really your fault. When you find them, you'll just tell them that, and everything will be just fine."

"I don't know where they are," Trillig moaned. "And if I find them, they'll probably shoot me before I can explain."

"There ain't no rascals gonna come shoot you while you're protected by us," said Basil. "You gots nothin' to fear. Them Navy folks ain't likely to be a messin' with us. Let's put it like as how it is, Hornblower. We be fearsome pirates."

Trillig stared at him through heavy, swollen eyes as if facing an apparition created by delirium tremens.

"It be the God's awful truth."

"Don't you know where your fleet was heading after they blew us apart, Hornblower?" Remy asked.

"They're heading south to latitude something-or-other. It's got a number but I can't remember it. Then they're going to an island, tomorrow maybe – or is it today – but what island? Oh, I should know. Darn! I can't remember. My head hurts. I think maybe I'm going to be sick."

"Just breath deep, dear," said Peaches. "And maybe have another cup of coffee." Trillig groaned. "Poor boy," mumbled Peaches as she headed back to her morning chores.

"You just relax for a little while," said Remy. "Maybe before long you'll be able to remember. And we'll help you find them."

"You'd really do that?" Trillig sniffed.

"Seamen always does for other seamen," said Basil gravely.

"Sure," said Remy. "Basil, would you see if you can find Stout and tell him we'll be going out again tomorrow morning. It's probably getting too late to go today. I'll see if I can find

186

Christian. Hornblower, you stay here and rest. Don't try to go anywhere, and don't fall off the chair."

Terry exited his room early, hoping to avoid Anna and Mrs. Lovejoy. He walked slowly through the still quiet hallway, just as he had last night, past Room 8 and Room 9, stopping at Room 10. It was here he had stood last night staring at the worn plastic number for fifteen endless minutes before turning back to his own room without ever reaching Room 11 and the temptation therein. Now he picked up his pace as he passed Room 11, made a sharp turn in front of Room 12 and bounded down the stairway to the street below.

After a ten-minute apology and a solemn promise to pay better attention to the airline's schedule, he had been rebooked on a morning flight to Martinique where he would be able to make connections to New York. He had been instructed, several times, to arrive an hour before the scheduled departure, a requirement generally not demanded of passengers who could be trusted. At close to two hours before his departure, Terry wandered into the nearly deserted L'Orient Airport terminal, through Security such as it was, had breakfast from a vending machine, and waited for the flight that would take him away from Remy forever.

As Terry sat in the matchbox waiting area, his only companions were the middle-aged couple in matching shirts with floral prints and the young woman who stood behind the Hopeful Air counter, shuffling papers. Although Terry was ticketed to Martinique and then on to New York aboard another airline, his mind stubbornly boarded flights back to Soleil – back to Albert and Peaches, Basil, Mutton and Christian – and yes back to Remy.

In time, a young man joined the few inhabitants of the terminal. He slumped into a spot at the other end of Terry's bench and quickly fell asleep. The counter attendant paid the sleeping newcomer no attention, and Terry speculated that he might be a local drunk who slept off his previous evenings on a regular basis, an itinerant whose only need in life was a warm beach, a cold bottle and an airport waiting room. He had long sun-bleached hair and a deep tan, and he wore wrinkled khaki pants and a white shirt that were once part of a uniform of some sort. Was it just Terry's current state of mind or did he in fact envy the young tramp and his (Terry guessed) carefree existence.

Finally, the middle-aged woman uttered the first words

spoken at the airport that morning. "When will our plane arrive?" she asked, addressing the young woman behind the counter.

She looked up. "Arrive? It's been here all night, actually. That's her right out there." She pushed her thumb in the direction of a small two-engine plane standing twenty feet beyond the doorway. It looked as if it had always stood there and always would. An expression not unlike that of a newly caged animal spread across the inquiring woman's face. Terry could empathize; the aircraft was tiny, capable of seating six, including the pilot, uncomfortably, and it had seen better times. Terry scrutinized it for signs of patched-over World War II bullet holes but found none; either it had survived all its dogfights unscathed or had been cleverly repaired.

Terry shuddered and asked: "When are we leaving?"

"Don't know," said the attendant without looking up from her paperwork. "Tommy, when you plan to leave?"

The beach bum stirred at the other end of the bench but did not open his eyes as he spoke: "Everybody here?"

"I guess so."

"Couldn't scare up a fourth, huh?" The beach bum now known as Tommy sat up, opened his eyes and shook his head a bit. "Well folks, I guess Hopeful Air flight 21 is ready for boarding. Why don't we introduce ourselves. First names are fine. I'm Tommy, your pilot."

Terry, Herbert and Wanda introduced themselves. "Okay, let's weigh in."

"Baggage is one twenty," said the attendant. Tommy pulled a clipboard from the side of the bench and made a notation. Then he looked to Terry and said: "How much you weigh, Terry?"

"One seventy," said Terry, confused by the question and just a little worried about its pertinence.

"And how about you folks?" Tommy asked the couple.

"Two hundred," Herbert answered.

"Wanda?" Tommy prodded.

She looked to her husband as if he could somehow make this easier, then quietly said: "One fifty . . . seven."

Tommy scratched at his clipboard with the air of an evil mathematics genius calculating the imminent explosion of the entire Earth, while the others looked on, fearing that the calculations would somehow prove that danger lurked within their combined weights. Calculations completed, he set the clipboard down. "I hope we're not too heavy," said Terry.

"I guess if we all push hard, we'll get her off the ground," said Tommy with a grin. Wanda let out a low, painful squeal.

"Just kidding, ma'am. Well, I guess it's all aboard time. No, that's train talk. Let's all hop in and take her for a spin." He opened the door to the runway, received a pinch on the behind and a salacious look from the attendant, then led them out to the plane. They followed slowly, meekly, as if approaching their final judgment. After the passengers themselves had loaded their luggage into the small compartment to the rear of the wing, Tommy locked the compartment, jumped up on the wing, and opened the single door.

"Step right up, ma'am," he said, extending a hand to the white-faced woman.

"On the wing?"

"I'm afraid that's how we get in, Wanda," said Tommy. "They don't make those roll-about stairways in our size. Just take my hand. It'll be fun."

With the help of her husband pushing from below and Tommy pulling from above, Wanda climbed up across the wing and forced her way into the cabin, taking the seat just behind the pilot's. "I've never been on one of these before," she explained as she passed Tommy.

"Your first time?" said Tommy. "How did you folks get here?"

"Catamaran," answered Herbert, climbing onto the wing. "Thought it might be exciting."

"Hey, if you're looking for excitement, you've come to the right place," said Tommy.

"Ooooh," came Wanda's plaintive reaction. As her husband took the seat next to her, she imbedded the nails of her right hand in his left wrist.

Terry climbed up, and Tommy motioned to the front seat. "Guess who's my copilot today?"

"I was hoping for God," said Terry.

Tommy laughed. "Good, Terry. *God Is My Copilot*. 1945. Must have seen it a dozen times on TV. Hell, that's how I learned to fly." Terry heard the gasp from the rear seat as Tommy grinned and jumped down from the wing. Tommy walked slowly around the plane, making a quick inspection as he went, then hopped up on the other wing and climbed in next to Terry.

"Comfortable?" he asked.

"I've been in Buicks bigger than this," said Terry.

"Yeah, but they didn't have all these nifty dials, did they? Actually, the dials are all just for show. We do everything by leaning – lean back to take off, left or right to turn, forward to land. See that little warning light over there? That's your job. If it goes on, scream." He twisted a key, and a moment later, the left engine jumped into action; the right engine limped slowly to life. "Now if you wouldn't mind holding that door open with your leg. Otherwise, it gets damn hot in here. That's just while we taxi. You can close it when we take off."

"Thanks," said Terry, pushing his leg out the opening and planting it firmly against the door. The plane began to move slowly toward the end of the runway.

"Welcome to Hopeful Air service to Martinique," said Tommy theatrically. "Let me assure you that our name does not refer to our prayers for individual flights but to our overall corporate goal. We hope to grow up to be American Airlines. Those are flotation devices you're sitting on. You'll probably find seat belts nearby; please buckle up. The emergency exit is the door you came in through. To open it, turn the handle – works just like a Buick. We'll hit Martinique in about an hour – bad wording – we'll arrive in about an hour. From there, I imagine you'll be continuing on aboard a real airplane. Until then, enjoy the flight."

They reached the upper end of the runway and reversed direction. The entire runway stretched out ahead of them, twice the width of the plane itself and hauntingly short. It ended abruptly where the ocean began.

"Okay, Terry," said Tommy, "you can bring in the old leg and slam that door tight. You might want to lock it, too. Keeps intruders out. Here we go, folks, just like in the movies. Everybody cross fingers. Just joking again, Wanda."

Rattling a bit, the plane moved down the runway, picking up speed, and just before the runway disappeared, rose above the ground, hung suspended for a moment, then climbed upward in a large arc. Terry unclenched his fists and relaxed; it was like launching a paper airplane, easy and effortless. In fact, it was the most comfortable take-off he'd ever endured, almost fun. The plane climbed steadily through blue skies that crackled with purity, past a few puffy clouds hanging in stark white contrast, until it finally leveled off at a height that still enabled Terry to easily identify everything below. Terry looked back to see how his fellow travelers had fared through take-off. Herbert was intensely flushed, his additional depth of color probably stolen from his wife who was so completely white and rigid that Terry wondered if she were still alive until the little plane bounced across an air pocket and brought forth a muffled gasp.

"There's Pointe Francoise, off to your right," said Tommy.

"Then that must be Soleil," said Terry, pointing to a small land mass jutting out of the ocean just beyond it.

"Hey, you're good at this," said Tommy. "Maybe I'll take a nap."

"I've just come from there – Booby Bay."

"I guess I've never been there."

"That's a pretty impressive yacht down there," said Terry, looking down at a large craft just below them.

"It certainly is," said Tommy. "The Esperance. Belongs to a wealthy dude named Keyes. Some folks say he got his wealth by running drugs, illegal immigrants, you name it. Really nasty sort."

"I can't go to Martinique," said Terry, suddenly.

"Beg pardon," said Tommy.

"I can't go. I have to go to Soleil."

"I'm sorry. But I can't turn back at this point."

"Can you land this thing on Soleil?" Terry asked.

"Why is he talking like that?" said Wanda. "Don't let him talk that way, Herbert."

"No way," said Tommy. "There's nowhere to land."

Terry thought for a moment, pushing aside his feelings of foreboding. "Can you fly very low over the water and slow enough so that I can jump?"

"He's crazy, Herbert," said Wanda.

"I could get low," said Tommy, "but anything less than sixty and we'll stall."

"Then I'll jump at sixty."

"My God, Herbert. He's a maniac. He's escaped from one of those asylum places. Do something."

"You'll just kill yourself," said Tommy.

"Don't let them slow down, Herbert. We'll all be killed. We'll drop into the ocean and drown."

"Maybe I will," said Terry. "But I've got to try."

"Look, Terry. Why don't you go on to Martinique, then just fly back. Chances are you'll be back by tomorrow morning."

"There isn't enough time," said Terry. "I don't like to be nasty but if you don't do it, I'll start pushing buttons and pulling levers."

"Herbert, don't let them. Kill him, Herbert. Kill him."

"Okay, buddy, I'll slow her down as much as I can."

Terry wondered why he heard no further protests from the rear-seat passengers and, looking back, realized the merciful silence was a result of their both having fainted.

"Better take one of those flotation cushions," said Tommy, as he banked the small plane in the direction of Soleil. "Maybe I can get her down to fifty-five, but you're still going to hit the water mighty hard."

"Thanks," said Terry. "I appreciate it."

"Don't thank me," said Tommy. "Even at fifty-five, it's still going to kill you."

As he opened the door and inched his way out, Terry mused momentarily that this arrival at Booby Bay might be even more dramatic than his first arrival, aboard the flotsam cruise line. "At least this time it isn't raining." He jumped.

Remy bounded down the beach to the water's edge where Christian and Peaches stood mesmerized by something out across the water. They stared without speaking and didn't acknowledge Remy's arrival. "We'll go out after Keyes again tomorrow – bright and early, okay?" she said.

"Okay," Christian answered mechanically without turning his head.

"What are you two so interested in out there?" Remy asked.

"A plane just flew by," said Christian.

"You're staring at a plane that's come and gone? I know we don't see many planes here, but still . . ."

"It came in very low over the water," Christian explained. "Very low, and it slowed down as if it were going to attempt to land. Then it dropped something and picked up speed and altitude again."

"Something or someone," said Peaches. "And maybe it wasn't dropped. Maybe it was a someone who was pushed out."

"Or jumped," said Christian.

"Come on," said Remy. "What fool would jump out of a plane? It's probably a bag of garbage some jerk generously dropped off at the Booby Bay landfill. There's nothing there now, so it must have sunk."

"Yes, there is," said Christian. "I can see it now."

"Where?" Remy began to stare as intently out to sea as the others.

"There." Christian pointed to a barely discernible object bobbing in the water.

"Okay," said Remy. "I see it now. It does seem to be floating in."

"Me too," said Peaches. "You don't suppose it's another stranger floating in?"

"I've lived most of my 25 years on this island," said Remy, "and in that time exactly one stranger has floated in. I should think it would be another 25 years before we got a second."

"We'll know soon," said Christian. "It's getting bigger."

Six eyes remained frozen on the approaching object as it continued in its direct path toward them.

"It's a someone," said Peaches. "I can see its arms moving. It seems to be swimming."

The object was indeed a human form, and it continued to paddle closer and take on a mortal appearance until finally the paddling stopped, and it stood up in the water, although only a head and shoulders showed above the surface. As it walked through the water, it became a man, fully clothed, and then, at about twenty feet out, a familiar figure. In less than a minute, Terry, thoroughly soaked, a flotation cushion wrapped across his chest like a baseball catcher's chest protector, stood grinning at them.

"Hi," said Terry. "Remember me?"

Remy laughed. "You insist on arriving with a splash, don't you?"

"Did someone push you out of that plane, poor boy?" said Peaches, helping him out of the cushion, trying to dust the water off him and generally fussing.

"No, I guess I jumped."

"That was a very foolish thing to do," said Peaches. " You might have been killed."

"Well, when I hit the water, I thought I was. I always

thought water was supposed to be softer than that."

Remy studied him as he spoke. "Why did you leave?" she asked, her voice sounding more accusatory than she had intended.

"I just figured it was time to go home," said Terry. "I'm sure the American public is suffering from acute yellow journalism deprivation. And I was just starting to get in the way here."

"Well, you certainly weren't in anyone's way," said Peaches.

"Why did you come back?" asked Remy.

"Because I . . . do you suppose I could have a cup of coffee?"

"Of course, of course," said Peaches. "You just come right up to the cafe, and we'll fix you up good. Albert will be happy to see you, I'm sure. He hasn't said anything, but I think he was sorry you left. I think we all were." Peaches glowered at Remy who quickly looked down at the beach to avoid the reproachful glare.

When they had settled themselves into chairs at the cafe and Terry sipped at his coffee, Remy said to him: "You didn't tell us why you came back." Her voice had softened, and she looked at Terry in that way that had rendered him helpless many times before. For a moment he might have thought she was hoping for a certain answer, if he had not known better.

"I heard about your pirate adventure," he said, careful not to let an I-told-you-so creep into his voice. "Last night, from two of your victims. And this morning on the plane I heard some things about Murchison Keyes, and I had to come back."

"What things?" asked Remy.

"He holds a mean grudge. I don't think he's going to be content to let things drop. He knows how to get even. He buys people to do it for him. According to Tommy, my pilot, he even got to someone in the U.S. Navy. They're down here on maneuvers. His guy switched some numbers so that the Navy would fire on an inhabited island. Just to settle a score with one person. Quite a guy, huh? And now you're out looking for him."

"That one person was Albert," said Remy. "And this was the island."

Trillig had lifted his head from the table and was staring at Terry as though he were the Angel of Death. "My God," he said. "I . . . "

Not really understanding why Trillig was babbling or even who he was, Terry went on: "Keyes is in the neighborhood. And sooner or later you'll find him. That's why I had to come back."

"That . . .that was me," Trillig stammered. "They gave me the wrong coordinates so I'd destroy this island. I knew I didn't make a mistake."

Terry looked at him, bewildered, and Remy said: "This is Hornblower. He's with the U.S. Navy. He was the one shooting at us, but he didn't mean to. He's very sorry."

"Pleased to meet you, Hornblower," said Terry. "Where's the rest of the Navy?"

"They went away," said Peaches, "and they forgot to take poor Hornblower with them."

"Phony numbers, on purpose," said Trillig, flushing with anger. "That no good scoundrel."

"Who be's a scoundrel?" Basil, with Mutton in tow, had just joined the party. He spotted Terry. "Oh, there be's the scoundrel. Who drug the rogue back?"

"He came back himself," said Peaches. "He's not a scoundrel."

"He came to our rescue just like the cavalry," said Christian. There was no sarcasm in his voice. "If you heard very much about our first adventure, you know how much we need you." He turned to Remy and, now with sarcasm, said:. "Isn't that right, Remy?

Remy blushed and looked down at the table.

"Actually," said Terry, "I was going to try one more time to convince you that you should let the authorities handle this."

"We can't," said Remy without looking up. "I can't. I never thought I could actually hate anyone. I didn't think I had it in me. But I do. Hate is really quite simple. I hate Keyes; I want him dead. It's a nice straightforward emotion. It's not like other emotions that can get cloudy and complicated."

"He's a son of a bitch," said Terry. "I'm afraid he'll hurt you . . . all of you, I mean. And Albert. Anyway, I'm here again. And, well, I'm ready to do whatever I can, even if it's chasing after Keyes. If you still want me, that is."

Remy looked up. "I'm the captain," she said, her eyes suggesting that, if anyone were a potential mutineer, it was he.

"You're the captain," said Terry.

Remy smiled at him. "I still want you." Terry looked back at her directly, causing her to blush again. For just a moment, he thought – hoped – that maybe – but then Christian spoke.

"Tell him now, Remy," said Christian firmly.

Oh shit, Terry thought, *they've made it official.* "No need to tell me anything," said Terry quietly. Then with forced cheerfulness, he added: "Except which end of the boat you want me to stand on, captain."

203

"So ol' Bonney be's back t'buccaneerin' with us," said Basil, once again effectively steering the conversation and the possibility of Remy's revelation off the road and into a ditch.

"Did you go somewhere?" asked Mutton.

"I'd like to go with you, too," said Trillig. "I want to get that son of . . .uh . . . of a bee, too."

"Thanks Hornblower," said Remy. "But I don't know if you want to get involved in this. After all, you're a pacifist and we have no peaceful intentions."

"I want to," said Trillig with a sudden loud burst of determination. "I want to be a buckaroo, too."

Basil roared with laughter. "Whoa, laddie. A buckaroo is one what rides around on horses like Buffalo Bob Hickock. We's buccaneers, and that's a right different thing. We be goin' after scalawags, not injuns and cowpokers."

"But I still want to go," said Trillig.

"We'll need all the help we can get," said Terry. "Keyes isn't alone."

"Okay, Hornblower," said Remy. "Consider yourself conscripted. This should really please your father – my son, the pirate."

"Oh we's be gettin' a jolly good piratin' crew," said Basil, heading for the bottle of rum that stood on the bar. "We'd best toast seafarin'."

Remy stared intently at Terry, then finally spoke. "Thank you for coming back.

I . . . we . . ."

"What my sister is ineptly trying to say is . . ."

"What did you say?" said Terry with a sudden shudder.

"My brother was just reminding me that I forgot to tell you that I missed you and I'm glad you're back." She looked at him with the same eyes that had captivated him that night on the beach so long ago, and even at midday, the stars were shining there.

The table and all those sitting around it – except Remy – grew smaller as Terry floated above them, cavorting in the air like a drunken Icarus. Mutton's voice was barely audible from the ground below: "Half a brother. Just half a brother. The same father but not the same mother."

Chapter 8

Three-inch-high letters spelling Esperance (each pirate checked the spelling several times) loomed above on the stern of the shining steel-clad luxury yacht. Murchison Keyes' yacht almost dwarfed the galleasse, reinforcing its image as a bygone anachronism in a twentieth century Caribbean Sea.

"Jesus Christ," said Christian. "It's monstrous."

"Do you have to talk like that?" Trillig asked. "Blasphemy won't help make this any easier. Prayer would be more likely to help."

"I prays I can straightaway look eyeball to eyeball with that rogue Murchison Keyes." Basil stared at the Esperance through crimson eyes. "But I won't be eyeballin' him for long. One quick look then I runs the bastard through like a friggin' shish-ka-bob."

"I didn't think it would be so big," said Christian.

"The bigger they be, the faster they sinks," said Basil.

Remy shushed them. "You're making too much noise. We don't want to announce that we're coming."

"We certainly don't," said Terry. "When you attack the QE II in a rowboat, you need all the element of surprise you can get. They've probably got semi-automatics and assault rifles and God knows what other fancy weapons. We, by the way, are unarmed." Except, of course, Basil's sword, Stout's shotgun, and Remy's brace of ancient pistols without bullets, surreptitiously borrowed from Albert. "Let's just hope they think it's a joke until it's too late."

"They'll find out soon enough it's no joke," Remy growled.

"You be right, lass," said Basil. "They be laughing from the other side of their faces right soon."

"How are we going to get up there?" asked Mutton surveying the obstacle above and looking confused.

"A rope and a hook over the railing," said Remy, matter-of-factly. "Simplicity itself." She picked up the heavy rope with the large iron hook attached to one end. "Mutton, throw this up and make it stay there."

The others watched spellbound as Mutton followed Remy's instructions to the letter, tossing the rope in the right direction and hooking it properly on the first throw as though he'd been performing this feat his entire life.

"Let's board this mother," said Remy, grabbing hold of the rope. Terry stepped in her way.

"May I make a suggestion, Captain?" he said.

"Okay," said Remy.

"Let me go first. If they spot us coming aboard – which they probably will – I might be able to talk my way on and keep them occupied for a moment. Basil and Mutton should follow me so that if I don't succeed we'll have some brawn. Then Christian and Trillig, and you're last, because you're the captain and you should make a proper entrance."

Remy thought for a moment then said: "Okay, I guess I can live with that."

"Can I say one more thing before I go up?"

"If you must," said Remy impatiently.

"I haven't had the opportunity to tell you how sorry I am about the things I said. I know they hurt. I didn't want to hurt you – well, at the moment, I guess I did – but I was just – well, I'm sorry and I want to be friends again for real."

"And you want to kiss and make up," said Remy, "here and now?"

"Just make up. You don't have to kiss me. But it's important to know you forgive me."

"Why?"

"I guess I'm just insecure."

"My God," said Remy. "We're in the middle of boarding an enemy vessel to plunder and kill, and you're telling me you're insecure."

Terry grinned and Remy had to laugh. "Okay," she said, "we're friends. I'm sorry too. I said some pretty mean things myself."

"Are we gonna do some piratin' or are we gonna jabber all day long?" said Basil.

Terry grabbed the rope and started to climb, but Remy grabbed his arm, pulled him back and kissed him. "Be careful," she said. With a pirate song in his heart, Terry bounded up the rope. As he climbed over the rail, Mutton started up the rope, and then Basil. Terry looked down at them and shrugged his shoulders to indicate all was quiet on deck. But, as Terry stood alone on the deck and Mutton peered over the railing, two amorphous goons suddenly appeared.

"Hey, who the hell are you?" one of them shouted.

"Good morning, gentlemen," said Terry as they approached. "Doctor Terrence Bonney. Sorry to disturb you like this but we've had a peck of trouble with our boat. She seems to be taking on water. Our cell phones don't work, and we were hoping that you might have a ship-to-shore on board." Mutton climbed over the rail and stood next to Terry; Basil followed. "And these two gentlemen are Mormon missionaries. We were on our way to the leper colony to see what we might do."

"Why's that missionary fella dressed up like Captain Hook?"

"Brother Brigham is just a bit eccentric," said Terry maintaining his innocent smile. "But he's very sure of his calling." Christian climbed over the rail followed by Trillig. "This young lad has just come from an orphanage; he's on his way to meet his new foster family. And the other gentleman is a social worker."

"Hmmm," growled the talking thug as he looked to his silent companion. "Are there more of you down there?"

"Just the schoolmarm," said Terry as Remy swung over the railing and onto the deck.

"Schoolmarm?" said the goon as he and his companion both let their eyes sweep the length of her body. "Don't look like no schoolmarm I ever seen."

"You'll change your mind when I take a ruler to your

knuckles," growled Remy. "Now why don't you run along and sit in a corner."

At that moment, three more men started across the deck toward them. Remy and Terry both quickly recognized them as Sammy Apollo and his burly blonde bookends. "I think this is it," Terry whispered.

"What's going on here?" shouted Apollo. "Who are these people?"

"My name is Remy Lafitte," Remy shouted back, jumping on a wooden box to give herself added height and, hopefully, menace. "Remy Lafitte, the pirate. We're here for Murchison Keyes."

"Pirates?" Apollo chuckled but his two men tensed. Apollo stared at her for a moment then recognition crossed his face. "Hey. You're the broad from that old guy's cafe, what. What the hell's going on here?"

"That old guy is Albert Lafitte," Remy continued. "And we're here on his behalf. To repay the favor."

"Now," said Terry quietly to Christian. The two of them flanked the large goons. As Terry spoke, the goons, who had been concentrating on Remy, looked toward him. The closest looked just in time to see Terry's fist, propelled by all the strength he could muster, coming at his face. It was a lucky, well-placed blow and it sent the larger man sprawling across the deck.

At the same time, Christian jumped onto the back of the other, riding him around the deck like an unmanageable horse, unable to pull him off his feet. Basil moved in and brought a big knee into the man's groin. "How's your balls, matey?" he chortled.

With a quick surprised look at Basil, the goon doubled over, shaking Christian loose. Christian crashed to the deck and sat there groaning as Basil, chuckling all the while, brought his knee up into the hunkered man's face. The momentum of this blow carried him back upward, and Basil followed up with a fist to the side of the head.

Sammy Apollo and his two men had been standing back, comfortable with the two goons' handling of the intruders and content to avoid getting mussed themselves. But now Apollo snapped his fingers and motioned in the direction of the intruders. Instead of joining the fray, Apollo's men moved quickly to the railing of the yacht and reached down into two large wooden boxes. From his seat on the deck, Christian spotted them, realized they were going for firearms and shouted: "Hey, Mutton. Those two Penn State linebackers just called you a has-been wreck from Sissy Tech."

Apollo's men managed to grab hold of their weapons but had no time to use them, for Mutton rumbled toward them like a bowling ball lobbed halfway down the alley and scored a perfect pocket hit that sent them both flying overboard at forty-five degree angles. Seeing the tide turning against them, Apollo slithered past the action and grabbed Remy in a move calculated to bring the others sheepishly to bay. He threw an arm around her from behind but discovered that she was more than an armful. Writhing and kicking, she quickly loosened herself from his grip and sent him sprawling back into Basil's open arms.

Basil had not expected Apollo to drop in unannounced, but he welcomed him anyway – with a hand around Apollo's throat. "Who are you, little man?" asked Basil.

"Who are you?" Sammy hissed, his voice straining to pass through the large hand clenched around his skinny throat.

"I be a fearsome pirate. Bad Basil Ringrose by name; killin' rogues, by game. I'm just gettin' you ready to meet up with your maker. The old mighty and me got a rangement about rogues. He makes 'em, and I takes 'em out. Now what rogue are you? Be you Murchison Keyes?"

Even though Basil's grip had reduced his voice to a squeak, Sammy answered: "Let me go, you stupid blockheaded asshole." Basil tightened his grip, lifting Apollo off the deck.

213

"Y'know how pirates deal with rogues. Ever hear of old Lollynoise? Why he just up and tore his victim's 'eart right from outen his chest and ate it up. Maybe you wouldn't be so much for namecallin' if Bad Basil was to do the like. Or maybe I just cut you up into little bitty pieces and feed you to the fish."

"I'm . . .not . . .Keyes."

"What are you doing with that piece of garbage, Basil?" asked Terry, joining them.

"He followed me home," said Basil. "Can I keep 'im?"

"God no," said Terry. "You don't know where it might have been. Just toss it overboard." Basil dutifully carried Sammy Apollo by the neck to the starboard side of the yacht with Terry following.

"Thar she blows," huffed Basil as he flung Apollo over the rail and off to sea.

"Hey, Sam," Terry yelled. "That's for your pal Al."

Just as the pirates were about to congratulate one another, armed reinforcements came scurrying down the deck — four men, two of them waving guns in the pirates' direction. They took aim, and the sound of gunfire echoed across the empty sea. But the sound had come from a different direction and the two armed men were suddenly on the deck groveling and screaming. Barnaby Stout looked over the railing at them and smiled; his shotgun rested on the railing. The other two men looked in horror at their fallen comrades just long enough for Mutton to bring them both down with a running tackle.

"What's the meaning of this?" said a heavy-set man in flowered pajamas as he rounded the cabin from the other direction. "Who's shooting? What's going on?" He was bald with a grayish face and a thin mustache. Quickly, he surveyed the scene before him; a half dozen of his bodyguards lay scattered lifelessly around the deck while a half dozen intruders roamed at will. "Who are you and what are you doing on my yacht?"

"You must be Murchison Keyes," said Remy stepping toward him.

"I am," said Keyes haughtily. "And I demand to know why you're on my yacht, fighting with my men."

"I'm Remy Lafitte and this is my crew of cutthroats. We're from Booby Bay."

"Booby Bay," said Keyes. The puzzled look on his face turned quickly to recognition. "Ah, Booby Bay. And what are your intentions?"

"We've come to rape, pillage, and plunder," answered Remy. "And kill."

He looked at her, and a thin, malicious smile spread

215

underneath the pencil mustache. Remy continued to glower back at him as fiercely as she could but she hardly instilled fear. At 5'3", towering over her six-foot adversary was a flight of buccaneer fancy; her face was clean and fresh; her snarl was more of a kittenish pout; and her firm, unpiratelike breasts gave new meaning to Terry's white shirt. Murchison Keyes leaned casually against the cabin wall, ogling her, and said: "Rape your little heart out, my dear."

Remy gave him a black look, then turned to Basil and said: "Rape him."

Keyes self-confident smile disappeared as Basil, thoroughly confused by his captain's last command but nevertheless duty-bound to obey her, stumbled toward Keyes. Fear quickly overwhelmed Keyes, and he bolted toward the chest of armaments. But just before he reached his quest, he tripped over a prostrate goon and fell headlong into Trillig who had been leaning against the rail handling one of the weapons, as if trying to figure out how it worked. Keyes and Trillig were equally surprised by their sudden encounter and even more surprised by the gun's discharge. Surprise remained Trillig's expression but not Keyes'. A look of profound shock stole across the once smug face as he staggered back and saw his own blood seeping through the pajamas. He fell against the railing, and his momentum was enough to carry him easily over it and to the sea below.

Basil staggered over to the trembling young man with the smoking gun; Trillig dropped the weapon as though it were burning his hand. Basil threw big arms around him and said: "So you be the lucky one who got old Murchison Keyes. Who'd a thought? Shiver me timbers, who'd a thought?"

Remy, nonplussed, stood silently as the others watched, awaiting further orders. Finally, the pirate captain found voice and instructed her motley crew to search the yacht and toss overboard anything that looked even vaguely like drugs. "But don't take things," she added. "We're pirates, but not thieves."

Terry snapped a salute and winked, then he and Christian headed around the cabin and down the starboard deck. Basil, leading a dazed Trillig, took the port side, Basil muttering in awe: "The little pacifier lad. Shiver me timbers." Mutton stacked goons.

With her crew occupied, Remy strolled to the railing and looked out across the tranquil sea. She shouted into the silence: "And how do you like that for a daughter, Albert, you old fart. Yo ho ho and a bottle of fucking rum."

After the bloodthirsty pirates had stuffed themselves on Peaches' elaborate celebration dinner, Remy raided the Booby Bay Cafe bar and found a bottle of fine French champagne. Ceremoniously popping the cork, she emptied the contents of the bottle into disparate glass tumblers. When the champagne had been distributed to all present, Remy raised her glass and said: "To the swarthiest, scurviest crew of swashbucklers ever to sail the high seas, the scourge of the Murchison Keyeses of the world. Thank you. Thank you for being my friends . . . my family."

They all drank except for Trillig who sat staring blankly at his glass.

"What's the matter, Hornblower?" asked Remy.

"I killed him," said Trillig. "I actually killed a man. I don't believe in killing, but I went and did it. Cut him down."

"It was really kind of self-defense, Hornblower," said Christian. "You couldn't help it."

"Besides," said Remy. "We're not really talking about a man. He's a predatory animal. He wouldn't have thought twice about killing you, or any of us. He didn't think twice about burning us out or blowing us up. Did he ever think about the victims of his drugs? There's no reason for shame, Hornblower. You're a hero."

"And another besides, matey," said Basil with a wink. "You gots the reward."

"Where's Albert?" asked Terry in a transparent attempt to shift the conversation elsewhere.

"He's sleeping," said Peaches.

"Does he know about today?" Remy asked.

"Yes, I told him. He acted kind of funny about it. I think he couldn't decide what to think. He did have a cigar and a glass of sherry but mostly he just sat there staring and thinking. He smiled once though and said 'Remy.' But then he went to bed."

Remy sighed.

"Give it some time to sink in," said Terry. "Albert has to reflect on things. And it certainly is a lot to digest all at once. In a day or two."

"You're right," said Remy, brightening. "Let's give it a day or two. And let's have some more champagne."

"Tell me all about your adventure," said Peaches.

"And adventure t'was," said Basil. "First we storms the ship, fearsome and belligerent and reckless, cuttin' down black'earts left and right, tossin' some to the sharkies. And then there be the blackest of the rogues, Murchison Keyes hisself, standin' afore me tremblin' as like to give up the ghost right there. And there be our own Bad Basil makin' ready to do my

219

duty and colleck my reward, figurin' to toy with the scalawag for a bit afore runnin' 'im through. Maybe poke 'im here and there with my sword and scratch 'im up a bit. But the rogue turns and runs off like the coward he is and straight at old Hornblower who shoots 'im right proper – an I ain't sayin' he hadn't no right to. Rogues is fair game, and old Basil just lost out on 'is reward. But I'd a killed him prettier."

"There's a reward for Mr. Keyes?" said Peaches.

"Not really," said Remy quickly. "Basil's just confused."

"Well, there should be," said Peaches. "After all you had to go through." That said, Peaches excused herself and went to check on Albert. Basil, his tale splendidly told, pulled a little box out of his pocket and began to turn it over and over, studying it.

"What's that, Basil?" asked Christian.

"It's offen the boat," said Basil.

"Basil," said Remy, "I said we wouldn't take anything."

"It ain't anything really," said Basil, fondling the box. "Just a itty bitty treasure chest. Sorta looks like a real one though, don't it? It ain't really plunder; it's just a momentum of the occasion. An I be giving it to you, 'cause you be the captain." He handed the box to Remy.

"It's all right, Basil," said Remy. "You can keep it. Do you know if there's anything in it?"

"Don't know," said Basil. "She's locked. Don't rattle none though."

"Here, let me try," said Christian. He took the box and began to work at the little lock with a table knife while the others looked on in fascination. After a few moments of fiddling, the lid sprang up with a little pop, and Christian pulled out a piece of paper that had been folded several times to make it fit in the box. He carefully unfolded it and smoothed it out on the table.

"Holy jibbers," cried Basil. "This here be a treasure map." The drawing on the paper did resemble a map – various lines, symbols and directional arrows, all within an amoeba-like outline.

"Treasure map?" Terry scoffed. "This is the 21st century. They don't bury treasure any more; they put it in Swiss bank accounts."

"It does look like a map," said Remy.

Barnaby Stout, who had been standing behind them staring at the paper with interest, suddenly spoke: "Hey, ho. I think I recognize that shape. See how it sort of looks like a dog's head."

"No," said Mutton, straining his eyes at the picture. "It looks more like a duck."

"I'd say a horse," said Christian.

"Duck, dog, cow, grizzly bear," said Basil impatiently. "What's it matter? You knows it, Stout?"

"Yes," said Stout, now emphatic in his certainty. "It's part of a string of tiny islands near the Virgins – kind of an archipelago – known as the Isle of Black Misery because a hundred years ago the few people that lived there all died of some disease. They're still uninhabited because of that and because most of the low-lying areas are underwater at high tide. Some of the islands even disappear entirely. The parts that don't get flooded are pretty rocky. There are better places to live. This island is called Hairless Cay. From a distance, the rocks poking out above the trees look like a bald man's head."

"Sorta like old Albert's head," said Basil. "Well shit in me drawers if we don't have us a treasure map. An where there's a treasure map they's gotta be treasure. Whoop de do."

"Basil," said Remy quietly. "If there is a treasure there, it's drug money. We can't take it."

"But it be's Murchison Keyes' now," said Basil. "An there ain't no more Murchsion Keyes."

"It doesn't matter," said Remy, pouring some rum from Basil's bottle into her tumbler. "I think we should turn it over to someone."

"She's right," said Terry. "How about Hornblower? He's the U.S. Navy."

Remy, seeing the look of disappointment on Basil's face, said: "Let's sleep on it."

"In the meantime, why don't you let Remy keep the map," Terry suggested. "She is the captain."

"Okay, cap'n" said Basil, handing her the map. "We sleeps on it." Then he suddenly grinned and poked Trillig with an elbow. "Least as how most of us be sleepin', but not them what's collectin' rewards, right Hornblower." Trillig blushed and gulped down the rest of his champagne.

"It must be gettin' nigh on to rewards time," said Basil.

"Knock it off, Basil," said Terry. He turned to Remy and continued quietly: "You don't have to go through with it. The whole thing was a dumb idea. And you were upset at the time. I'm sure no one will hold you to it."

Remy put her hand on his arm, squeezed it briefly and said: "I know it was a dumb idea, and my agreeing to it was stupid. I'm sure my anger had something to do with it. But I did agree. And everyone else here, for whatever reason, kept his end of the bargain. I've got to keep mine; I hope you can understand that. I'm sorry. I wish . . ." She stopped and downed her rum. "Well, Hornblower, I guess you're the man of the hour."

Terry stood and without saying anything further walked out of the cafe. Remy watched his departure, also silent. She poured herself another glass of rum after which Basil poured one for Trillig and one for himself.

"Here's to Hornblower," said Remy, taking a big gulp.

"Hows about the others of us which almost kilt that rogue gets to watch?" said Basil.

"What are we watching?" asked Mutton.

"Nothing, Mutton," said Remy. "Why don't you just watch Basil here while Hornblower and I go for a walk." She stood, extended her hand to Trillig and smiled. "Come on, handsome. Let's do pirate things."

Terry paced the beach in agitation, smoking his first cigarette in ten years – and his second and his third. It was all so idiotic, he told himself. Remy with Trillig – to imagine, an idea spawned by the questionable mind of Basil Ringrose coming to lunatic fruition. Folly. He stopped and stared out to the darkened sea now unsure if he really wanted to be here alone. Finally, he decided he would return to the cafe for one drink then take his shattered psyche to bed. As he started to turn, however, he was grabbed from behind by strong arms. He struggled momentarily against his silent assailant but a sharp prick in his back instinctively brought his protestation to a halt.

"You're absolutely right," his captor said dispassionately. "That is a knife in your back. A very sharp knife."

"What do you want?" said Terry.

"Me? I don't want anything. However, Mr. Keyes wants to speak with you, and I'm here to see that you do speak to him. If he wants me to kill you during or after the conversation,

I will. Nothing personal, of course."

"Keyes is dead," said Terry.

"Let me assure you," said another voice somewhere behind him, "that, as Dickens said, the reports of my death are greatly exaggerated." Murchison Keyes stepped out of the darkness to face Terry. He didn't look particularly dead. Patting the right side of his rib cage, he said: "A minor injury – and an unpleasant swim."

"That's unfortunate," said Terry.

"Ah yes, one of our tough-talking pirates. "We'll see how tough the talk remains. Now let me point out that the knife at your back could easily be imbedded within your back. I would prefer it that way. Your unwarranted intrusion has aggravated me deeply. You attempted to kill me; even now one of my men lies near death from his wounds. Killing you would be a

225

pleasure actually, but at the moment I have more important concerns. You have a document of mine; I want it."

"Document?" said Terry. "What document?"

"Don't play the idiot with me. I'm not going to stand here and play a silly cat and mouse game. I'll just tell you once. You or one of your playmates bring the map to the harbor by 6 a.m. and, as much as it disappoints me, I'll let bygones be bygones. If you don't, we will find the document, killing you all in the process. Fair enough?"

"I still have no idea what you're talking about."

"Rather than playing Indiana Jones and getting a lot of people hurt, why don't you just remain silent for now. Take my message to your friends; discuss it with them. Perhaps clearer heads will prevail, and you'll choose to keep them. 6 a.m." Keyes backed away and started to turn.

"It wasn't Dickens, by the way," said Terry. "It was Twain." As he spoke, he saw Keyes turn back and nod his head, then Terry felt a blow to the back of his head, and he fell to the sand.

Terry slowly raised his head from the beach, spitting the sand from his mouth. It was comparable to his worst teenage hangovers. He didn't think he'd passed out, felt certain that he'd only been lying face down for minutes, not hours. Murchison Keyes, alive and angry – a chilling thought. Murchison Keyes alive, not dead. He was abruptly struck with a thought that carried more force than the recent blow to his head. It wasn't Keyes threat nor the danger of continuing to play this suicidal game with him. Remy! Remy and the man who hadn't killed Keyes after all. He had to get to Remy. Dizzy, his head both throbbing and spinning, Terry forced himself to stand, to walk briskly, then break into an agonizing run.

Rushing into the cafe and seeing Christian, Basil and Mutton but neither Remy nor Trillig, Terry shouted: "Where is she? Where are they?"

"They be settlin' up their affairs," said Basil.

"We've got to stop it. I've got to find them. You and your damn fool ideas."

"Be a sportin' fellow," said Basil. "We's all disappointed. But Hornblower, he won fair and square, sorta. Those of us what lost just gotta accept the spoils."

"I know how you feel, Terry," said Christian. "But she won't change her mind. She considers it a matter of honor."

"That's a strangely inapplicable way of putting it," said

Terry. "But it doesn't matter; she doesn't have to. Keyes isn't dead."

"Keyes isn't dead?" Christian looked at him skeptically. "What makes you think that?"

"I don't think; I know. I just had a brief encounter with him on the beach. He wants his map. But right now I want to stop Remy."

"You're right," said Christian, jumping up. "Let's find her."

"Keyes not dead," mumbled Basil as he watched them disappear. "Why, the rogue must have him nine cat lives."

"Maybe he's twins," offered Mutton.

"Don't be a lardhead; rogues is allus one of a kind."

"Want to go for a quick swim?" asked Remy.

"I don't think so," Trillig answered nervously.

"It'll do you good, Hornblower. You seem a little on edge."

"Do I? I guess I am a little. Everything that's happened today has been so unexpected. First that man on the boat . . ." His face twisted into revulsion at the thought. "And now. Well, I guess I'm sort of filled with butterflies."

"You've just got to relax," said Remy gently as she unbuttoned his shirt. "It'll be fine."

"Okay, but let's not go out very far," said Trillig. "It's so dark and it's probably cold."

"Whatever you say, Hornblower," said Remy, stepping back and unbuttoning her own shirt, which wasn't actually her own shirt, she realized with a flash of guilt, but the one she had borrowed from Terry. Trillig lowered his eyes as Remy slipped out of the shirt and let it fall to the ground. Then, quickly slipping out of the rest of her clothes, she stood watching as Trillig fumbled with his belt. Slowly, he loosened his belt and, slowly, he slipped his pants down and over his feet. He knelt on the beach and carefully folded his pants, then removed his shirt, folded it, and placed it carefully atop the neat little pile. He looked up at Remy with hesitation and, upon seeing her, lowered his head again.

"It's okay, Hornblower," said Remy quietly. "You're allowed to look. I think it's part of the package." He raised his eyes, gulped when he saw her, and continued to stare with a look almost of disbelief as though he had never realized such things actually existed. Remy turned toward the water, saying: "Come on. Let's get wet."

Trillig stood and asked: "Can I leave my shorts on for

now? I don't like to go in the water naked."

"Sure you can," Remy said with a laugh as she waded into the water. "But how do you take a bath?"

"That's different," said Trillig, following her. "That's inside, behind a door."

"Locked of course."

"Of course," said Trillig, edging into the water after her. They swam briefly in water that was slightly warmer than the night air. The moonlight played across the water, creating as romantic an environment as the island provided, meant to aid and abet such activities, but Remy selfishly wished they weren't here or, more accurately, that Trillig weren't here.

After a moment, Remy waded back to shore with Trillig faltering behind. She dropped to her knees on the beach and watched Trillig as he struggled to walk through the water, then as he pulled frantically at his shorts which had been baggy before he entered the water but which now clung aggressively to his skin. Finally, he reached Remy and sat down on the beach facing her. She sat silently for several minutes, looking out across the water, as Trillig fidgeted uncomfortably and stared self-consciously at her wet body glistening under the moonlight.

"I think it's time, Hornblower," Remy said finally, almost whispering.

"O-Okay," Trillig answered. "What d-do you want me to d-do?"

"First, I think you want to finish undressing."

"Yes, that's right," he said. "Okay." He stared down at his wet shorts as if he were attempting to will them off. Finally, he began to fumble with them.

"Have you ever been undressed with a woman?" Remy asked.

"I . . . I guess not."

"I'll turn my head," said Remy. "If you want, I'll keep my eyes closed."

"No, that's all right," said Trillig. He pulled the shorts down across his thighs, then suddenly pulled them up again. "I don't think I can."

Remy gave him a reassuring smile. "The problem is," she said softly, "we can't do it while they're on."

"I . . .I mean I d-don't think I can do anything."

"Are you afraid of me? There's no reason to be."

"No, no," Trillig stammered. "It's not that at all. I really wanted to . . .uh . . . you know."

"Make love to me?"

"Yes, that. At least I think I did. You're the most beautiful woman I've ever known."

231

"Thank you," said Remy.

"But you see, there's this other person. She's a woman, too. She's not really as pretty as you are, but she is in another way. I mean . . ."

"You love her?"

"Yes," said Trillig, apparently relieved that someone other than he had said it. "I do. And I've sort of promised myself that I'd wait, that I wouldn't . . . I know it sounds silly."

"It doesn't sound silly at all," said Remy.

"Thank you," said Trillig. "I'm sorry I didn't say something sooner. You know, before you took all . . ." He finished his sentence by motioning at Remy and looking at the scattered pieces of clothing. "I wanted to, but I couldn't. I wanted to see you, and I'm sorry." He dropped his head.

"There's nothing to be sorry for," said Remy, slipping Terry's shirt over her bare shoulders. She leaned closer, pushed his face up and kissed him on the cheek.

"Do you suppose . . ." Trillig started, then stopped. Remy thought she could see the emotional battle behind his eyes. Finally he said: "That maybe we could sort of . . . uh . . not tell the others about what happened. You know, pretend that we really did . . . that's asking too much isn't it? It's just that they might tease me. I wouldn't say that I did it unless you said that was all right. It wouldn't be fair."

"Sure," said Remy, "We can pretend – except for one person – I need to tell him the truth. He won't tell anyone else, and he won't tease you. As for the others: My God, that Hornblower is a raging bull. Who would of thought?"

Trillig laughed and looked comfortable for the first time, but as Remy continued dressing, he once more averted his eyes. When she had finished dressing, Remy leaned over and pulled at his chin until he was facing her again. "I hope I didn't make a mistake I'll regret later," he said.

"You didn't," said Remy.

Trillig smiled, stood up and quickly dressed. "I guess we should get back," he said.

"You go ahead," said Remy. "I'd like to sit here for a while."

"Okay," said Trillig, "See you later." He turned and headed up the beach, a noticeable bounce to his step.

Trillig stopped to compose himself when he was out of Remy's sight. He stood, looking out to sea, and relived the past half hour with Remy. He had already decided that when he

233

returned to the cafe he wouldn't tell any boastful lies about the experience; somehow he couldn't. He knew he had done the right thing, the thing that made him feel comfortable with himself, and he didn't regret it, but . . .

A sudden blow to the small of his back forced him painfully to his knees. It was followed by another blow and another. And then he was being kicked, again and again. He could see no one and his only physical realization was the pain. Then he was lifted and propelled through the air. The water that had been so warm and pleasant before now seemed cruel and cold as it enveloped him.

Sitting alone, Remy couldn't help laughing. It wasn't Trillig's discomfort; it was her new comfort and just how relieved she was at how it turned out. She had been fully prepared to do what she had to do and would have done it without remorse. The act of revenge she had undertaken came with baggage, and a brief interlude with a befuddled Hornblower paled in comparison. She sighed and pulled the wrinkled map from her pocket. Staring at the strange notations, she was struck by the absurdity of the entire day; it was like an early morning dream, from the raid on Murchison Keyes to the aborted affair with Hornblower – and the map, a fucking modern-day treasure map.

A familiar voice sliced the silence: "Well, well. If it isn't little miss buccaneer and her treasure map."

Chapter 9

"Do you think you can find that island without the map?" Terry demanded as Barnaby Stout labored to keep his weary eyes from slamming shut. It was 4 a.m., and Terry had shaken Stout out of a sound sleep, a sleep that had been made all the more sound by the large quantity of rum that he had consumed during the celebration that had ended a few hours ago. Terry's celebration had been cut short, first by Trillig's "reward" and then by Murchison Keyes and an all-night search for Remy.

Terry and Christian had been unable to find Remy or Trillig on the beach. For his part, Terry was ready to tell Remy that, even though he didn't like it, he understood her commitment to the affair with Trillig, ready to tell her straight out how he felt about her whatever her feeling toward him, ready to tell her that he wanted to stay nearby in case she needed him as a friend, plaything or whipping boy to sympathize, empathize or just hand her a hankie when necessary.

Finally, Terry suggested that Christian return to the cafe on the chance that she had returned there. He continued to search the beach, eventually discovering two sets of footprints he guessed would be theirs. With a wrenching little knot in his stomach, Terry looked at the spot where Remy and Trillig had sat, where they had made love, and where the impressions in the sand gave stark testimony to the zest of their liaison, recording it, if not for future generations at least for Terry and anyone else who might stroll along the beach before the high tide erased the evidence. They had really kicked up the sand. But as he stared at the sand, transfixed, something nagged at him, disturbed him even further. He wasn't sure what it – yes he was! – the footprints; why were there so many now? They led up the beach and into the trees, down the beach toward the harbor. They all converged at this spot, as if half a dozen people had joined in the fun. Could Remy and Trillig possibly have made all the prints? And where were they now?

He followed the footprints up the beach to the trees, but where the palms and hibiscus began, the sand ended, and the footprints were lost. He rooted around in the foliage for several minutes then started down the beach to the harbor. But why

237

would they have gone to the harbor? (As a precaution, the pirates, when they returned from their last voyage, had moored the galleasse in a small cove down the beach from the cafe in the opposite direction.) The harbor was, as expected, dark and deserted. Two small sailboats tied to the pier rolled lazily in the water. Only the sound of the water slapping their hulls broke the silence. He didn't know if the footprints had even come this far; the water had already erased most of them. He paced back and forth along the pier, unsure about where to look next. Back to the cafe. Maybe Remy was already home and in bed. But wouldn't Christian have come back to tell him?

When Terry passed the original starting point of his quest, he found that it was almost underwater, the tide having reached nearly its highest point. He continued on, the hope of finding Remy consigning to forgotten history all thoughts of Trillig's reward just as the water eradicated the physical evidence of it. He spotted something up ahead at the edge of the water, a lumpy mound, motionless except when shoved by an aggressive wave. His heart leaped when he recognized it as a human form, and he ran toward it. As he approached, he saw that it was Trillig, waterlogged and looking very much the same as he himself had looked on his first arrival. Terry knelt down next to Trillig and studied him for signs of life. The sailor's otherwise washed out, ashen face was highlighted by purple welts and bruises and several cuts that were already fading from red to grayish-brown. But Trillig was still breathing.

Terry pulled Trillig to a standing position, wrapping an arm around his back and under his arm. Trillig's water-soaked uniform had added a good twenty pounds to the weight of his slender figure. Terry hobbled along attempting to keep his burden upright but finally picked him up and carried him in both arms. As he trudged back to the cafe, Terry felt certain he knew what had happened. Murchison Keyes had found Remy and Trillig on the beach. And she had what he wanted. He had taken Remy and the map and beaten poor Trillig and thrown him into the water to drown. Somehow he was certain that they hadn't done the same to Remy, that she was now Keyes' prisoner.

Terry and Trillig reached the cafe where Terry deposited his burden, and the cafe was soon buzzing with activity. Peaches and Mutton put Trillig to bed while Terry, Christian and Basil went off on another fruitless search for Remy. Finally, Terry woke Barnaby Stout.

"Find it without the map," said Stout groggily. "Hell, I can find it with my eyes shut, which is what I'd rather do." He tried to put his head down and hide it under a pillow, but Terry persisted, carefully prodding Stout into alertness with his story and an occasional shake.

"Will your workmen come with us?" asked Terry.

"If they get paid," answered Stout.

"Can they be trusted?"

"If they get paid."

"Okay," said Terry. "We need them. I want to be ready to sail promptly at six a.m. How long will it take us to reach the island?"

"A day," said Stout. "Twenty hours if the wind's right, longer if it's not."

"How long will it take Keyes?"

"Not as long. And the wind doesn't matter to him. But chances are good he won't arrive until after dark. So he probably won't go ashore until daybreak tomorrow."

"Then we've got a chance?" said Terry, looking at him hopefully.

"A chance," said Stout, getting to his feet.

An hour later as the morning sun peered over the horizon, the pirates waited nervously on the beach, watching for any sign of Keyes but not really expecting to see him. They were now all convinced that he already had what he had come for. The crew was short one Trillig, who remained in bed suffering mightily, but they had gained the services, for whatever they were worth, of Zack, Ghost and the Carib. Like Stout, most of the crew were suffering from hangovers as a result of the previous evening's reckless pleasure, but they would have a full day at sea to recuperate. Terry didn't know if the three workmen actually had hangovers since they had not been part of the celebration. They had remained on the island since the completion of their duties, appearing at the cafe only to be fed. Looking at them, Terry hoped including them wasn't a mistake. The Carib looked particularly menacing, and Terry wondered for a moment if he had truly forgotten the culinary predilections of his ancestors.

At six a.m., Terry said: "Keyes isn't coming. Let's sail."

"It would appear that you're not much of a morning person," said Murchsion Keyes as the two men hauled Remy toward him. She struggled against them just to be disagreeable without any real hope of tearing herself loose. When the two men had deposited her in front of Murchison Keyes, she stopped struggling, stood squarely and said: "You'll be sorry, you bastard."

"Come now. I believe that a person in your position

would do well to be civil to the man who holds all the aces." Keyes held a small rod that resembled a maestro's baton, which he alternately waved and tapped against the palm of his free hand.

"Fuck off," said Remy.

"Such a sweet face and such a sour tongue. That's piracy for you. It makes one terribly disagreeable. And headstrong enough, I imagine, to attempt something foolish. Men, I think you had best restrain her." He pointed to the yacht's railing, and the two men quickly and efficiently tied each of her wrists to the railing. Then they tied her legs together at the ankles and departed, leaving her to stare angrily at her captor.

"Now that's better," said Keyes. "Being bound hand and foot does tend to make a person a tad more cooperative." He took up a position directly in front of her, standing too close for her liking. "Well, Ms. Blackbeard. It looks as though your reign of terror on the high seas is over."

"What are you going to do?"

"Do?" said Keyes indifferently, as though he hadn't given the matter any thought at all. "Get rid of you eventually, I guess. As soon as I've secured my treasure. Actually, digging it up will leave a nice hole unused. Even large enough for a person, with a little shoving and pushing."

"You won't get away with it," said Remy. "They'll come after me."

"But they have no map. Nevertheless, they may find their way somehow. That's the primary reason you're alive at the moment. A little insurance." He grinned darkly. "And, in the meantime, we can have us a little pirate fun."

Remy didn't answer.

"Now what was it that pirates do for fun? Let's see, they pillage and plunder, but there was something else. You mentioned it yesterday, but it slips my mind momentarily." He paused theatrically and stared at the sky as though searching for the answer within the puffy clouds. Then he looked back at her and sneered. "Ah, yes, I remember now. Rape."

"Try it, asshole."

"Me?" said Keyes with an insulted look. "I'm the captain. Like you, I'll simply have one of my men do it." He pushed his baton into the opening of her shirt just above her waist and pulled it steadily and forcefully upward, popping each button along the way, and opening her shirt. "Yo ho ho on a dead woman's chest. I half expected to see a baroque tattoo of some sort – a naked man, perhaps. I must say, however, I don't miss it at all. You have lovely breasts for a pirate. I'm sure you'll serve as an inspiration to the men. But as for our pirate fun, I hope

243

you won't be too disappointed, but I must go tend to other things right now. You needn't worry about the men. They may stare but they're under strict orders not to touch you – at least not for the time being. We will, of course, have to reward them for their patience eventually. Well, *a bientot.*"

"*Va te faire foutre.*"

"We'll get her back," said Terry as he started to board the galleasse that now stood next to the pier, Stout having brought it out of hiding. Peaches looked back at him, hope and fear blended in her eyes. She forced a weak smile to break through her cloudy visage.

"Or I be not Bad Basil Ringrose, a terror to behold," Basil thundered from the deck.

"You'll tell Albert what's happened?" said Terry.

"Yes," said Peaches, "I will. He really does love her, you know."

"I know he does." Terry paused and added: "I do too."

"Bring my baby back to me. Please." The tears welled up in her eyes again as she kissed Terry briefly on the cheek. Terry, feeling tears form in his own eyes, hurriedly climbed aboard and joined the other members of the rescue party as they scurried about the ship making last minute preparations for sailing. They worked quickly and quietly, seemingly afraid to break the heady silence of the morning, so that the scuffling on the gangplank, which they might not otherwise have heard, commanded their attention. All hands watched in awe as the small man strode onto the galleasse. He wore a ruffled white shirt, blue trousers that were just slightly bell-bottomed and an admiral's hat only slightly too large for his head, complete with a long white plume that drooped to one side and tickled his neck, forcing him to continually swat at it.

"Albert is here," he said, poking a finger into the air above his head and marching straight to the helm.

"It's good to see you up and about, Albert," said Terry, following him. Christian and Basil also joined the procession. "I guess you heard about Remy. We're going after her, and we're just about to sail." Terry paused, hoping Albert would realize that this was not the time to take a stroll about his galleasse. "Why are you here?"

"To sail, of course," said Albert. "Albert is taking charge."

"You are?"

"*Mais oui*. If such a mission is to be undertaken, it must be undertaken properly. And who better to lead it than Albert?"

"The French is here, the French is here," said Christian,

245

dropping to his knees. "Hail to the frog prince."

"Now laddie, that be insubordination," said Basil. "Wouldn't want to keelhaul a fine young boy. But whats gotta be, gotta be. We needs order on a ship. We got to follow the chin of command."

"And what better chin than a French chin," said Terry. "I'm ready to follow Albert on our quest. I won't get my Roman nose out of joint over it."

"Call me Lafitte," said Albert.

"Aye, aye, Cap'n Lafitte," said Basil. "Why you old sea dog. Devil take me if this ain't gonna be a pretty adventure."

With her original captain standing proudly at the helm, the galleasse pulled out of the Soleil harbor on her perilous mission of rescue. Albert guided his sailing ship with a firm hand, and he followed Barnaby Stout's navigational directions unerringly. A brisk wind benevolently filled the sails, promising a speedy journey.

"It was good of you to take command of the ship during my absence," Albert told Stout when they were well underway and the two men stood alone together on the main deck.

"It was my pleasure, sir," Stout answered.

"It was also kind of you to lend your expertise to the restoration of my ship," said Albert.

"My pleasure again," said Stout. "Of course I was paid to do it."

"Quite handsomely, as a matter of fact," said Albert. "But you did a good job. I've found only a few irregularities. Minor, to be sure. But an irregularity robs us of perfection, does it not? I'm not criticizing, mind you. It's just that there are certain levels of workmanship. I imagine you were just not familiar with some of the innovative French modifications to the traditional sailing ship. Well, no matter. I'll attend to them when we get back."

"As you say, sir," said Stout, bristling at the new captain's arrogance. He mumbled a few words about a rigging that needed attending to and excused himself, passing Terry who was just approaching as he left. Terry thought he heard Stout muttering something under his breath about a "pompous little asshole" as he passed but wasn't sure.

"How are we doing, captain?" asked Terry as he reached the deck. "Are we making good time?"

"*Magnifique*," answered Albert. "*La mer est amicale.*"

"The Caribbean Sea is magnificent," said Terry. "I'm always amazed at how plain old colorless water can be so vibrant and colorful – dark blue, turquoise, flaming orange at sunset, black at night. *C'est magnifique.*"

"*Oui, c'est magnifique,*" said Albert, smiling.

"It's good to see you up and in command again," said Terry. "We've all been very worried about you, you know."

"Have you?" said Albert with a look of surprise. "I can't understand why."

"You were so . . . so despondent. Like you'd lost the will to live."

"Aren't we being a bit melodramatic? I was merely thinking."

"I guess you did have a great deal to think about," Terry offered.

"A thinking man always has a great deal to think about."

"What I meant was the new developments in your life," Terry pursued.

"I know what you meant," said Albert. "What is it you would like me to say? Do you object to the way I have lived my life? Do you want me to express regret? Very well. I express regret."

"No, that isn't what I wanted."

"Then I retract my expression of regret."

"It's just that . . . Remy," said Terry. "It's been a rough time for her."

"Discovering that her father is a finicky Frenchman, becoming a pirate and swashbuckling about the West Indies, staying out late at night and getting kidnapped – it sounds like a normal childhood to me."

"She's not a child," said Terry.

Albert looked at Terry as though he were trying to decide which vicious crimes Terry was guilty of. "I realize that," he said. "She has grown to adulthood. Without a father."

"You were there."

"But I didn't know."

"And what would you have done differently if you had known?" asked Terry.

"I don't know," said Albert. "Nothing, perhaps."

"You've always been a father to her. Even without the knowledge that you were biologically her father. I think the new situation is just awkward for both of you. But you'll work it out."

"Thank you for your confidence," said Albert, removing the oversized hat and once again exposing to the sun the shiny dome that had grown pale during the past week. He concentrated momentarily on the ship's wheel. "I'm sure you'll note how much steadier Albert is at the helm than that Dutch jackal, Stander."

"You know about my trip then," said Terry.

"Of course. I have been thinking; I haven't been in a coma."

"I care about her, you know."

"Care about her?" said Albert, derisively throwing Terry's words back at him. "That's somewhat nice that you care about her. I myself care about a lot of things – the weather, the tides, climate change ."

"I love her," said Terry, almost angrily.

"*Voila!*" said Albert. "He declares it."

The sun stood just above the western horizon, and Remy stood tied to the railing of the Esperance where she had spent the entire day enduring the ogling of Murchison Keyes' parade of lackeys and goons, their laughter, their crude remarks. Sammy Apollo was the worst of them – thoroughly churlish behind his Brooklyn charm school manners. His disgusting jokes about her body, his masculinity and contemplated sexual acts were always preceded with a "Nice day, what?" and followed by a "You'll be seeing more of Sammy later, sweetheart." He frequently acted as though he were about to touch her and once, when she swore at him, raised his fist as though he were about to hit her. But he always caught himself, and Remy realized how very much in control Murchison Keyes was.

She saw little of Keyes after their initial meeting, spotting him only a few times at a distance. But as the sun began its final descent, he paid her another visit. "Beautiful day for a sea journey, isn't it?" he said. Remy turned her face away and ignored him. He stood watching her, sipping at what appeared to be a martini.

"Not very talkative, are we?" said Keyes, leaning against the railing next to her. "You've had a good long time to think things out though. See the error of your ways, perhaps. You'll be pleased to hear that we are nearing our destination. We'll be laying anchor off the island within the next few minutes. Tomorrow morning we'll go ashore and I'll retrieve my belongings and move them to a new safekeeping spot. All will be normal again, except that there will be one less meddlesome pirate in the world."

"We had no designs on your money," said Remy. "Your ill-gotten gains were never in danger, even though you were stupid enough to bury them."

"Bury my money? How naive. My money is buried in bank vaults – in Treasury bonds, Walmart stock, various off-shore accounts – buried treasure earning interest, my dear. No, the treasure to which the map refers is completely different. It is your typical buried treasure. Gold doubloons, pieces of eight, that sort of nonsense – worth a couple of million perhaps. It's all about the sentimental value, at least so I'm told. If you believe the stories, it once belonged to none other than Captain Kidd. Since then it's been passed from dirty hand to dirty hand, buried and reburied. It's tradition. It's all about the bragging rights. I came to it as the result of a tawdry little affair a few years ago. A scurvy little man who owed me money, a pirate, I guess – but you know what lowlifes would-be pirates are."

One of his men appeared with a full drink, which Keyes quickly traded for his empty glass. Once again, he sipped silently at the martini for several minutes and stared at Remy who stubbornly refused to make eye contact.

"Are you terribly uncomfortable?" Keyes asked finally.

Remy looked at him for the first time, hatred in her eyes. "Yes," she said.

"If I untie you, will you act responsibly and not make a nuisance of yourself. You realize that making a nuisance of yourself is the worst you can do. There's nowhere to go."

"Yes," she said. "I will."

Keyes finished his martini, knelt down on the deck and untied her feet. Remy fought hard the temptation to kick him in the face. He stood and untied her hands. Remy rubbed her wrists for a moment, then edged a few feet away from him, again fighting her natural impulse which was to run.

"Would you care for a drink?" Keyes asked.

"Yes," said Remy. She continued to look away from him. His very presence was disgusting, the sight of him almost too much to bear. Keyes raised an arm in the air, extending two fingers upward; almost immediately one of his men appeared with two martinis. Keyes took one and handed it to Remy, then traded his empty glass for the second.

"I don't know why we can't be pleasant with one another," said Keyes. His voice was slightly slurred.

She spun around to face him and said angrily: "Because you burned Albert's ship and his cafe. You had us shot at. I'd say that's reason enough. And you're going to kill me tomorrow."

"But that's not until tomorrow," said Keyes as though he couldn't understand why that future event would have any bearing on the present. "And the old man wasn't very nice. He said some terrible things about me."

"He says terrible things about everyone, but everyone else just ignores him."

"Murchison Keyes is not everyone else. I don't take criticism well. And look what you did. You boarded my yacht, beat up my friends, tried to kill me and stole my property. I'd say that, in the area of transgressions, you've more than equaled mine. So if I'm willing to forgive you for the time being, you should be willing to put my transgressions aside so we might be civil with one another – especially since we're probably the only two intelligent people on this ship. I'm really quite a likable person, you know. People have always said that."

"You kill people," said Remy.

"But that's business," said Keyes. "And those people aren't worthy of your sorrow. I realize that you don't approve of my career choice. But it isn't as though I create the demand for the services I provide. I'm simply a distributor of services whose need was created by archaic blue laws meant to protect people from themselves. I don't see that as such a terrible thing."

Remy wanted to laugh at him derisively, to show her utter contempt, but she didn't; she held her emotions carefully in check. Instead she concentrated on how she might free herself from his clutches. The sun had disappeared, and the sea around them was cloaked in that half-light, half-darkness of dusk. Behind her, far off the starboard railing of the Esperance, Hairless Cay lay dark and gloomy sucking in the last light of the day. Forbidding. A place of death, Death for you know who. *Here lies Remy Lafitte. Thought she could be a pirate.* She turned her attention back to her captor who was preoccupied with his martini and her body. Unaware, perhaps, of anything else.

"Perhaps you'd like to join me for dinner," said Keyes.

"I don't know," said Remy. "I'm not hungry. I would like another drink. Being tied up in the sun all day makes you thirsty." Keyes eyes lit up a bit, and he beckoned his dutiful attendant who once more produced two martinis.

"I can be an excellent host and . . ." he added slowly, ". . .an agreeable companion." *The son of a bitch thinks he can seduce me. Not only is he a drug dealer and killer, he's a fucking high seas lounge lizard.* She turned away from him, stared out to sea toward the island and sipped at her drink. Keyes stepped closer, and she felt the clamminess of his hand on her shoulder. She fought the shudder within her and turned to face him again.

"You're hoping to make it with me tonight," she said. "Even though you plan to kill me tomorrow." Keyes was unabashed by the direct statement about his intentions; in fact, he looked quite pleased that she understood his intentions and that they were now discussing them straightforwardly rather than dancing around the subject.

"I don't think you'll be entirely disappointed," said Keyes. "Possibly even amused. And as far as that unpleasant business tomorrow goes – well, perhaps we can give that further thought."

"You mean if I put out tonight, I survive tomorrow," Remy summed up for him.

"It's not a matter of quid pro quo. There's no linkage here. However, it is fair to say that the former would certainly be an inducement toward the latter."

Lying bastard, Remy thought. "Do you really mean that?"

"Murchison Keyes has a reputation for being quite harsh with those who cross him. But he also has a reputation for rewarding those who please him." Keyes slowly pulled her shirt open again, and she breathed in quickly. She felt his hand caressing her breast but fought back the urge to bolt.

"Could I have another drink please?" she asked. "It will help me relax." Keyes signaled again. As the attendant approached with two more drinks, she pulled her shirt closed again. "Thank you," she said and sipped slowly at the drink. Keyes gulped at his then hovered over her. The remains of his drink sloshed in his glass as he began to weave impatiently, leaning so close that she felt his breath on her face, then swaying back again. He slipped his hand under her shirt again, but was leaning on her more than fondling.

She downed the rest of her drink, placed the empty glass on a nearby box, and gave Keyes what she hoped was her most seductive smile. He was now caressing her clumsily with both hands, and she realized with an almost giddy sense of conquest that she was now in control of this drunken, horny, despicable beast. But, she reminded herself, there were others nearby. She unclasped Keyes' pants and pushed at them until they dropped to the floor around his ankles. Then she stepped back and gently pushed his hands away from her, still smiling with the promise of better things about to come. Reaching beckoning arms toward him, she shoved him backward with all the strength she could muster. As he lost his balance and tumbled backward, she vaulted the railing without a second thought and plunged to the water below. She hit the water and immediately began swimming furiously toward where she had seen the island a few minutes earlier, but where now there was only darkness. She could barely hear the shouts from the yacht.

The dramatic highlight of an uneventful day at sea was Mutton's recitation of the *Rime of the Ancient Mariner* in its entirety throughout which Zack, Ghost and the Carib listened dispassionately while the others occasionally dropped in for a stanza or two. To his credit, Mutton delivered the poem flawlessly except for his substitution of "wedding guys" for "wedding guest." Now, the sun having disappeared, darkness spread quickly over the seascape, and dark sky merged with dark sea, eliminating any perception of a horizon. The galleasse floated through a huge, black void.

"It's kind of spooky out here at night, isn't it?" said Christian. The crew had formed a large circle, sitting on boxes or the deck itself, except for Albert, who stood at the helm, and Zack, Ghost and the Carib, who sat off at a distance in complete silence other than an occasional hushed word or two.

"They's been many a sailor what's gone mad from too many nights at sea," said Basil. "Ain't that right, Stout?"

"Aye it is," said Stout. "There's something about the sea at night that puts the shivers on a man's soul. They say that the spirits arise from their underwater coffins and seek revenge on those who would disturb their eternal sleep."

"You mean like us?" said Mutton, wide-eyed.

"Aye lad, like us," Stout answered.

"It's because people like telling ghost stories in settings like this, Mutton," said Terry. "It's like sitting around a campfire in the woods at night."

"Tis true," said Basil. "Tis true. Why, there's been whole ships what've disappeared at night never to be seen again all through these here Indies. Ain't that right, Stout?"

"Aye," said Stout. "The man speaks the truth. The Gaspary, the Marie Hellene and the Treacle, just to name a few.

Disappeared with never a trace. Ships, goods and entire crews never seen again."

"Superstitious prattle," said Albert, passing by on one of his hourly circumnavigations of the deck. "Most seamen are gullible louts who believe this nonsense and pass it on as truth. Any man of knowledge would dismiss its authenticity as quickly as he'd dismiss the contradictory notion of an English nobleman." Albert didn't wait for agreement or rebuttal; he strutted off sternward.

Terry chuckled quietly. God, what a wonderful sight and sound. He was anxious for Remy to see this walking, talking, opinionated French sailor, this wonderfully obnoxious little man.

"Oh, ol' Albert don't know it all," said Basil. "When it comes to the sea, there's others what know better. Right, Stout?"

"Aye," said Stout. "Take the ghost of old Jack Twickham, for instance. He's been haunting these parts for a good three centuries now, hunting down and killing the descendents of the crew of his ship, the ones that mutinied and killed him. They threw him to the sharks in 1660 and thought it was the end of him. But it wasn't, not by a long shot. He's been hunting the sons and daughters and grandkids ever since. I've even encountered the ghost of Jack Twickham myself. Probably lucky to be alive."

"A rogue as ever 'twas," said Basil, savoring Stout's monologue. "Both alive and dead, a real black'eart."

"Tell us about it, Stout," said Christian, sensing a good ghost story about to unfold.

"I always figured they were old sea tales," said Stout. "Like the old man there. Not being a fearful man myself and not being a believer of occult jabberwocky. But I changed my mind one night back in '72. I was on a small ship that sailed out of Jamaica carrying sugar cane. We were really just a skeleton crew. Me . . ."

"You mean skeletons with bones and skulls?" asked Mutton.

"No Mutton," said Christian. "Just listen."

"There was me and Jimmy Glitten, Merle Sykes, the captain and a Jamaican that didn't have a name. It was a cloudy night, not a star, and the fog rolled over the water all around us. Nothing felt right that night. It was eerie, I want to tell you. You don't often see fog in these waters. And there were low, mournful sounds, like lost souls wailing out there in the fog. Jimmy Glitten was a young fellow, sort of our mascot. It was his first night out at sea, and he was really scared. Finally, he couldn't take the eeriness and the moaning anymore so he asked me if I'd come below to his bunk and stay with him for a little while.

"We shared a bunk in a little room, with Sykes and the Jamaican in another room, and the captain in the big captain's room. Well, we sat for a bit, and Jimmy was getting a little more comfortable, but then the moaning started getting louder and louder, and there were strange sounds all over the ship. I decided to go check what was going on. I opened our door and I'll be damned if the fog wasn't right outside the door, right on the ship. Jimmy shut the door behind me and latched it. I started to look around the ship."

Terry noticed Basil looking back and forth between Stout and his empty glass as if trying to make a difficult decision. A second later, he stood quietly and wandered off into the darkness. Stout looked after him momentarily but no one else took any notice.

"I looked over the entire ship," Stout continued, pausing now for effect. "And no one was there, not a soul. The fog was everywhere, thick as gruel, and there seemed to be ghostly eyes staring out of it – from here, there, everywhere." His eyes darted back and forth as he spoke, and the others found themselves looking as well. Terry noticed that Mutton was as white as any ghost Stout was likely to bring up, and even Christian had lost his calm and youthful bravado. The mood was right, Terry admitted, and even he had to fight the impulse to look back over his shoulder.

"They were gone – the captain, Sykes, and the Jamaican – all three of them. I went back down below and rapped on the door to our bunk. But Jimmy didn't answer. I tried the door but it was still locked. I pounded and yelled to him, but still he didn't answer. Then I heard a thin, little voice say: 'Not me.' Then it was silent. I pounded on the door again, and then I put my shoulder to it. When the door broke open, there was so much fog in there I could barely see. But when I did, what a sight! There was little Jimmy Glitten hanging from the ceiling by his feet, his throat cut open."

Stout leaned back to see the effect his story was having on his audience, and he was pleased. He went on: "Strange thing was, Jimmy was descended from folks in Europe who'd never been to sea. He couldn't have been descended from any one of Twickham's crew. Nope, he wasn't. It seems this cruel, bloodthirsty ghost, when he went hunting and couldn't find someone he was after, couldn't let be. He had to kill to satisfy his thirst for blood. He always slit somebody's throat." Stout spoke the words with a low, dramatic voice and then dropped almost to a whisper. "He always slit the throat of the youngest man on board."

Christian gulped, and suddenly a voice boomed from behind him: "I be's the bloodthirsty Jack Twickham, come to slit your throat."

Mutton buried his head between his legs, and Terry had to hang on to Christian to keep him from leaping overboard. Stout rolled on the floor with laughter, and behind Christian, Basil jumped up and down with glee, chanting: "The ghost of Jack Twickham is gonna slit your throat. Hee, hee, hee."

Albert walked by, shaking his head, and said: "The ghost of Jack Twickham. *Merde*."

Remy was wet and cold, but far more comfortable than she had been in the last twenty-four hours. She didn't know how long she been huddled here in the brush near the beach. The swim had been long and tiring, but she hadn't been pursued and could have swum farther if necessary. She didn't know how long she had been swimming, and with the sun down, time had become a mystery. She guessed a few hours had passed. But what did it really matter now? Daylight was what mattered; Keyes would surely be back in pursuit. She tied to convince herself that she'd probably have time to get familiar with the island, and maybe there would be a way to avoid being caught again.

The island was almost as clammy as Keyes' touch. A mist had crept in, and smoky wisps clung to the bushes around her, masking and distorting their shapes. Clouds must have filled the sky for there were no stars, just darkness everywhere. It made her uneasy – the mist, the total darkness and the unfamiliar surroundings – but nothing this island could produce would equal the last hour she had spent with Murchison Keyes.

With no competition, the few night sounds there were took on added clarity and emphasis. To pass the time and reassure herself about them, she tried to isolate each sound and identify it. Several, however, were unrecognizable and therefore all the more ominous. She began to sing softly a song Peaches had frequently sung to her as a child: "James James Morrison Morrison Weatherby George Dupree took great care of his mother, and she took great care of he."

A new sound interrupted her song. It was entirely different in character from those she had been listening to for the past hours. It was a rustling, as though something were being physically disturbed. The islands had no animals that posed any danger. Keyes wouldn't bother to come ashore at night. He'd have no need to. And he had been quite drunk. Everything was all right. She forced herself to continue: "Don't ever . . . go down . . . to the end of the town . . . if you don't . . . go down . . . with me."

The rustling continued, and it was louder now. She turned and looked behind her. There was nothing there. Not at first, but as she stared an apparition began to solidify within the mist. It became a man – a tall, gaunt man with a long gray beard and sunken eyes. He looked like Death.

Chapter 10

Remy stared at the ghostly figure, wanting to scream but finding no voice.

"So you came back, did you?" He growled the words, but his voice cracked, and its anger had no strength. "Come to see if I'd rotted yet, eh Keyes?"

"I - I'm not Keyes," Remy answered feebly.

"No, I reckon not, Keyes. The apparition stepped closer and stared through Remy, who huddled on the ground. "I reckon it's just for the treasure, isn't it. You've probably long forgotten your old pal. But I haven't forgotten you, partner. No indeed, I haven't forgotten you."

"Please look at me," said Remy. "I'm not Keyes. My name is Remy."

"Go ahead, squirm," said the man, a grin splitting his beard and spreading across his face. "So the efficient Murchison Keyes finally made a mistake. Thought you left old Sylvester dead." He laughed, a high-pitched, cackling laugh. "Oh, you came close all right. Tried your best. But my hate, it wouldn't let me die; it's kept me alive. Because I knew you'd be back and that I could repay your kindness."

Remy stood and her movement startled him. She had the sudden fear that he was about to spring at her, but after a quick, abortive gesture, he remained frozen. "Can you see me?" asked Remy. "Please look at me, and you'll see I'm not Keyes. Can you hear my voice?"

The man who called himself Sylvester stared at her, studying her appearance and her words, turning them slowly in his mind. But would they register on him? Remy realized his grip on reality was weak and hoped he wasn't entirely mad. He continued to stare, reality battling his delusions.

Reality lost. "Trying to save your worthless ass with trickery," said Sylvester. "It won't work. Because I'm going to kill you, Keyes."

"Damn it," Remy screamed. "Listen to me. I'm not him. I hate Keyes as much as you do. I want to kill him, too." Once again he stopped and turned her words over in his mind. His eyes gave no indication of the reasoning process, if any, going on behind them. Suddenly he took two steps forward and, hovering over Remy, pushed his hairy face down toward hers.

He grabbed her arm and held it tight, once again freezing in position for several long, painful minutes.

Finally he spoke: "You're not him. You're a gal."

Remy sighed and went limp. "Yes, yes," she cried.

But he continued to hold her tightly enough to keep the twinge of pain racing up and down her arm. If he had started on the road to reality, it was still bumpy going. When he spoke, the anger remained in his voice. "Why are you here?"

"Keyes kidnapped me," said Remy. "I escaped. Please let me go. You're hurting me. I'm not going to run away, I promise." Sylvester continued to hold her as though he hadn't heard her or had heard her and didn't care. Finally, he released his grip, and Remy took a slow, cautious step backward. "He's out there," she said. "In his yacht. He'll be coming ashore when it gets light. I'm sure of it."

"Keyes is out there," Sylvester echoed dumbly.

"He's coming to get his treasure," said Remy, "and to kill me."

"Kill you?"

"Yes, the way he tried to kill you. Can you remember that and talk about it? Maybe it will help. *Part-time pirate attempts to psychoanalyze mad hermit on deserted island*, Remy thought and could immediately see Terry's face, the roll of his eyes, the look that said poor, naive child.

"Kill you?" Sylvester repeated, grabbing her arm again. Remy hoped her words hadn't inadvertently triggered the very action she sought to avoid. But this time Sylvester's grip, though firm, was not tight, and he began to pull her along with him as he moved with sure foot back into the mist from which he had emerged. Remy followed, frequently losing her footing as she bumped, stubbed and tripped, rocks and other unseen objects jumping at her out of the blackness.

After stumbling through the darkness for several minutes they arrived at a crude shelter made of rocks and sticks, and Sylvester released Remy's arm. He sat down cross-legged in a small clearing in front of the shelter. Remy sat near him, noticing the remnants of past fires and a nearby pile of small, dead lizards. She looked quickly away from the lizards, not wanting to think about what she was certain they were used for, and stared instead at her new captor. Sylvester's look suggested he was ready to talk, awaiting only a cue.

"Tell me what happened," said Remy.

Faltering, with frequent, often long pauses, as if trying to remember, Sylvester told his story. "Keyes and me, we first came to this island back in'05. I had me the map. Got if off of Growler Nelson. Off his body anyway. You saw, it wasn't me that killed him. Some other guy stabbed him in a fight. I leaned down to see if he was dead, and he told me to take the map. 'Kidd's gold,' he whispered, and I knew exactly what it was. Did you know what it was? I slipped the map out of his pocket and into my own. Bet you didn't see me do it, did you?

"I had this here map, but no way to get to the gold. Keyes and me had done some stuff together in the past, but you know all about that, so I went to him and told him all about it. We agreed we'd partner up, fifty-fifty like. And we did. I'm sorry we didn't share with you, but you weren't there, were you? Well we went and found the gold and moved it to this island. We made us each a map, but agreed we'd only come back together. Which we did a couple of times just to check on it.

"Couple years ago, we came back again, dug her up. It was a ceremony like. We'd share a bottle of rum, look at it a bit, then bury it again. This time we'd just covered it and I was down on my knees patting the dirt in place – I like to do that, keep it tidy – when I looked up and there was Keyes with this funny look on his face and a gun in his hand. He says to me: 'You know, I never did like you,' and with not another word shot me. That was all I remembered until I woke up later, hurting bad. Got to get to the water. Salt water. Maybe that will save me.

"The salt water and the devil, he saved me so I could kill Keyes, wants me to kill Keyes. Did he send you to find out if I done it yet? I would have but he han't been here yet."

"He's here now," said Remy. "He's come back. But he has a lot of men with him."

"It doesn't matter," said Sylvester. "I'll kill him. I was meant to. They won't be able to kill me until I've killed him. After that, I'm meant to die, and I'm ready."

Sylvester closed his eyes and spoke no further. Remy thought. The yacht from which she had escaped was beginning to resemble the proverbial frying pan. Her most likely option still had to be avoiding Keyes and his men, not confronting him in a suicidal partnership with Sylvester. But if Sylvester were somehow to kill Keyes, maybe the others would just forget about her and leave. Leave her to end up like Sylvester. "But someone will come for me," she said aloud. "Someone will come."

"Sailing directly from Soleil," Albert explained to Terry, "Keyes would most likely approach the island from the southwest – according to Stout, whose analysis we must accept at face value." Accepted grudgingly, Terry was certain. "Therefore," Albert's finger was once again in the air as he continued, "I have approached the island from the east, even though it is a slightly longer journey."

"Sounds smart to me," said Terry.

"Of course it is," said Albert. "Nevertheless, I believe that when the sun appears, the island will likewise appear before our eyes so that we should be able to go ashore just as early as Keyes probably will."

"That's great," said Terry. "Even if Keyes is expecting us to follow him, he probably won't expect to find us already on the island. We need that advantage. He has Remy."

"I am aware of that," said Albert quietly.

"When we gonna storm them beaches and catch us some rogues?" Basil hollered as he approached. "The sun's just startin' to peep up at us, and this seafarer's itchin' to kick some scalawag ass."

"We're not going to storm anything," said Albert. "We are going to move surreptitiously ashore and remain in concealment until the opportunity presents itself. Then we act swiftly and boldly."

"You mean we's gonna sneak up at 'em," said Basil with disappointment.

"Yes, Basil," said Terry.

"Everybody's always wantin' to sneak up. Don't that be sort of sissylike? If we do it piratelike, they be just as surprised. If we goes screamin' and whoopin' at 'em, they probably be so bloodcurdled they'll run and jump in the ocean."

Albert glared at Basil then looked back to Terry, exasperation blanketing his face. *"Il est bete comme ses pieds."*

"That's our old Albert," said Basil with a grin. "Makin' frog talk again, just like old time's sake. What's say, Albert? Can't we attack 'em pretty?"

"No Basil, we can't," said Albert. Basil harrumphed and wandered off, talking to himself about how pirates by all rights ought to attack rogues outright.

"Merde," said Albert, but his expression softened and an uncharacteristic smile crept onto his face.

"Think we can do it?" said Terry.

"Of course I think we can do it. "You're familiar with the French Resistance during the Second World War, I presume?"

"Yes, somewhat," Terry answered.

"We can do it because it's got to be done," said Albert. "And we'll do it soon now." The sun had pushed above the eastern horizon, and the darkness had drifted away during the past few minutes. As Albert had promised, Hairless Cay – the field of battle – loomed directly ahead.

Murchison Keyes marched stiffly up and down the deck in front of his assembled troops, barking orders and issuing assignments in a dizzying display of autocracy. He designated Apollo and seven other men as members of the landing party. The others would remain aboard the yacht, watching for approaching vessels. Were one to approach, it would surely be a rescue party from that bothersome Booby Bay.

"Our first priority," said Keyes, "is to find the bitch. I want her. Do you understand?"

"Dead?" Apollo inquired.

"No," said Keyes. "Murchison Keyes will handle that assignment personally. After that, we'll retrieve my box and leave quickly. Does everyone understand?" Affirmative mumbles in reply. "And remember the Ms. Pirate is mine, alive."

Apollo grinned and winked at Keyes.

"Don't ever wink at Murchison Keyes again," said Keyes, glowering at him. Then he turned and said: "Let's go ashore."

Stout looked up with amusement as Christian and Mutton stood at something close to attention while Albert lectured, explaining as patiently as he could that one might moor a ship, anchor a ship or lay to, but one did not park it. As he completed his lesson, Terry and Basil returned from their task of readying the small boat that would carry them to shore.

The galleasse lay a quarter mile off Hairless Cay, an island aptly named. Rocky masses jutted from the tangle of sea level foliage like a bald man's weathered dome. The island's flora clung tenaciously to its existence. From just below the rocks, sloping down to the beach, short scrubby palms, their fronds slapping each other in the breeze, fought for space beneath the leathery green canopies of windswept sea grapes. The coarse sand of the beach was littered with pebbles and frequently gave way to large marshy areas where the aerial roots of red mangrove clawed at the mushy earth like huge, stubby fingers and the sharp blades of bulrushes pointed skyward from murky water. It was no wonder that the island remained uninhabited; it was no tropical paradise. It was unfriendly, maybe even forbidding, although much of the air of hostility could, in this case, be attributed to the eyes of the beholders.

"We'll have to make two trips," said Terry. "The boat's pretty small."

"Why don't I take the five of you in first," said Stout, "then I'll come back for my men." Albert considered the idea for a moment, looked briefly to Terry, who shrugged, and agreed to Stout's plan, feeling the need, however, to assert his captaincy by building upon the plan.

"Very well," said Albert. "And since we have two landing parties, let us continue that arrangement once we're ashore. My party will move off to the left, your party off to the right. That will increase our chances of discovering the enemy."

"An we surrounds the rogues, right Albert?" said Basil.

"Something like that," said Albert.

"Aye aye, sir," said Stout, heading off toward their landing craft with the others following.

Stout climbed down into the small boat first. Albert followed, quickly claiming his position at the bow where he assumed the stance of General Washington in The Crossing of the Delaware. Terry, Christian and Mutton climbed down and stepped carefully into the rocking boat, but Basil, excited at the adventure that lay ahead and anxious to get on with it, leaped, landing heavily and awkwardly in the craft, not quite capsizing it but successfully throwing General Washington into the Delaware. Christian and Terry quickly pulled him from the drink, the sodden captain letting loose a spate of French invective.

They rowed toward the beach, silent except for the swishing of Basil's sword as he waved it through the air in anticipation and an occasional *"merde"* from the bow. Once they had been deposited on shore, they watched as Stout, without stopping to chat, rowed back toward the galleasse.

"I hope that man can be trusted," said Albert.

"Trusted," said Basil. "By gar, he be a seafarer. If you can't trust a seafarer, why you can't trust your own momma."

Albert shrugged, turned and started to make his way through the shoulder-high palms. They hadn't traveled for more than five minutes, however, before he announced that a short visit to a friendly tree was imperative, that the others should keep going and that he would catch up with them in a moment. Before anyone could reply, he disappeared into the foliage.

Remy awoke with a start. The sun had come up and was now just beginning to bathe the unfamiliar terrain, making it just a bit more benign than it had been during the night. She had fully intended to stay awake, still unsure of Sylvester's stability and her own safety in his company. She had just been too tired.

Fortunately, she had awoken alive, untouched and alone.

The last words she remembered from the conversation that now almost seemed a dream were Sylvester's, his vow to kill Murchison Keyes. Remy guessed that he had ventured off for just that purpose, and she hoped he would succeed. For her own part, she hoped to keep out of sight, to avoid being discovered on what she knew was a tight little island. She had no idea where on the island she was, but with the sun off in one direction, she knew Keyes was off in very nearly the opposite direction. If she headed east, she should be moving away from Keyes and would presumably find a beach. Even though she had spent more than enough time in the dark sea the night before, she felt the need of a quick, refreshing swim. She'd just move very cautiously, keeping herself well-concealed.

Remy circled Sylvester's rustic living quarters and found a path that led off through a tangle of bushes. She crouched low and moved cautiously, stopping every few steps to listen for any unusual sounds ahead. There were none; even the sounds that had taunted her last night were no longer there – only a silence that was itself overwhelming.

After she had followed the path for several minutes she heard something; it was barely audible and she wondered if it were the sounds of the sea ahead of her. She stopped, knelt down and listened. The sounds grew more distinct; they seemed to be off to her right, but at some distance. It sounded as though several people were moving through the foliage. She also thought she heard the sound of voices, but couldn't be sure. As the sounds began to recede, she heard something much louder on the path ahead of her. Someone was coming down the path from the opposite direction. She crouched, listening, as it grew closer. She felt certain it was only one person, and there were no voices to indicate otherwise. Maybe it's Sylvester, she thought, on his way back to the lean-to. She hoped it was Sylvester.

Picking up a softball-sized rock that lay conveniently near her right hand, she stood and moved back from the path where she was hidden by a clump of palms. She waited. If it weren't Sylvester, she might be able to strike a first blow and overwhelm whoever it was. She stood frozen, her arm in the air ready to hurl the rock at the first sight of someone who wasn't Sylvester coming along the path.

But the sounds had deceived her. The person who approached was not on the path. Instead he stepped out of the bushes across the path from her, just six feet away. The two of them shared a moment of shock, then an instant of recognition, as Remy checked the motion of her arm just as she was about to throw the rock. *"Mon Dieu!"* shouted the man on the other side of the path.

"Albert!" Remy cried.

"Let she who is without sin cast the first stone," said Albert.

Remy looked momentarily at the rock she now held motionless in her hand, dropped it quickly, and ran to him.

Terry heard the sounds, grabbed Mutton, who was about to lumber into the clearing ahead of them, by the seat of the pants and pulled him back behind a clump of tall grass. Christian and Basil, also hearing the sound and seeing Terry's reaction, crouched in the bushes nearby. The sounds grew louder, and they watched as three men stepped out of the bushes at the far end of the clearing. Terry recognized two of the men from the battle aboard the Esperance; the third he didn't remember. Terry guessed that Murchison Keyes and Sammy Apollo, as well as additional henchmen, must be nearby. It would be best to remain concealed until some of the others showed themselves, with the hope that Stout's party was near at hand – as well as Albert who was presumably somewhere behind them. Terry turned toward Mutton at his left, putting a finger to his lips as a direction to remain silent. He turned to his right to give the same instructions to Christian and Basil just in time to see Basil jump up from his concealment, wave his sword, and shout: "Them three be's mine."

Basil stormed across the clearing toward the three surprised men, whooping and hollering: "You's seen the last o' your rogue days. Down t'yer knees if you wants to save your asses. Bad Basil's all over you."

The three men had no time for measured response as the wild-eyed pirate thundered into their midst. Two of the three instinctively fell to their knees as told. The third attempted to raise a gun toward Basil, but Basil swung his sword, catching his arm with a heavy blow. In shock, the man dropped the gun, grabbed his wounded arm with his other hand, and with Basil's sword swinging back through the air like a returning pendulum, fell to his knees. The sword whistled through the air, where a second earlier his neck had been. The sword's momentum took even Basil by surprise as he was pulled awkwardly backward, dancing to keep his footing. One of the men crawled toward the gun lying in the dirt, as Terry now raced across the clearing, muttering: "Goddamn it, Basil." Mutton and Christian were a few steps behind him.

Spotting the charging reinforcements, the goon had

second thoughts about the gun; he backed away and meekly resumed his kneeling position. Terry, unarmed himself, bent over, scooped up the gun, and waved it back and forth in front of the three praying figures.

"Good doin', lad," said Basil. "Notes how I softened 'em up for ya."

"I noticed," said Terry. Christian and Mutton stood by his side attempting to look menacingly enough at the three men to hide the fact that they too were unarmed.

"Right pretty little battle to get things started," said Basil. "Warms us up for the other black'earts. The old hot blood's just aswooshin' through this here body, I'll tell ya. How 'bout you mates?"

"I guess so," said Terry, relieved at the outcome of this first battle, but knowing full well it wasn't the war. He just hoped that Basil's premature attack hadn't been a grievous tactical error. "I just hope . . ."

"Please be so kind as to drop that gun," said a familiar voice from behind them. "And that hideous sword." Terry turned, just to make it official that the speaker was Murchison Keyes who now had the advantage. Keyes was flanked by Sammy Apollo, his two blond warriors and two additional strong-arms Several guns were pointed in the pirates' direction.

Terry obediently dropped the weapon from his hand; he hadn't much cared for it anyway. Basil, on the other hand, held his sword tightly, refusing to let go of it and glaring back at Keyes. Terry, realizing that Basil was on the verge of staging a one-man kamikaze attack on the lot of them, said quietly: "Drop the sword, Basil. It won't do any good."

"Wise words," said Keyes. He stood fifteen feet away from them and made no move to get any closer. The other three thugs got to their feet behind the humbled pirates. "I guess I should be surprised to see you here," Keyes continued. "But somehow I'm not. You do keep turning up, don't you? Where's the old man? Isn't he with you?"

"Albert?" said Basil. "He be's taking a . . . "

"Taking what you've done to him pretty hard," Terry interrupted. "He barely gets out of bed anymore." Basil looked at Terry in confusion; so did Mutton. Terry prayed that one of them wouldn't try to correct him.

"That's unfortunate," said Keyes. "He should have been more cooperative."

"He should have been more a gentleman, what," said Apollo.

"Shut up," said Keyes.

"Where's Remy?" Terry demanded. "Have you . . ."

283

"I thought maybe you would have seen her," said Keyes. "She seems to be on the loose for the moment. I'm sure she'll be pleased that you came for her. Unfortunately, you'll all be dead before she knows."

Terry was about to respond, when Albert stepped quietly out of the bushes behind Keyes and Apollo. He grinned and waved. Terry and Christian both shuffled slightly trying to block the view of the men behind them. Basil didn't move, but he already effectively blocked out the man behind him. Terry saw Mutton out of the corner of his eye and his heart jumped. Mutton was raising his arm to wave back at Albert. But Mutton didn't wave; one of Apollo's bookend bullies, seeing Mutton's movement, didn't pause to question it. He fired, and Mutton let out a little cry then doubled over as though he were a quarterback protecting a football as he plunged through the enemy line. But this quarterback made no forward movement; he collapsed to the ground.

Basil fell to his knees next to Mutton and rolled him over, inspecting him through blurred eyes. "They kilt him," said Basil. "They kilt my little lad. He be's a dear one, too." He looked up, tears streaming down his cheek, as if waiting for someone to tell him why. Then the pirate caught even Terry by surprise as in an instant he scooped up his sword, jumped to his feet and charged the villain who had fired the shot. The man fired again as the pirate rushed toward him, but he was wide of the mark. He fired a second shot as Basil lunged, but this one went wild, nearly hitting one of his compatriots. He didn't fire a third time. Basil had hold of his arm. The gun flew through the air, and Terry heard the sickening snap as the man's arm broke. The man screamed as Basil let go of his dangling arm, lifted him, even though he was Basil's equal in size, and hurled him ten feet, where he came crashing to rest.

His counterpart had been attempting to take aim on Basil, but before he could fire, a wiry little Frenchman had tackled him from behind. He fell face forward, but rolled onto his back and attempted to take aim at the annoying little man wrapped around his legs. Apollo watched in confusion, pointing his gun first at Basil, then Albert, then toward Terry and Christian, unable to select any one target. Murchison Keyes was less confused. He backed slowly away from the action and left his men to handle it as he disappeared into the bushes.

Terry and Christian had jumped the men who were guarding them just as Basil had made contact, and Terry now wrestled on the ground with two of them and Christian with the third, not convincingly but enough to keep the men occupied. Basil now turned his attention toward Albert's plight. With one swing of his leg, Basil's foot connected with the gun, which sailed through the air. He then pinned the man to the ground with a big pirate foot on his face, as Albert extricated himself. The two remaining thugs had joined the melee; one now jumped on Albert and the other attempted to pull Basil from his face-stomping stance.

A gunshot brought all action to a momentary halt. It was louder than a pistol shot, and they looked up to see that it was the blast of the shotgun wielded by Barnaby Stout and his cavalry – Zack, Ghost and the Carib. They all stormed into the clearing and the battle resumed. The Carib grabbed the goon from Basil's back and casually tossed him against a tree. He pulled another off Albert by the neck and tossed him into the clearing. Christian was underneath his thug taking a good beating until Zack stumbled over, plucked the aggressor from his prey and sat on him. One of Terry's two thugs broke loose, kicking Terry's head in the process, and ran toward heavy cover; a blast from Stout's shotgun felled him a few feet short of his goal. Terry, now able to concentrate on just one opponent, managed to land an elbow to the bridge of his nose and a knee to his groin, rendering him bloodied and helpless.

Terry sat up and surveyed the battlefield through aching eyes. Three of Keyes' men lay motionless; the others had run or hobbled off in the direction of Keyes' yacht. Only Apollo stood his ground, but now stripped of his bodyguards and seeing the wreckage of their forces around him, he was stunned. He waved a pistol recklessly in the air, unsure of whether to fight or flee. The decision was about to be made for him, however, as the Carib glided relentlessly in his direction. Apollo waved the gun at the Carib and shouted; "Get back." He fired once at the rather large target, but missed, and the Carib maintained his steady approach.   Apollo fired again, missed again; he was no marksman. In exasperation, he threw his gun at the Carib.

Basil, who had been watching with glee, grinned and shouted to Apollo: "That big fella there, he be a Carib. He gonna eat ya." That was enough for Apollo. He turned and ran into the bushes, the Carib on his tail. Basil roared with laughter, but then, seeing Albert and Christian kneeling next to poor Mutton and remembering his dear little comrade's fate, fell silent.

On his feet, Terry stumbled across the battlefield, only half realizing they had prevailed and noting for the first time that Keyes had disappeared. "I've got to find Keyes," he mumbled as he passed Christian and Albert.

He passed by Basil, Zack and Ghost and left the clearing. As he pushed through the bushes in the direction he guessed

Keyes must have gone, he heard Christian's voice. "Basil, you've got a lot of heart and courage, but I'm afraid you don't have an ounce of brains."

Remy wished she had not let Albert convince her to remain hidden while he and the others took on Keyes and his men. She had argued with him, pointing out that she was as capable as any one of them – and more capable than some – to take on the task at hand. Her argument was sound, but in the end she was forced to bend to Albert's point of view, shallow though it was: "I am your father, and I want you to wait here." It was the first time she had heard him utter such words, and upon hearing them could no longer persist.

She had remained concealed, once again listening to the few island sounds, real and imagined, trying to interpret their cause and their meaning. Then she heard the gunfire. She knew its cause and was frantic about its meaning. Leaving her concealment, she wondered about Sylvester, whom she still hadn't seen since their conversation in darkness. She wondered if maybe it were he that was involved in the gunfire. If he were, maybe Albert, Terry and the others weren't. She crept along quietly and slowly, although she was certain any rustling sounds she might make in her journey would be lost among the sounds of battle she now heard in the distance. She paused momentarily to listen, leaning against a large rock.

"Shhh," said a voice. "You don't want them to hear you."

She turned quickly and found the barrel of a revolver pressed against her cheek. She gasped as Keyes spoke again: "You've been a very naughty girl. Very naughty. I'm afraid our earlier agreement can no longer be honored. I think you were playing me for a fool, that you really didn't want to make love to me."

"I'd rather suck face with a moray eel," Remy said, staring directly at him in disgust. "So where does that leave us?"

"I'm going to shoot you, of course," said Keyes almost pleasantly. "I don't like my affections being played with. Then after I shoot you, I'm going to fuck your dead body while it's still warm." Remy gagged. Keyes, with a sneer, continued to taunt her: "One way or another I always get my way. I thought it important that you know, that you take that thought to your death."

He grabbed Remy's arm and pushed her roughly ahead of him. They pressed through a thick grove of tall grasses and palms, leaf blades slashing at them like thrusting swordsmen,

289

Keyes shoving Remy every few steps, to keep her moving at a steady pace.

"Where are we going?" asked Remy.

"We're going on a treasure hunt," said Keyes cheerfully.

"I thought you were going to shoot me."

"In due time, in due time," said Keyes. "You're not getting anxious are you? Looking forward to a little post mortem sexual activity. I'm afraid I need you alive for a few moments longer, on the slight chance some of your friends escaped my men. I think it best to have a hostage until we get to my goods. See those rocks up ahead. We need to climb up over them."

They reached a rocky hill, and Remy stopped momentarily. Keyes shoved her impatiently, causing her to lose her balance and fall. "Damn you," she screamed, looking up at him from the ground.

"Get up," said Keyes.

"Fuck you," Remy answered.

Keyes reached down and pushed the gun into her face. "I'd prefer not to blow your pretty face apart," he said angrily. "But if I have to, I will. Now stand up."

Remy struggled to her feet and started climbing over the rocks, holding on to the trunks and branches of the skinny trees that jutted from cracks in the rocks and curved upward toward the sky. "Just don't shove me anymore," she said. "I'm moving as fast as I can." They continued climbing until the rocky hillside leveled into a plateau, which overlooked a perfect Caribbean vista of blue sky and turquoise water, then they walked to the edge of the plateau where the world suddenly dropped sixty feet to a rocky coast. The water energetically slapped at the grotesquely shaped rocks below them.

"Quite pretty, isn't it?" said Keyes, holding Remy uncomfortably close to the edge of the cliff. "It looks more like an English or Scottish coast." He stepped back a bit from the cliff's edge and continued. "This spot is pretty in more ways than one." He pointed toward a large tamarind tree, its location among the rocks defying both reason and nature. "At the base of that tree is my little treasure, the one you're dying for."

Keyes loosened his grip on her arm and stepped back a few feet away from her, but he kept the gun pointed directly at her.

"Now strip please," said Keyes icily.

"No," said Remy, crossing her arms and staring back defiantly.

"You seem to forget who has the advantage here," said Keyes, waving the gun. "Now do what I tell you."

"Va te faire foutre," Remy shouted. "I know you're going to kill me no matter what I do. And that's liberating. "I don't have to do shit for you, asshole."

Keyes grew red with anger and sputtered: "Bitch. Okay, have it your way." He raised the gun and stepped closer, but Remy ducked, threw her entire 110 pounds against him, knocking him off balance, and ran toward the lone tamarind tree. Keyes quickly regained his balance and fired at her. She heard the bullet whistle past her and, at the same moment, caught her foot on a rock and went flying through the air, landing hard on the rocky surface six feet from the tamarind tree. Keyes fired again, and the bullet hit the ground next to her, spraying her with tiny rock fragments. Seeing Remy frozen to the ground, Keyes paused to aim more carefully. But he was unable to pull the trigger before Terry had rushed from out of nowhere across the plateau and jumped him from behind, riding him piggyback in an erratic pirouette.

Keyes danced only momentarily before Terry's weight pulled him to the ground. The gun shot out of his hand and bounced across the rocks toward Remy. Terry and Keyes rolled on the ground, each holding the other as tightly as if they were lovers whose passion had got the better of them. Twice they rolled close enough to the edge of the cliff that Terry could look directly down at the rocks below before reversing their direction. Finally Terry got the upper hand and, with Keyes pinned on his back, delivered a strong blow with his clenched fist that landed squarely between Keyes eyes. Keyes looked at him blankly, then went limp. Terry looked up to see Remy scrambling for Keyes' pistol, but as he did, he felt Keyes moving beneath him. Terry turned back just in time to see the rock in Keye's hand swinging directly at him. He took the blow on his forehead and fell back to the ground inches from the edge of the cliff.

Keyes crawled to his knees before looking up to see Remy standing ten feet away from him, brandishing his pistol. He stood slowly and brushed himself off, never taking his eyes off the pistol-packing pirate. Terry groaned once from below, but didn't move. "It would seem the tables have turned," said Keyes. "Now, I'm your hostage, and I have this strong suspicion that I no longer have reinforcements ready to spring from the bush. Shall we bargain?"

"Strip," said Remy, glaring at him with hatred.

"Do you plan to kill me," said Keyes, slowly removing his shirt.

"Yes," said Remy.

"But first you'll humiliate me. Is that it?" Keyes removed his pants and stood facing her in shorts, shoes and socks. "I guess I can understand that." He spoke calmly and obsequiously, but didn't cower. He didn't even look afraid.

"All of it, asshole," said Remy.

"Knowing what I know now and how it feels, I probably would have acted differently before." Keyes removed his shoes and socks. "I apologize for that. Does that make any difference to you?"

Remy shook her head and motioned at him with the gun. Keyes sighed and dropped his shorts. They stood staring at each other, neither apparently certain what the next move would or should be.

"I've killed a few people in my life," said Keyes, hushed as though he were in a confessional and the possibility existed that Remy would let him off with nothing more than a few Hail Marys. "I've seen others kill, too. For most people, it's very difficult. Even after they've done it a few times. It's not an easy thing to do." He took a cautious step forward. "Granted there are those to whom it means nothing, those who actually enjoy it. But most of us are thoroughly intimidated by the prospect." He took another step.

"Stay back," said Remy.

"I myself don't really enjoy killing people," Keyes continued, searching her face as he spoke. "I've ordered it done, but that's not the same. To do it myself . . . well, that's possibly why you're now holding the gun. Do you find that strange?" He took another step, bringing himself within three or four feet of her.

"Don't move again," Remy said nervously. "I mean it."

"Now if a famous hard heart like me doesn't like to kill, I imagine a novice such as yourself would be mortified by it. I can see it in your eyes. Frankly, I don't think you can pull that trigger." She hesitated as he suddenly leaped at her, then pulled the trigger. But she had waited a moment too long. Keyes had her arm before she could squeeze the trigger. The bullet grazed his shoulder but didn't stop him. He twisted her arm sharply, forcing her to the ground. With his free hand, he took the pistol from her as she released her grip. He stepped back.

"Quite the game of changing fortunes, isn't it?" said Keyes. "But enough is enough. You and yours have shot me twice. It's become rather annoying. Time to be done with it. By the way, that nonsense about my not enjoying killing was really just that. It doesn't bother me in the least. And this one I'm going to particularly relish. But first let's dispense with your nuisance of a friend." With his foot he began to push Terry's motionless body toward the edge of the cliff, never taking his eye or the sight of his gun off Remy. He strained as he pushed and somehow looked vulnerable even though he was in complete command of the situation; nakedness can do that. As Terry hung stubbornly on the edge of the cliff, his body refusing to be nudged easily over, he stirred and opened his eyes. Feeling nothing but air under the left side of his body, he instinctively grabbed to hold on to something. The something was Keyes' white, hairless leg, and Terry held it just as tightly as he had held the piece of flotsam that had carried him to Booby Bay, enduring Keyes' stomping and kicking.

Then they heard the wild, animal-like scream and turned to see a figure streaking crazily across the rocks toward them. "Ke-e-e-eyes," shrieked Sylvester. "Now we die. Together again. Til death do us part." Keyes shot at him, and Sylvester took the bullet midbelly but didn't stop. He leaped at Keyes and took another shot point blank in the stomach as his arms encircled the now terror-stricken Keyes. Sylvester's momentum carried both of them, in a surrealistic aerial embrace, over the edge and into space. Terry loosened his grip on Keyes' leg just in time to prevent his making the company a crowd. Keyes screamed momentarily before he and Sylvester hit the rocks below.

Remy ran to Terry who had inched away from the precipice. They peered over the edge and watched as several people approached the still bodies below, and they heard Basil

shout: "Old Keyes be as dead as a doornail, that's for sure."
Remy put her arms around Terry, held him tightly, and cried.
They both cried.

Chapter 11

Self-satisfaction engulfed Hairless Cay after the battle between the pirates and the rogues. Pirate patted pirate back and grinned when the compliment was returned. The mission had been a complete success: Remy had been rescued; Keyes (and Sylvester) lay dead on the rocks; and Keyes' men had been routed and chased back to the yacht in which they had sailed off, not waiting for word of their boss. Mutton had been the pirates' only casualty, but Basil's pronouncement of death had been a bit premature; Mutton now lay uncomfortably against a mangrove root, nursing his bullet wound.

Sammy Apollo, however, was still missing, and so was the Carib who had last been seen in pursuit of him. The question of their whereabouts, however, was answered within minutes as the Carib pushed his way through the heavy bushes and into the clearing. His huge body spilled out of what looked to be a child's jacket but which, on closer inspection, proved to be Sammy Apollo's overcoat. They all stood watching him as he strode to the center of the group. Finally, Terry tried to voice what they were all wondering: "You didn't . . .?" The Carib grinned, the first time they had ever seen a smile on his face.

They had easily found Murchison Keyes' treasure chest as promised at the base of the tamarind tree, and it had been loaded onto the small boat. "Two trips again, captain?" said Stout, looking to Albert for his approval. "Why don't I take my men out. They can unload the box, and stow it while I return for you."

Terry interrupted: "I think we should get Mutton aboard first. Perhaps you should go as well, Albert. And maybe Basil and Christian. The rest of us can make the second trip."

"Yes," said Albert. He gave Terry a satisfied smile. "Mutton should go first. And Basil and Christian can certainly unload the box."

That afternoon, the galleasse sailed away from Hairless Cay, reversing its course of the previous day and heading home to Booby Bay. The pirates were more solemn than one might have expected, given their successful foray and their high spirits immediately following the battle. They attended to their shipboard duties silently, and it wasn't until they were well underway that each member of the crew found his eyes and thoughts frequently drifting toward the wooden chest that stood on the deck of the galleasse. . It looked just like a treasure chest should look – imposing and mysterious, lacking only the booted foot of a Captain Kidd or a Long John Silver atop it. Visions of the riches within permeated the mind of every pirate passerby.

"Okay," said Remy, reading the looks of intense curiosity in the eyes around her. "We'll open it just to take a look. Basil, would you like to do the honors?"

Basil's eyes lit up, and he hurried to the box before Remy could change her mind. Kneeling in front of the box, he began to pry at its lid with a small crowbar. Terry, Remy, Christian, and Barnaby Stout looked on with fascination, and even Albert, who had attempted to ignore the entire scene, leaned closer as, after minimal coaxing, the lid popped open. An eye-popping collection of glittering gold coins, gold cups and other artifacts gleamed up at them.

"According to Keyes, this treasure belonged to Captain Kidd," said Remy. "It's gone from pirate hand to pirate hand for the past three hundred years."

Basil ran his hands through the gold pieces. "My oh my," he said.

"Hogwash," said Barnaby Stout, picking up a coin and looking at it. "The stories about Captain Kidd's treasure is what's been going from pirate hand to pirate hand. This stuff is worthless junk." He tossed the coin back into the chest and started to walk away.

Terry picked up a coin and said: "I'm no expert, but I think Stout is right." He put the coin down and began to paw through the remaining contents. "Odd. There's only about six inches of stuff here before you hit bottom. Yet the chest is two feet deep. This is just a shallow box. Let's see if we can lift it out."

After a few minutes of exploration, they found two indented handles and were able to lift the smaller box out of the large chest. A look of disappointment spread across Basil's face as he stared at the remaining contents of the chest. "It just be papers and stuff," he said. "This ain't no treasure."

Terry leaned down next to Basil and picked up a handful of the papers about which Basil lamented. "This piece of paper is a certificate for one hundred shares of IBM," said Terry. "Here's one for Apple, Coca Cola. A $50,000 U.S. Treasury Bill, a stack of them. There's a fortune here in negotiable securities, mostly American. It does my heart good to see that Keyes invested in the American economy instead of burying baubles."

Basil had burrowed under the remaining papers, and once again his face lit up. "What ho," he said. "Here be the real money, hidin' down there in the bottom." Basil was right. Underneath the stock certificates and treasury bills, they found cash, stacks of bills. Terry immediately recognized the U.S. bills with Benjamin Franklin staring up at them, a sly half-grin suggesting he guessed what was now going on. Keeping Ben company were various French statesmen, English monarchs, other Europeans and even a few Japanese dignitaries.

"Oh, would ya just look at it," said Basil, fondling the bills. "Such a treasure, my oh my. There must be hundreds of these pretty little things."

"Basil," said Remy sternly, "remember we're just looking. It's not ours." Basil stopped rummaging and Terry replaced the securities, and he and Christian lifted the smaller box of gold coins back into place before closing the lid of the chest itself.

"I still says maybe we ought keep it. For all our good deedin'. Seems right to me."

"No, Basil," said Terry. "We decided before."

"What says we vote on it," prodded Basil. "That be fair. That be the democratic way. You believes in the democratic way, don't you, bein' American and all?"

"This isn't a democracy," said Remy. "The captain is the law."

"But that be fair," whined Basil. "You be captain, Albert. Shouldn't we be fair?"

"He's right," said Albert after a moment. "This was a perilous undertaking. No one was forced to come along other than Remy. Everyone here has a right to vote."

"I always know'd you was a good cap'n, you lovable little Frenchie. Okay, I'll take us a real vote, fair and square like. Stout, what say you to this here vote?"

"I'm for keeping it, of course," said Stout.

"An hows about your men?" asked Basil, registering Stout's vote with the index finger of his left hand.

"They want to keep it, too," Stout answered.

"Okay," said Basil. "That be one, two, three, four votes what say let's keep the treasure." Basil had now extended the four fingers of his left hand. "Albert, what says you?"

"I want no part of it," said Albert. "It should be turned over to the authorities. It's ill-gotten gains."

"Right," mumbled Basil, straightening his right index finger. "Albert says return it."

"Lass, how you gonna vote on this here matter?"

"Return it," said Remy.

"Bonney, what say you? Now think 'pon those IBM papers, you was holdin'. Weren't they handsome little fellas?"

"Return it," answered Terry.

"An what say you, lad?" said Basil, looking to Christian. Christian stood silent, thinking hard.

"Christian," Remy prompted.

"Return it," said Christian.

"Now, let's see here." Basil studied the eight extended fingers on the hands he held before his face. "Okay, that be four for keepin' it, and that be four for givin' it back. That there be a tie." A big grin spread across his face. "But Basil ain't voted yet. That old seafarer, Basil Ringrose, gots the vote to break the tie – the winnin' vote. Whoop de do."

Albert glared at him silently, steely French eyes burning into the buccaneer's countenance. "Stop lookin' on me, Albert," said Basil. "I gots to vote my conscious." Albert glared on, the intensity of his gaze mesmerizing the other observers as well as his target. "Get your froggy evil eye off'n me, Albert. It ain't right to try at influenciating how a person votes. Tis my vote, so look somewheres else." Albert continued his hypnotic gaze, and slowly the glee drained out of Basil's face. He sighed a heavy, pirate sigh. "Oh damnation. I votes to give it back, too."

Albert smiled at him innocently and said: "It looks as

though democracy has decided to give the money back." Basil stomped off, dejected; Barnaby Stout shrugged and walked off in the other direction.

"Weren't you worried about voting on it?" asked Terry.

"Not at all," said Albert. "We French consider every individual's vote sacrosanct."

"But what if we had lost?"

"We could not lose," said Albert.

"I guess I really expected Basil to vote for keeping it," said Terry. "I was surprised."

"I had no doubts," said Albert. "Nevertheless, Mutton didn't vote. And he would certainly have voted to give it back. So the worst we could have is a deadlock, and the captain breaks deadlocks." Albert smiled with satisfaction and departed in the direction of the bridge.

"Knows it all, doesn't he?" said Terry.

Remy laughed. "But of course."

Even though a great deal of time had seemed to elapse during their adventure on Hairless Cay, the sun had barely reached its high point in the sky. Nevertheless, the celebration on board the galleasse was well underway, the matter of the treasure having been settled and most hands now willing to forget about it. Even Basil, who had had his earlier dreams dashed, had put it out of his mind and now took an active part in the singing and the exaggeration of individual exploits during the earlier battle. The celebrants included everyone except Mutton, who was sleeping, and Stout's three men, who once again sat off by themselves. Even Albert had joined in, although he mostly harrumphed and rolled his eyes at the lies being so casually tossed about, then finally left to resume command of his ship.

After they had sung another verse of a bawdy song that was worse than the other verse, Remy stopped and turned to Terry. She gave him the same smile that had first conquered and made a prisoner of him. "Thank you for rescuing me," she said softly.

"It wasn't just me," said Terry. "It really was a group effort."

"But I'll bet that you were the leader," she said, leaning closer. "The spark plug."

"Well, not really," said Terry, grinning. "But if you insist on giving me the credit, I'll take it."

"I'm very grateful again," said Remy, giving him a look

that coupled innocence and worldliness, purity and lust. "And I want to make love."

Terry choked a little, looking down from her gaze only to be confronted by the buttonless shirt doing little to hide the real pirate treasure within. "Me too," said Terry. "Why don't you slip off and go below, and I'll wait a few minutes, then join you."

"Don't be a jerk," Remy said with a laugh as she stood and pulled at his hand. "Excuse us, please," she said to the others. They paid no attention, continuing to sing about a fair young thing from Havana, as Remy led Terry away and down below deck. Remy pushed open the door to one of the cabins, and Terry pulled it shut behind them. Sitting on the edge of the small bed, Remy folded her hands and rested them demurely in her lap.

Terry stepped toward her and she said suddenly: "I'm glad you didn't kill Keyes. I mean I'm not sorry he's dead. But somehow I'm just glad that you didn't do it. I'm glad none of us actually killed anyone."

"But we did," said Terry. "The Carib killed Apollo. Stout shot a couple of Keyes' men. And Zack squashed one."

"No, I mean us," said Remy. "They're not really us."

"And I'm one of us?"

"Of course you are," said Remy, smiling.

"That feels good," said Terry. "I really appreciate that."

"You were right all along, you know. The idea of becoming pirates was very foolish. We're lucky we weren't all killed."

"Maybe it was foolish," said Terry. "But look at what it accomplished. And particularly with Albert. Just look at him."

"Right now I'd rather look at you," said Remy, the mischievous, wanton look returning to her eyes. "Now what was it we came down here for?"

"You realize that's my shirt you're still wearing," said Terry.

"Is it?" Remy answered, looking down at the shirt as if surprised. "I'm afraid all the buttons have fallen off it. Are you sure you still want it back?"

"Yes," said Terry.

"Okay, if you're going to be so selfish." She stood and dropped her arms to her side. Terry untied the knot at the bottom of the shirt and slowly pushed it back over her breasts and then her shoulders. She wiggled a little and it dropped to the floor. Terry dropped to his knees, letting his hands slide off her shoulders and down across her breasts and stomach until he reached the buckle of her pants. "Are those yours too? she said, as he worked to open them.

"I'm not sure, but I'll check ," he said as the buckle snapped open. As he pushed the pants over her hips, he heard a small gasp and felt her body tighten. It didn't sound or feel like sexual excitement. He looked up and saw that her eyes were wide with fear as she stared beyond him. He turned, rolling back off his knees and into a squatting position on the floor. There, just inside the door to the cabin, filling the room with his presence, stood the Carib, looking at them blackly.

"Well, Mr. Stout," said Albert, holding the wheel steadily as the galleasse plied southward through friendly Caribbean waters. Hairless Cay had now entirely disappeared from view.

"This fair ship has performed admirably on our little quest, wouldn't you say?"

"Aye, it has, sir," said Stout. "It's a fine ship indeed."

"Some small part of the thanks for that belongs to you, sir," Albert said magnanimously. Stout forced a smile in answer to the compliment. "And why are you not back continuing in drunken revelry with the others, Mr. Stout?"

"I came to relieve you, sir," said Stout.

"That's very kind of you," said Albert with a wave of

dismissal. "Very kind. But as you can see, all is well here, and I'm perfectly happy to remain at the helm. A captain should set a certain standard for restraint and moderate behavior since the others all look up to him. Perhaps I'll take a short rest later."

"What I mean, sir," said Stout slowly and rather forcefully, "is that I'm relieving you of your command."

"I beg your pardon," said Albert, looking at him suspiciously.

"I'm taking command of the ship."

"Does the word 'mutiny' have an application here?" asked Albert, now gripping the wheel tightly as if his holding on to it would prevent its transfer to Stout.

"I'm afraid it does," said Stout. Albert now saw that Barnaby Stout was backing up his incendiary words with a small pistol that was pointed directly at the captain who was about to give up his ship.

"Why are you doing this?" asked Albert.

"My men and I feel that it's not in our best interests to give the money over to the authorities. We feel that it was justly earned and could be better spent elsewhere. And since you folks wouldn't agree to such a course of action, it became necessary to adopt this course of action."

"We outnumber you," said Albert.

"The others are already in our custody," said Stout. "It really wasn't very difficult. It's time for you to join them. I'm now the captain."

"*Si vous etes assez idiot pour le faire,*" said Albert. He reluctantly released the wheel and stepped down from his position of authority at the helm. With Stout following close behind, he marched, head held high, to the stern of the ship, where Zack, Ghost and the Carib stood pacing in front of their hapless prisoners who sat on the deck, hands bound behind their backs.

"What are your plans?" asked Albert as Stout bound his wrists and forced him down into a sitting position next to the others.

"I'm afraid we're going to have to part company," said Stout.

"He means he's going to kill us," said Remy.

"I'm afraid we haven't much choice," said Stout. He was perspiring and did look genuinely uncomfortable with the task. "We're not exactly going to kill you. I haven't the stomach for it, myself. I guess we'll just let the sea handle it."

"You're going to toss us overboard?" said Terry.

"Yes, I'm afraid so," Stout answered.

"Why not set us adrift in the rowboat?" suggested Terry.

311

"You'd be long gone before anyone found us, if anyone ever did."

"I considered that," said Stout. "But I just couldn't bring myself to do that. I'm afraid that if you were found – no matter how long it took – you'd report the incident to the authorities, and we'd end up on the run. Isn't that right?"

"Of course it is," said Albert, casually destroying Terry's next bargaining ploy – a pledge of eternal silence.

"You be a filthy rogue, Barnaby Stout," Basil growled.

"Yes, I guess I am," said Stout. "But you've always known me to be a filthy rogue. I've never pretended to anything more."

"It be unfair to just fling us overboard," said Basil. "We got the rights to walk us a plank with pirate honor."

Stout thought for a moment. "I guess that can be arranged."

"Thankee," said Basil. "You be's a true gentleman even if you are a filthy rogue."

Terry shook his head in disbelief with what Basil had just accomplished, and Albert muttered: *"Espece d'imbecile."*

Stout nodded to the Carib who disappeared below deck. As the prisoners sat silently contemplating their fate, they heard him banging around below. The reality of this latest threat and the realization that Stout had no intention of relenting gnawed at them as they sat helplessly and listened. Each sound from below was like the unexplained thump on an airplane that knots one's stomach and fills the imagination with impending doom. But this time no reassuring flight attendant would come by to explain that the sounds were nothing to be afraid of.

A few minutes later, the Carib emerged from below deck carrying a long board that was actually Christian's surfboard but that would serve admirably as a plank in a pinch. Zack assisted him as he placed the front of the board over the edge of the railing and stacked two wooden boxes near the railing to support the other end. Once the plank had been laid in place, they positioned a third wooden box next to it to serve as a stepladder to assist the condemned as they climbed to their end.

"Let's get on with it," said Stout nervously, obviously anxious to be done with the dirty business, unlike Murchison Keyes who would have savored every moment.

"We needs blindfolds," demanded Basil. "It be the proper way. You know that, Stout." Had Terry not been tied, he could have easily strangled Basil, who worsened their plight every time he opened his mouth. Although, Terry realized, it probably didn't matter that much. The only thing they would be able to see without blindfolds was each other drowning. Basil might have been the captain speaking, so quickly were his orders acted upon by Zack, Ghost and the Carib. Sadly, the blindfolds were created by tearing into strips the pirate flag that had once waved proudly, if somewhat oddly, over the galleasse.

"Anyone care to lead the way?" asked Stout. No one answered, until Basil finally stood and said: "Bad Basil Ringrose be ready to take his leave of this here ship." Zack wrapped the blindfold around his head, and the Carib helped him find the box and step up onto the plank. "Hi ho, Davey. Basil's comin' to see ya." They prodded him with an oar from the small rowboat and Basil disappeared with a splash.

Terry watched as in quick succession Mutton and Christian disappeared over the side. Then he was lifted to his feet, and the blindfold turned his world black. He faltered and fumbled his way up onto the plank. He was not certain how far along the plank he was until he felt the prod of the oar and found himself falling. With a sudden slap he hit the water and immediately went under but, by steadily kicking his legs and holding his breath, he was able to reach the surface just in time to hear Albert's voice firmly saying: "Vive la France," followed by a splash. A few seconds later, he heard another splash; that would be Remy.

Kicking gently, Terry attempted to steer himself in the direction of the final splash, yelling: "Remy!" He wanted to be near her before the end. Finally, he bumped into someone and said softly: "Remy? Is that you?"

"It is Albert," came the reply.

"I've got to find Remy," said Terry. "I need to be near her."

"Ah," said Albert. "And you are seeking her father's permission. That is good."

"For God's sake, Albert," we're drowning," said Terry.

"Very well, you have my permission."

"Hi sailor," said Remy from just behind him. He felt her hands down near his, pushing and tugging.

"What are you doing?" he asked.

"Untying you," Remy answered.

"How did you get yourself untied?" asked Terry.

"Jesus, look a gift horse in the mouth," said Remy, working his hands free. "I studied under Houdini. I mean with Houdini." Terry removed his blindfold and turned to see that beautiful wet face that he thought he'd never see again smiling at him. She worked at Albert's knot as she spoke: "Zack didn't tie me all that well. He was preoccupied with peeking under my shirt. I was untied before I hit the water"

Terry, Remy and Albert quickly found Basil, Christian and Mutton bobbing nearby in the water and freed them as well.

"Okay," said Remy. "Now what do we do?"

Terry searched the seascape and found it even more menacing than it had been the day he'd been dumped from his boat. Off in one direction was the faintest gray image of a land mass hugging the horizon. In another direction, the retreating galleasse was growing smaller. Everywhere else, nothing but water. "Tread water as best we can," said Terry. "For as long as we can. And hope for a miracle."

"I've got an idea," said Remy. "Let's make love before we drown."

"Here?" said Terry. "In the water? With people all around?"

"My God," said Remy. "We're all going to drown within fifteen minutes, and you're worried about what people will think?"

Mutton groaned a little before Terry could answer, and they all turned toward their wounded comrade. "Are you all right, Mutton?" asked Christian.

"I think so," said Mutton. "Just tired."

"You lean on Basil for a few minutes, lad," said Basil, slipping an arm around him. "Just to rest up."

"How long do you think we can tread water?" asked Remy.

"I don't know – a few hours, maybe," Terry answered.

"Magnifique," said Albert. "Our lives don't have to flash before our eyes; they can parade by leisurely."

"Look!" said Christian. "I think it's a shark. They all turned in the direction Christian indicated, a new fear now gripping them.

"They groaned, they stirred, they all uprose," intoned Mutton.

"Merde," said Albert. "What does a man do so wrong in his life that he must leave it by drowning or being devoured by sharks while someone recites poetry."

There was indeed something in the water about twenty feet away. But it was something floating, not a shark. "I think it's a piece of wood," said Terry. "It's the plank! They threw it overboard." Terry swam to the floating plank, and the others followed. They each grabbed hold of it until it began to sink under their weight.

"We've got to take turns," said Terry. "While one of us rests, the others tread water. Let Mutton take the first turn." The others helped as Mutton climbed onto the board and straddled it.

"This is really a break," said Terry happily.

"I forgot," said Remy laughing. "You're an old hand at

this. This is the way you cruise the Caribbean. So what do we do, float back to the island? Or maybe to Jamaica. I think it's over that way." She pointed across the empty sea.

"We do something," said Terry. "We don't just wait to die. Let's head toward that island." He pointed toward the unknown island that lay barely visible in the distance. "Maybe someone will find us. There's always a chance."

"There's something funny about Albert's boat," said Mutton who lay on the board staring off in the direction of the galleasse. "It should get smaller and disappear."

"Maybe the world is actually flat," said Albert without looking. The others looked toward the galleasse and found that not only was it no longer getting smaller, it actually appeared a little larger.

"It's coming back this way," said Terry.

"Why would they come back?" asked Remy. "That doesn't make sense."

"Maybe they changed their minds," Christian suggested.

"I doubt it," said Albert. "They probably just want to make sure we're dead."

"Black'earts!" thundered Basil. "You just come back here, Stout, if ya dare."

They watched intently for the next few minutes, barely

cognizant of the fact that they were still treading water and getting tired. "It's not alone," said Remy suddenly. Two large gray vessels had appeared on the horizon at either side of the galleasse, and within minutes appeared to be close alongside. They continued watching, the ships no longer getting larger, apparently having stopped in the water.

After a while the galleasse appeared to be moving again, but this time it proceeded alone, the two large gray ships remaining stationary. Time passed slowly as the galleasse continued in their direction, and it was another ten minutes before the galleasse was close enough that they could make out figures standing on board. The man standing at the bow had Barnaby Stout's build, but it was not Stout. It was a stocky, bronze-faced man in a white uniform. The gold that decorated his hat, shoulders and arms and the kaleidoscope of colorful ribbons that adorned his chest suggested that he was not a newcomer to the navy and that he was a man used to command.

Standing next to him, waving wildly at the wet pirate heads that bobbed in the water, was Peaches.

One by one they were pulled out of the water and onto the deck of the galleasse, where Peaches began talking at once.

"So this nice navy realized that they left Hornblower behind and came back to find him." The Admiral beamed as she told the story. The soggy pirates noted his name tag – Trillig. "Yes," said Peaches. "This is Hornblower's daddy, and he's the general in charge of this whole navy. So I figured since we took care of Hornblower while the rest of them were lost, maybe they could help us. I asked him if his navy would come and get you, so it did. I was worried about you. Isn't that nice of them?"

"How did you know where to look?" asked Terry.

Admiral Trillig began to speak but Peaches cut in. "Hornblower. That dear boy is so smart." Lieutenant Trillig, who had joined them, blushed. "Hornblower remembered that the island looked like a cow or something, so he checked hundreds of maps and found it."

Trillig and his father both coughed, twin signals of modesty. Trillig looked at the pirates and grinned but blushed upon seeing the one survivor on whom being soaked to the skin was the most flattering.

The Admiral reasserted command of the story: "Met the jackanapes head on. At first, they tried to tell us that you'd all been killed by this Murchison Keyes and that they were returning the money to the authorities. But their story fell apart

320

quickly, and they confessed straightaway. They're in the lock-up aboard one of our ships now."

Most of the talk was now beginning to buzz by Terry's head as he too stared at Remy, unable to think about or see anything else. She stared back at him as well, and Terry realized they shared the same depraved thoughts. As one by one the other pirates drifted off in different directions, Terry walked to where she stood shivering and put his arm around her.

"You look cold," he said. "Not to mention fantastically beautiful. Walking the plank does you well."

"I think it's just my wet clothes," said Remy.

"Maybe we should go below and get out of them," said Terry, attempting to be nonchalant and worldly but coming across more like a nervous kid contemplating a cigarette behind the garage. Albert, who Terry had forgot was standing next to them, glowered.

"Sir," said Terry boldly. "I'd like to ask permission to go below deck with your daughter."

"For what purpose?" asked Albert.

Terry stammered, and Remy said: "Albert!"

"Hmmm," said Albert. He stared at Terry in a silent, but probing, cross-examination, causing Terry to quickly redden.

Peaches grabbed Albert's arm and said: "Leave them

alone, you old fool; they just want to talk."

"Parler," said Albert, mockingly, as Peaches led him away. Remy giggled and pulled Terry below deck, dropping her wet shirt along the way.

The sun departed with a dramatic display of bright, hot color, and the galleasse glided silently across the dark glassy waters under a star-filled sky. Terry and Remy witnessed none of this. They had cloistered themselves within a small cabin below deck. There they had made love and fallen asleep in each other's arms, oblivious to the world outside their door. They slept through the night, awoke with the sun and made love again. Afterward they lay in the small bed, unwilling to quit their hidden little island.

"I want to be honest," said Terry. "I'm going to have to go home."

"I know," said Remy.

"I hope you don't think that I'm leaving now because I finally got what I wanted, like you suggested before. I hope you know that's not the way it is."

"I know," said Remy.

"I'll come back. I promise."

"I know."

"I love you," said Terry.

"I know."

"Aren't you going to say anything?" said Terry peevishly.

"Goodbye," said Remy.

"That's it?" said Terry, frowning.

"I hate long goodbyes," said Remy with a playful smile.

"But don't you . . . don't you . . . I mean . . . even a little?"

"Love you?" Remy asked innocently.

"Yes, that's what I mean," said Terry.

"I don't think I'm going to tell you. I'll let you sit up there in cold, cruel New York and worry about it."

"You're a mean, spiteful person. Do you realize that?"

"I know," said Remy, laughing. "Piracy does that to a person. Why is it so important for you to know if I love you anyway? You're leaving."

"I don't know why it's so important," said Terry. "It just is."

"Okay, I love you," said Remy.

"Really?" Terry jumped up, banged his head on a sloping beam and, in a daze brought on not by the bump but by Remy's words, began to babble. "Do you mean that? You're not just saying it? You really do mean it?"

"No, I'm lying," said Remy. She laughed and shook her head. "You're impossible."

"Come to New York with me," said Terry.

"I can't."

Terry darkened again. "After all we've been through together, it just seems like we deserve a happy ending."

"Personally, I don't think I'm quite ready for an ending – happy or otherwise."

"That's not what I meant. I . . . Well, I'll be back. Count on it.

"I'll be here," said Remy.

From outside the door they heard Albert's voice, thick with sarcasm: "We're approaching L'Orient. Have you finished talking, yet?"

The small plane turned on the runway, and Terry pulled his leg in and slammed the door.

"You're getting to be a real pro at this, Terry," said Tommy. "Maybe I should start worrying about my job."

"It's safe, believe me," Terry answered.

They started down the runway and picked up speed, but

just before the plane lifted off the ground, Terry shouted: "Stop the plane. I can't go."

Tommy skillfully aborted the takeoff, bringing the plane to a bumpy stop just a few feet from the end of the runway and the beginning of the ocean. He turned to Terry, gave him a look of admonishment, and said: "You promised me you were really going this time."

"I know," said Terry. "I'm sorry. I thought I could go. But I can't."

Tommy shook his head and taxied the plane back to the terminal. "I don't think this is what they meant by frequent flier," he said, killing the engines and leaning back. "She must really be something."

"She is, Tommy," said Terry, opening the door and jumping out. "She is."

Excerpt from the Booby Bay Chronicle by Basil Ringrose, retired buccaneer, with additional material by Terrence Bonney, retired buccaneer

Just as the entrance of Murchison Keyes and Sammy Apollo into the tranquil Booby Bay culture gave rise to the new age of piracy, so their demise brought that age to an end. The tiny band of brigands returned to their remote island paradise and hung up their pirate flag, never again to sail the seas with plunder and adventure in mind. The US Navy never officially recognized the existence of Keyes treasure and therefore did not take possession of it. Peaches had convinced Admiral Trillig that the money should remain in the West Indies and be used to "help folks who aren't as well off as we are." Several humanitarian organizations throughout the islands shared the swag.

Lieutenant Trillig promised to return to Booby Bay, but thus far hasn't. Through an extensive Caribbean grapevine that few know or understand, we learned that he had at last married his true love and taken an exit from the navy. Proving what a small world the West Indies can be, Christian, on a trip to L'Orient met one of the pirates' early victims, Anna Lovejoy. He returned to Booby Bay a week later, a much older young man. Tommy the pilot visited the island once for a few days and, upon leaving, said to one of the former pirates: "I'd have jumped, too."

Albert Lafitte corrected the few remaining deficiencies he had found in the reconstruction of the galleasse and christened her the Remy. Shortly thereafter Albert, Remy and Christian took her on what Albert insisted was technically still her maiden voyage. Peaches stayed behind to mind the cafe, Basil and

Mutton. Terry and Remy have not had a happy ending – nor, so far, any ending.

"We can't sail all the way to France," said Remy. She and Albert sat in a small Martinique cafe. Christian prowled the streets for a fair young tourist looking for a little Caribbean romance.

"The galleasse is capable of sailing anywhere," Albert answered.

"I'm sure she is. I guess what I'm trying to say is that I can't sail to France. I need to get back home."

Albert stared at her intently. "You miss the bustle and excitement of Booby Bay. Is that it?"

"You know damn well what I miss. And I'm not going to give you the satisfaction of admitting it."

"Very well," said Albert with a sweeping gesture. "We return to Booby Bay."

Terry placed the pad of paper and pencil carefully in his lap and joined Basil, who sat in the chair to his right, and Mutton, at his left, as they stared out at the third consecutive day of rain. Barbie Dog rubbed a floppy ear against his leg, stood, walked around him, and settled in again against his other leg.

"Hope old Albert ain't out in this storm," said Basil. "The sea can be a friend or it can be your most fearsome enemy. Where do you reckon old Albert is about now?"

"I'd say about now he's sashaying down the main street of Basse-Terre or Forte-de-France or sipping wine and being argumentative in a beachfront cafe." Yes, Albert is stopping conversations, and Remy is stopping traffic. Christian is probably making a nuisance of himself with any young lady unfortunate enough to cross his path. Remy. I imagine she's broken quite a few French hearts by now. But her heart is here, and she'll return. She'll return.

Although the rain had finally stopped, Albert still wore an amazing yellow slicker and cap that made him look like a Maine lobsterman. Christian and Remy stood, watching Booby Bay come into view. Remy picked up a pair of binoculars to study the beach.

"We'll reach the harbor in a few moments," the man in yellow pronounced.

Remy put down the binoculars and said: "I'm not going to the harbor."

"What?" her companions said in unison.

"I'm going this way," she said, pointing off the starboard side.

Before either man could respond, Remy had dropped her shirt to the deck, swung over the railing of the galleasse, and dropped to the water below.

Terry sat alone on the beach. The return of the sun had lulled him into drowsiness and, eyes closed, he had not seen the galleasse as it passed. When he did open his eyes, it was to be stupefied by the vision emerging from the sea. Remy's wet skin sparkled; Terry's hair stood on end. He was reduced to reciting: "A speck, a mist, a shape, I wist! And still it neared and neared."

Finally, as Remy reached the sand and began approaching him, Terry stopped mumbling verses and stood. Remy drew close, and slipping her arms across his shoulders and behind his neck said: "Remember me?"

A year later, born to Remy Lafitte and Terry Bonney, a baby girl. They named her Alberta. She doesn't walk yet, but all the Booby Bay males stand ready to follow her around like puppy dogs when she does. Everyone is certain she'll grow up to be a pirate.